D0941328

AGGIE MORTON

MYSTERY QUEEN

AGGIE MORTON
MYSTERY QUEEN

THE DEAD MAN IN THE GARDEN

MARTHE JOCELYN

WITH ILLUSTRATIONS BY ISABELLE FOLLATH

tundra

Tundra Books, an imprint of Penguin Random House Canada Young Readers, a division of Penguin Random House of Canada Limited

Library and Archives Canada Cataloguing in Publication

Title: The dead man in the garden / Marthe Jocelyn ; [illustrations by]
    Isabelle Follath.
Names: Jocelyn, Marthe, author. | Follath, Isabelle, illustrator.
Series: Jocelyn, Marthe. Aggie Morton, mystery queen ; 3.
Description: Series statement: Aggie Morton, mystery queen ; 3
Identifiers: Canadiana (print) 20200408224 | Canadiana (ebook) 20200408240
    | ISBN 9780735270817 (hardcover) | ISBN 9780735270770 (EPUB)
Classification: LCC PS8569.O254 D43 2021 | DDC jC813/.54—dc23

Published simultaneously in the United States of America by Tundra Books of Northern New York, an imprint of Penguin Random House Canada Young Readers, a division of Penguin Random House of Canada Limited

Library of Congress Control Number: 2020951324

Edited by Lynne Missen with assistance from Margot Blankier
Designed by John Martz
The text was set in Plantin

Printed in Canada

www.penguinrandomhouse.ca

1   2   3   4   5   25   24   23   22   21

FOR TIM AND PAULA
I WISH YOU COULD READ THIS BOOK

Aggie Morton

Hector Perot

Mummy

Grannie Jane

George Bellamere

Sidonie Touati

Mr. Smythe

Eva Napoli

Dr. Peter Baden

Elizabeth Mc.Worthy

Inspector Henry

Alberto

CHAPTER 1

A SPLENDID HOTEL

THE NEWS THAT A WOMAN had died three days before our arrival was quite worrying for Mummy. We had come to the Wellspring Hotel & Spa for healing and serenity, not to learn that a previous visitor had departed for the Great Unknown. Hector and I did our best to empathize with Mummy's fears, but, truthfully, we were very much intrigued.

We heard the story only an hour after we arrived. Our first impression of Wellspring was one of marvel. I had never slept in a hotel and that alone was thrilling. Our suite had two bedrooms and a sitting room. The beds were high, the mattresses springy, and the covers made of quilted satin the color of blue smoke. Hector and I gaped at each other as we smacked the beds and poked the pillows and admired the bathtub that rested on porcelain claws like those of a griffin. We discovered bars of soap that smelled like attar of roses, and a welcome tin of short-bread from Farrah's of Harrogate. We drew open the silken curtains in the sitting room to reveal a view of the gardens, where the trees were lit golden in the late afternoon sunshine. Could it be more perfect?

"Off you go, then," said Mummy. "Explore the hotel for a bit while we unpack our things. Hector, they've put a cot for you here in the alcove behind the screen. Will that do, I hope?"

"Mais oui, madame!" Hector's smile suggested that an alcove behind a screen in the sitting room was the most wonderful thing to occur during all of April until now, and that included the chocolate mousse our cook had made last Sunday for Easter. It especially included not being left behind at the vicarage in Torquay, where he was living until his family could join him in England. Mummy had written to Hector's mother in Belgium, inviting him to come with us to Yorkshire. He would miss a few days of school, but the reply was, thankfully, yes. As I do my schoolwork with Mummy or Charlotte at home, my education could only be improved by travel.

Grannie Jane sat in one of the plump armchairs beside the little fire. "Please come back with news of when supper will be served," she said.

Hector waited at the door while I tucked my notebook into the sash of my dress, jammed a pencil into the thick hair behind my ear and saluted in readiness. Ready for adventure, and luxury! The corridor walls were papered in lush patterns of green and gold. Clusters of blown glass tulips shaded electric lights overhead. Carpets, like indoor forest paths, were strewn with woven leaves and wildflowers. We began with a stop at the dining room and learned that dinner was served from as early as six o'clock.

"That will please Grannie Jane," I said.

"Also, Hector Perot," said Hector, never shy about having an appetite.

"May I help you?" A man with a pointy nose above a pointy mustache peered down at us. He wore the hotel livery of a dark green jacket adorned with a gold crest on the chest pocket. His hat, shaped like a tea biscuit, sat slightly askew.

"No, thank you," said Hector. He knew it usually took me a moment to find my tongue when talking to unfamiliar adults.

The man sucked in his cheeks and narrowed his eyes. "I am Mr. Bessel, the bell captain. I must inform you that children from the village are not permitted inside the hotel."

"This is sad for them," said Hector. "Being guests, however, we are much appreciating our freedom to explore."

"Guests?" said the snooty man. "In which room?"

"Two oh one," I said.

"The Morton family," said Hector.

The bell captain made a *humph*ing noise and retreated, but only by two or three paces.

"Bessel, the buzzard," I whispered, "hovering over his prey."

"May our bones get stuck in his teeth," said Hector.

"What do you suppose made him think—?" I said. Hector was smartly dressed, as always, the collar of his sailor suit crisp and white. And I . . . well, now that I saw Hector's face, I realized that I was wrinkled and disheveled from the journey and had not made the slightest effort to repair myself.

It had been Grannie's idea that we should come here to the Wellspring. Attached to the hotel was a spa with Turkish baths. Mummy was to "take the waters" each day for two weeks, meaning that she would sit in rooms full of steam and plunge into pools filled with waters pumped from the natural chalybeate springs that flowed beneath the town. She would drink those waters too, loaded with iron, to restore her health and her spirits, still so low more than a year after Papa died. While Mummy was being cured, Grannie Jane would knit, and Hector and I would have splendid adventures.

The bell captain was still on our heels when I noticed a passage marked with an elegant arrow: To the Garden.

"Let's look outside," I said. We slowed down behind a

gentleman using a walking stick, and finally Mr. Bessel chose not to follow. We paused to give the doddery man time to turn the corner, but he paused too. An odd rumbling noise announced the approach of something heavy, *like a wave dragging across a stony beach. Like a galloping goat. Like a pram full of stones—*

And then, *whoosh!* A boy in a wheelchair hurtled around the corner and jammed to a halt, only a cane's length in front of us all. The gentleman gasped, leaning heavily against the wall. Hector, ever alert, jumped to assist by offering an arm for support. He guided the man to a handy seat that seemed placed there for the very purpose of allowing a startled old person to recover from a fright. The boy who had caused the upset watched us, looking not in the least bit contrite, but as pleased as if he'd won a race.

"You might have knocked him down." My scolding slipped out, though he was a stranger and an invalid. I felt the flush flood my cheeks. I guessed that he was two or three years older than I, fourteen perhaps, or fifteen. Being seated, his height could not add to my guess. I did not allow my gaze to linger on his dangling legs. His face looked healthy enough, pink skin with what Grannie Jane would call apple-cheeks because of being shiny and rosy.

"He might have tangled my wheels with that stick," he said. "You tell your grandpa—"

"He is not my grandpa," I corrected.

The gentleman was on his feet again, with Hector's help.

"You are mended, monsieur?" said Hector.

The man waved Hector away and jabbed a finger at the wheelchair boy instead. "*You* are a menace!" he said. "My heart is not as reliable as it used to be. Such a shock is most unhealthy. Why is a cripple permitted the liberty of tearing about like a hooligan? I shall have a word with the management."

"Oh, George," came a voice from behind us. "What have you done now?" The woman was brown-skinned, dressed in navy blue and with a nurse's crisp white cap. She shook her head wearily. "Sprints again?"

"You tell him, Sidonie," said the boy. "You tell him as it's part of my therapy and vital to my health. I'm taking these other ones outdoors." He performed an impressive turn, considering the size of his vehicle, and wheeled toward the garden.

"Come on!" he called over his shoulder. "Don't dally."

I looked at Hector. We shrugged in unison and followed, pleased to avoid the Cane Man's tirade. The boy named George stopped before the door, waiting. It took a moment to realize that a person sitting in a chair could not open a door and maneuver his way through it at the same time. This must be one of the tasks of the woman he'd called Sidonie. Hector was quicker than I, holding the door while George wheeled through into a lovely garden.

A brick path led us under flowering dogwood trees, with a wide smooth lawn on one side and benches nestled among shrubs on the other. A formal rose garden surrounded a tiered fountain, with scalloped stone edges featuring sculpted birds and cherubs on the top tier, prettily pouring water from enormous blossoms.

The wheelchair stopped and George performed another turn that brought him close to a bench beside the fountain. Room for us all to sit together.

"I'm George," said George.

"Hector," said Hector. "And this is Aggie."

"When did you get here?" said George. "How long are you staying?"

"We arrived an hour ago," I said. "We're here for two weeks."

"And you?" said Hector.

"I live in Harrogate," said George. "I come to the clinic for the sulphur bath, two or three times a week." He flicked a hand at his legs, as if we might not have noticed his plight. "There's no fixing them," he said. "I was run down by a tram nearly five years ago, and this is what I've got left." He glared at us, waiting, it seemed, for an expression of horror or commiseration. Both were blooming in my chest, enormous prickly stemmed weeds that I had no practice in holding. I hoped my face did not relay what I was feeling.

"And the sulphur bath?" Hector spoke before I'd turned my thoughts to courtesy. "It has some consequence?"

"No," said George. "No improvement. But it *feels* good while I am in the pool . . . I can float. My body moves in ways that cannot happen out of water." He banged the armrests of his chair, as if it represented all the limitations of dry land. "And it's *warm*," he added.

"Your sprints," I began, without knowing precisely what I meant to ask.

George's grin was so frank and humorous, I could not help but like him. "I have the strongest arms of anyone I know, and sprints are why." He bent his right arm at the elbow and told us to poke his muscle.

Hector obliged. "A boulder," he said, in admiration.

"Usually, people avoid me," said George. "They scuttle away like baby ducks when they see me coming. I'd much rather get a wigging, as I did just now, than be ignored."

"I imagine it is better to be noticed for any reason," said Hector.

George blinked and slowly smiled. "You're pretty sharp," he said, "for a Frenchie."

"This is perhaps because I am from Belgium," said Hector.

"Mrs. Shelton was different too," said George. "She paid attention. Makes it harder, somehow. *She'd* meet my eyes, but that's rare for an adult. She'd talk to me about how to mix colors or what sheep might think about. Things other than how I'm *feeling* today, or whether I've taken my tonic, and did I have a restful sleep?"

"Mrs. who, did you say?" I felt I'd missed something. "Was she another guest?"

"Mrs. Shelton," said George. "The one who died on Saturday."

CHAPTER 2

A LONELY CORPSE

"*DIED?*" I SAID. "Here? Three days ago?"

"Who died?" said Hector.

"She was a guest at the hotel," said George, "but she moved out last week, into a lodging house, and then she died." He pointed to a gate in the hedge that bordered the hotel garden. "In the park across the road."

"We certainly need to hear more about Mrs. Shelton," I said. "How did she die?" Wavering before my eyes were visions of the two dead bodies I had previously encountered. Our neighbor, in the autumn, under the piano in the Mermaid Dance Room, and the other, an actor, seeping blood all over the carpet in my brother-in-law's library on Christmas morning. "Did you see her?"

"I did not see her." George sounded regretful. "And her death remains a bit of a mystery."

"How can this be?" said Hector.

"She'd been ill, which is why she was at Wellspring, but then she got sicker. Maybe the hotel food was too rich? Or the waters disturbed her constitution? She and my nurse, Sidonie, became friends. She began to suspect that the hotel disagreed with her. She moved into a lodging house last week and improved after leaving the hotel, but then, she was found dead. In the park."

"So sad!" I said.

"Sidonie knows the landlady of the lodging house," said George. "That's why Mrs. Shelton moved there."

"Oh, hello." Hector stood as George's nurse came along the path.

"Here you are, George," she said. "Nice to see fresh young faces, eh? So many old people pottering about this place! I am Sidonie Touati. George's nurse."

"I am Aggie Morton," I said. "We are pleased to meet you, miss. This is Hector Perot. From Belgium." I added *from Belgium* because he was bowing from the waist, which seemed so foreign that I felt I must explain. Nurse Touati was also foreign, I guessed, as she, too, spoke with an accent, though slighter than Hector's. She must have lived in England longer than his few months. And where had she come from?

"We'd best be off, George. Your mother will be wondering. And you need to be considering your letter of apology to the gentleman you nearly clobbered back there."

Rather than looking apologetic, George produced a cheeky grin. "Dear Sir," he said. "I am woefully sorry to have distressed you by nearly ramming your knees with my wheelchair. Being a so-called *cripple*, I have no manners. I am—"

"As I said," Nurse Touati interrupted, "you will need to do some thinking before writing anything down." She took the handles of his chair and straightened the wheels on the path. "Watch your fingers, now."

George put his hands in his lap, away from where they'd been resting on the iron wheels. He wore gloves, the leather bald on the palms from the constant friction of maneuvering his chair.

"I don't come to Wellspring every day," he told us. "It rather depends . . ." He looked down briefly. "On how the night goes. But I'll try to be here tomorrow. Watch for me, will you?"

Yes, yes, we agreed. We'd see him tomorrow or the next day.

Mummy and Grannie Jane had not waited for us to return to the room but were in the lobby and in conversation with other guests.

"Oh dear." I saw that Mummy was merrily chatting to Cane Man, the gentleman who'd been so rude to George. With him were a younger man and woman: he ruddy-faced and big-eared; she rather creamy-skinned with a coil of honey-colored hair.

"We must first wash our hands and be tidy, I think," said Hector.

I caught Grannie's eye and signaled that I would brush my hair before joining the party. I wished it might take an hour to do so, for I truly loathed being introduced to strangers and compelled to talk politely. Particularly strangers who had just displayed impatience and growled unkind words. We hurried, though. We took turns in the fancy bathroom, washing our hands and splashing our faces. Hector plastered more water and discipline on his already flat hair, and changed the collar on his sailor suit, though to my eye it was already sparkling white. I brushed and re-plaited and retied ribbons in my hair, and, too soon, was generally presentable.

Back downstairs, my mother and grandmother had disappeared. A hefty man bustled up to ask whether we were the children with the Morton party. He introduced himself as Mr. Smythe, the hotel manager. My lovely mother, he claimed, had asked that he watch out for us and make certain that we joined her in the Champagne Lounge. He had the eyes of a stoat and a mustache so thin it might have been drawn with a quill pen. He insisted on leading us all the way to Mummy's side, as if we were Hansel and Gretel and had been lost in the forest. We now must sit with Mummy's new companions. The chandelier lighting was dim and twinkly, the tables oval-shaped and low, so that people's knees bumped into them instead of sliding elegantly under. Thankfully, Mr. Smythe retreated as the waiter approached.

"Dear ladies and pleasant gentlemen!" The waiter had a gleaming black mustache and nut-tanned skin. His voice was warm, his accent melodic and almost dramatic. "My name is Alberto. I am so happy to welcome you to the Wellspring Hotel." Grannie Jane was faintly horrified by his chumminess, but he was efficient enough in bringing our drinks.

The name of the rude gentleman was Mr. Hart, and he was not entirely a villain after all, nor so old as I'd thought because of the cane and the bad mood. He was closer in age to Mummy than to Grannie, though his overgrown beard showed some silver threads. Regrettably, he recognized us and was compelled to explain his side of the confrontation with George.

"I am here at Wellspring to address the matter of an

ailing heart." He put a hand on his chest, to remind us where such an organ might be found. "My physician has told me firmly to avoid anything that might cause undue surprise. To have a machine come rolling around the corner at such a speed . . . ! The boy might well have hit me! The shock was precisely against medical advice."

The young woman put a fond hand upon his sleeve. "Yet here you are, Uncle, as fit as a farm horse. All's well that ends well."

"Let us hope there is no end in sight for a while," said Mr. Hart.

"Uncle Benedict!" scolded his niece. "You mustn't be so gloomy. You'll go home from Wellspring a new man."

Mr. Hart's niece was named Mrs. Upton, and she had been married for six days. She and her new husband had come to Harrogate a week ago, for their honeymoon. Because her uncle had paid for the wedding and this trip afterward, he had joined them last evening, to take advantage of the healing waters himself for a few days.

"The boy's an artist," Mr. Hart told Mummy, though "the boy" must have been already more than twenty and was sitting right there.

"A designer, really," said Mrs. Upton. "An inventor. He's terribly clever, aren't you, Eddie? Almost an engineer. If you would take Eddie under your wing, Uncle Benedict, I believe he would flourish beautifully."

"What would be the benefit in that? An artist is an artist, not worth the price of canvas."

"He doesn't paint on canvas! He makes drawings of things that no one has thought of yet. He has a splendid idea for an umbrella that attaches to a chair—"

"I am sitting right here," said her husband, flushing. "I can speak for myself . . ."

"Why are we indulging in discord?" said Mr. Hart. "Here we are, in the company of so many beautiful ladies." He included Mummy—and even me—in his round of smiles. "How could any man complain, eh, Eddie?"

"Eddie has eyes for me alone, don't you, sweetheart?" said Mrs. Upton. Everyone laughed, including her husband. His ears stuck out from his head so far that light shone through them.

Alberto stopped by the table again, and Mr. Hart insisted that he would pay for all of us to have another drink. Grannie Jane declined, as she disliked anyone showing off about money, but the rest of us were happy enough to accept. Mr. Upton told the waiter he was expecting a telephone call and to please summon him and not just take a message.

"Oh, look," said Mummy. "The quartet is getting ready to play."

Four gentlemen wearing elegant tailcoats were settling themselves on a semi-circular platform at one end of the room. They took up instruments and began to play single notes to synchronize their tuning.

"Funny to see an African fellow playing a violin, eh?" said Mr. Hart.

The other musicians were all the more usual Englishman color of paste.

"You imagine that only drums are played in Africa?" said Grannie Jane. The violinist played a quick arpeggio that sang up the strings and back down. "Is he *from* Africa?"

"He is a brilliant player," said Mrs. Upton. "We've heard him more than once since we've been here. Ssh, they're starting."

I exchanged a smile with Grannie Jane as soon as the first notes were played. It was the famous minuet by Luigi Boccherini. I had learned a modified version for the piano and practiced so many times that Grannie had banned it if she was in the drawing room.

"A song as pretty as the ladies," said Mr. Hart. He patted his niece's arm, but he also looked at Mummy. A faint rose appeared in Mummy's cheeks. Was she *blushing*? I did not like this. Grannie Jane tapped my hand in warning. I bit hard on my lip to keep my growls inside. *How dare you speak so boldly to my mother, sir? What makes you think this manner of address might be welcome? Whyever would my lovely Mummy listen to such twaddle from a toad like you?*

17

I endowed him with bulging eyes, a warty nose and webbing between the fingers that held his wineglass. This was so satisfying a fantasy that I smiled, appeasing Grannie and myself as well.

Hector raised his eyebrow at me. I had missed a little of the conversation and found that Mrs. Lidia Shelton, recently deceased, was now our topic. Mrs. and Mr. Upton had met her on the evening of their arrival—and the night before she moved out of the hotel.

"She was a charming woman," said Mrs. Upton.

"A little odd, you know," added Mr. Upton. "She traveled about making paintings of birds and rodents. Not just portraits, but their skeletons as well!"

Skeletons? My interest perked right up. "Did you see any of her pictures?" I asked.

"She showed us one of her books. She'd had four or five published," said Mrs. Upton. "The illustrations were very delicate and realistic."

"I'd say she had a packet of money," said Mr. Upton. "Her clothing and jewelry were pretty fine stuff. Must have been family money, or an inheritance. I can't see a woman being financially independent from a few peculiar books."

"She may be famous, for all we know," said Mrs. Upton.

"It's just so very sad," said Mummy. "Had she any family?"

"It seems not," said Mrs. Upton. "She wasn't old, perhaps thirty-three or -four at most? She was a widow but had no children. Which is fortunate, under the circumstances."

"She was traveling alone?" said Grannie Jane. "A free spirit, then?"

"A bit too *free*," said Mr. Hart. "The sort of widow who was never properly married, if you take my meaning . . ."

I did not think I took his meaning.

"No more of that," said Mummy, quickly.

"I heard," said Mrs. Upton, "that she went out for a walk after lunch, to assist her digestion, and simply never came back. The landlady at her lodging house was frantic."

"With good reason, as it turned out," said Mr. Upton. "I expect the hotel feels very lucky she was no longer a guest."

"Just as we're lucky that we *are*," said Mr. Hart. "We are meant to be in Harrogate taking a cure, not dropping dead after dinner."

Naturally we all agreed with this sentiment, and left Mrs. Shelton—for the moment—to rest in peace.

CHAPTER 3

A PERPLEXING MOMENT

THE NEXT DAY, Wednesday, after lunch, I was to accompany Mummy to her first appointment at the Wellspring clinic. We were to have a tour of the Turkish baths, and the plan for Mummy's treatment would be devised. Hector announced—quietly and only to me—that he would walk into Valley Gardens Park to have a look at the bench beside the bandstand where Mrs. Shelton had taken her final breath. This was one of the reasons I liked Hector so much. He shared what Mummy called my Morbid Preoccupation and never tired of discussing the remarkable ability of the human body to die in many ways and places.

My Papa died in his bed, after a long illness, perhaps the dullest way to go. A short illness would have meant less suffering for Papa. But for a daughter with an aching heart, each extra day that he could talk with me, or hear me read, or simply breathe nearby . . . that was all I wanted. Why was it, then, that when a *stranger* was found dead, I did not consider the family or the loss but dwelt instead upon the death itself? How had it happened? Why in this place? Did the person feel pain? Was wrongdoing involved? And what happened now that a body had become a corpse?

"Aggie? Are you ready?" Mummy was pulling on her lace-backed gloves. She'd worn them since becoming a widow, whenever we were in company.

We easily found the sign directing guests from the lobby to the Wellspring Spa & Clinic, its arrow pointing down a passage that led in the opposite direction from the garden. Mummy was unusually cheerful in anticipation of a strange new experience. Between the hotel and the clinic was a covered walkway, as quick to cross as a drawing room—unless one encountered someone familiar and was obliged to exchange greetings. Which we did.

Mr. Hart and his niece had lingered there to gaze at the garden through a lattice of climbing roses, the buds ready and aching to bloom.

"Good afternoon, ladies," said Mr. Hart. "Here we are admiring the view, and with your arrival it has become even lovelier."

It would have been rude to shudder with distaste at this flirtation, but I allowed a slight shiver nonetheless.

"Isn't the fountain jolly!" Mrs. Upton hurried past her uncle's clumsy remark, and invited Mummy to comment on the stone cherubs sprinkling water.

"Very whimsical," Mummy said, "though perhaps a little ornate for my taste."

"You are receiving a treatment this afternoon?" said Mrs. Upton. "Uncle Ben also has his first appointment."

"I am quite nervous," Mummy admitted, "not knowing what to expect."

"Nothing to worry yourself about," said Mr. Hart. "I'm told it is agreeably soothing."

We would have passed by, but Mr. Hart stepped in front of us to open the glass-paned door to the spa, all while smirking at my mother. I marched right past him, my blood suddenly simmering. Mummy was obliged to follow me.

"How might we have managed that great brute of a door if the knight had not shown up on his horse?" I muttered.

"Aggie!" she scolded. But my unkindness was not overheard, for uncle and niece had allowed the door to close and could be seen through the glass, still admiring the garden.

We had arrived in a vestibule that opened into a busy wood-paneled reception office. A plump woman wearing a nurse's cap and apron stood behind a small desk that held a large appointment book. The customer she spoke with also wore a uniform, and I recognized her as being George's attendant, Nurse Sidonie Touati. I looked quickly about to find George waving at me from a corner of the waiting room beyond the desk.

"Hello, Aggie!"

"Good afternoon." I stepped away from Mummy, waiting her turn to register, and went over to talk with George.

"Sidonie is collecting a pot of quack balm," he said, "to rub into my legs."

"Quack balm?"

The nurse behind the desk shot him a severe look, but he merely shrugged at her. "Nurse McWorthy stirs up goopy pastes that are meant to soothe or even cure you, just as the quacks do, at village fetes. I don't know what she puts in mine, but it makes the skin tingle as if I'd stepped on a nest of fire ants!"

"Ouch," said the man sitting on a hard bench next to George's chair. "Fire ants are the meanest thing God put on this earth." He was the violinist we'd heard play the evening before. "I met a few hundred fire ants at a picnic once," he said. "In the Barbados, where I lived as a boy, in the Caribbean Sea."

George looked at him as if he'd claimed to have discovered a chest full of pirate gold.

"Did they sting or were they the biting kind?" he wanted to know.

"I did not stop to ask them," said the man. "I was running too fast and screaming too loudly. It felt as if they were doing both at the same time."

George grinned. "Do you have any scars?"

"That I do not. I spent the afternoon with my legs in a tub of ice and never went back to that terrible park again."

"They tried ice on these," said George, softly banging his thighs with his fists, "for days. But no luck. They wanted to cut them off, but my mother said no."

"You've been served a plate of rotten fish," said the musician, "as I have said before. And now must taste it the whole of your life."

"Have you met Mr. LaValle?" George asked me. I shook my head no.

Mummy, from her place in line, asked to be introduced to George, and he introduced us formally to Mr. LaValle.

"We heard you last night," said Mummy. "An hour of enchantment."

"Thank you, madam," said Mr. LaValle. He shifted his shoulder. "And now my tendons must pay for my vigor."

"Oh," said Mummy. "Your . . . tendons." Such personal information to be sharing with a stranger!

"One of the benefits of working at the Wellspring," said Mr. LaValle, "is that we are permitted treatments for what ails us, twice a month."

"That is benefit indeed," said my mother.

"Are you here to treat a troubled body or a troubled heart?" asked Mr. LaValle.

I heard her say, "Since my husband died . . ." and stopped listening. I let my eyes wander to the framed pictures and certificates on the wall. The Wellspring Spa had been awarded a place of honor on a list of similar facilities in the British Isles. Dr. Peter Baden had achieved Distinction in a Swiss clinic on Allergic Disorders. An oil painting showed pink blossoms and wide glossy leaves identified in graceful script: *Echinacea.* Nurse Elizabeth McWorthy had completed a course in Therapeutic Medicinals. Dr. Peter Baden had received Commendation from a clinic in Germany for Homeopathic Diagnostics.

"You have not yet tasted the waters?" asked Mr. LaValle.

"Today will be my first time," said Mummy.

"Yuck," said George.

"George," said Nurse Touati. "Your thoughts were not solicited." I moved out of her way as she tried to steer George's chair toward the exit, but Mr. Hart and Mrs. Upton arrived just then, causing more congestion. I found myself caught momentarily between Mrs. Upton's bosom and her uncle's hairy chin, but wiggled away to stand next to Mummy near the desk.

"Nurse Touati?" called the clinic nurse. "Don't leave without the ointment for George."

"Excuse me," said Mrs. Upton, not noticing that Mummy and Mr. LaValle had been waiting. "I was in yesterday to make this morning's appointment for my uncle, do you remember? I removed my coat because of the pleasant weather, and I seem to have lost a brooch that was pinned to the lapel."

"Could you wait a moment, madam?" said Nurse McWorthy. "I need to fill an order for this nurse here with her charge."

"Oh, I do apologize!" Mrs. Upton took in the scene around her more carefully, realizing how she'd spoken out of turn. Her uncle examined the certificates on the wall.

Nurse McWorthy stepped into the dispensary nook to find George's quack balm.

"If you don't believe me," George said to Mummy, "about how awful the waters are, then you're in for a nasty surprise."

"George!" said Nurse Touati.

But Mummy laughed. "I expect your opinion will ring in my ears when I take my first taste."

Nurse McWorthy returned from the dispensary with a blue-lidded pot. "I wonder you don't mix his balms and tonics yourself," she said to George's nurse, "though I suppose you daren't risk it."

"A weak joke, Lizzie," said Nurse Touati. "Please put the charge on his father's account."

A door behind the desk opened, and out stepped Alberto, our waiter from the evening before. Behind him was the doctor, whose name we knew was Baden. He was younger than I expected, with a brown beard trimmed to a point and light gray eyes.

"Please make another appointment for Alberto, Nurse," said Dr. Baden, glancing at the roomful of waiting guests. He looked straight at Mummy and smiled, and then at me, and smiled again. He waved hello at George, a regular patient, and beckoned to Mr. LaValle. The violinist wove his way through the crowd, which meant that I did not see how the new fuss began.

What I heard was Mrs. Upton's voice, unusually shrill. "Uncle?" she said. "Are you quite well?" His color was decidedly *not* well. "Will you sit for a moment?"

"No," said Mr. Hart, "I won't sit. I will go back to my room. I wish . . . I need to . . ." He blinked twice and gave his head a little shake, as if fighting off a moment of drowsiness or bewilderment.

"A rest will do you a world of good," said Mummy.

His smile held the gratitude of someone who wished to be elsewhere. "Thank you, Cora," he said. "We will find you this evening, I hope."

When did he begin to call her Cora instead of Mrs. Morton? It seemed a bold step on such short acquaintance, and not one that I found pleasing.

"I'll come with you, Uncle Ben." Mrs. Upton looked terribly worried. "I'll just . . ." She turned to the nurse, as Mr. Hart stumbled toward the door. "May I reschedule my uncle for tomorrow? If he is still unwell, I will inform you as early as possible."

"Yes, madam," said the nurse, making a note in the appointment book.

"And please, do keep in mind that my brooch is missing?" said Mrs. Upton. "It was a wedding gift from my uncle, just last week."

"Yes, madam," said the nurse, more brusquely this time. "If it comes to light, I will keep it safe for you. Good day."

Mrs. Upton hurried to her uncle's side, and very soon the hubbub of too many people died away. George was gone with his nurse. Mr. LaValle was with the doctor. Only Mummy and I remained at the desk, next in line for Nurse McWorthy's attention.

Mr. Hart had appeared healthy and jolly when we'd encountered him in the walkway. Was he so ill? Or had something in the room alarmed him? What had he been looking at that turned his face pink—and then as gray as dust?

CHAPTER 4

A Visit to the Underworld

"Mrs. Morton?" said the nurse. "Thank you for waiting so patiently through that busy moment! Would you and your daughter like a tour of the spa? The doctor will be ready for you in a few minutes."

"We'd like very much to look around," said Mummy. "And perhaps you will explain . . ." She hesitated. "The . . . logistics? Of how one gets from one place to another?" She was most nervous, I knew, about wearing her bathing costume in close proximity to other guests taking the cure also. Especially, I imagined, if Mr. Hart were one of those guests! What a horrible idea!

Nurse McWorthy's smile hinted that she was well-used to ladies being shy about having so little clothing on. "Women's hours in the Turkish baths are strictly separate from those of the men. Come this way," she said. "You'll soon see how it works."

I squeezed Mummy's hand as we were led into a whole new world.

"Goodness," said Mummy.

God's teeth! I thought but did not say. Only my sister's husband, James, was allowed to curse so brazenly. But this sight demanded an expression out of the ordinary. We were in a gorgeous, intimate cavern with vaulted ceilings and glimmering pools. Every inch of the walls, the floor and the graceful arcs above was tiled in a flowing mosaic masterpiece of color and pattern. We followed the nurse while information poured from her lips . . . *This is the Swedish sauna. Here is the pool with underwater jets. When you're ready for heat, the steam room is here. The doctor will suggest a particular order for your immersions. No, dear, the drinking pumps are by the entrance, there. These are the pipes that supply the steam rooms, and the hottest pool, the one with Epsom salts. Basins of ice chips over there. The lights are dim to encourage calm, and there are resting beds in the cubicles behind the curtain. This one is the frigid plunge, one minute recommended.*

Mummy shivered and the nurse chuckled. "Everyone reacts the same way," she said. "With a shiver! Believe it or not, you'll find yourself looking forward to the cold to recover from the heat of the sauna or steam.

"You are welcome to stay for any length of time, but we recommend that each visit begin with drinking the waters that come from the mineral springs underground, through these pumps, you see? They've made Harrogate famous. The doctor will discuss which best serves your particular needs. The sulphurous one is generally taken to treat gout or lumbago—which are not your complaints! We sit atop a well with the highest concentration of sulphur water in Europe. The chalybeate, or ferrous water, enhances the function of the brain and strengthens your internal organs."

"Goodness," said Mummy. These intimate matters were not her usual conversation.

"This door leads to the women's changing room. You'll be supplied each day with a fresh robe to wear between the hot rooms or pools. You see? Hooks on the columns beside every feature of the spa. It's a lot to take in, but you'll soon be comfortable making your way around. Any questions? The doctor is likely ready to see you now."

Dr. Baden made Mummy comfortable in the chair across from his own, at a grand desk of polished wood. The surface held one paper only, which the nurse had passed to him, with Mummy's name in tidy writing across the top. *Cora Eloise Morton.* One of my great talents was reading upside down. I'd taught myself this trick almost at the same time I'd learned to read the regular way. *Groveland, Barton Road, Torquay. 42 years. 2 daughters. Widow.* And so on.

"Welcome to Wellspring, Mrs. Morton." The doctor's palms were flat on the desk as he leaned slightly forward, giving Mummy a warm smile. I supposed he was quite handsome, with friendly eyes and a nice small beard—not one of those nasty, wiry nests one expected to see dotted with grains of rice and biscuit crumbs, like that worn by Mr. Hart.

"Nurse McWorthy is the mistress of all practical matters. I am here to attend the more serious afflictions, ailments of advanced age, and the guests like yourself, who want reparation after an interlude of illness or grief." He glanced at the paper in front of him and spoke his next words softly. "I am sorry to hear of your loss, Mrs. Morton. There is nothing more difficult to recover from than the death of a loved one."

I looked at Mummy to see whether suddenly expressed sympathy might upset her afternoon, but she accepted it calmly.

"Nurse has given you a tour?" said Dr. Baden. "Do you have any questions so far?"

"It all seems quite clear, Doctor, thank you," said Mummy. "I expect it will take a time or two for me to feel entirely at ease, but the facility is beautifully appointed."

"Your comfort is our main concern," said Dr. Baden. "I hope—I *know*—that after only two or three sessions, your dark mood will lift, your anxiety will lessen, and you will begin to bloom again." He twinkled at her. "After this afternoon's treatment, you'll eat a hearty tea and enter the evening with a spring in your step. This I promise."

Mummy glanced at me, as if embarrassed to feel optimistic that the doctor's words might come true.

"I have no doubt your daughter is eager to welcome back your good health and high spirits, Mrs. Morton. Isn't that true, miss? A spot of pink in her cheeks?"

I nodded vigorously, for that was just what I wanted. The pink-cheeked Mummy in high spirits had been in hiding for nearly two years, during the time of Papa's illness and then her hibernation after his death.

"Well, then." Dr. Baden stood to usher us out. "It is a genuine pleasure to welcome your family to Wellspring. I trust your first treatment will be splendid."

Mummy followed Nurse McWorthy into the changing room, and I hurried to meet Hector and Grannie Jane. We planned to visit the sunny garden while awaiting Mummy's report on the steam room and the cold plunge.

Grannie Jane settled with her knitting on a bench, which took longer than simply sitting. The benches were made of wrought iron and not particularly friendly to old bottoms, according to Grannie. The games steward loitered outside a small kiosk tucked under a tree. He turned out to be our waiter, Alberto. Except that he had changed—and not simply that his dashing white server's jacket had been replaced by a jaunty striped waistcoat with matching cap.

"What happened to your Italian accent?" I said.

"That's only for the dining room," he said. "Guests like a bit of continental flair, so I am Alberto when serving meals, but out here I'm plain old Bertie Barker, master of games." He efficiently tucked cushions in the right places to aid Grannie's comfort, and then concerned himself with us.

"What'll it be, kiddies? Shuttlecock? Croquet? Hoops and sticks?"

Hector did not hesitate. "Croquet, please."

"Righty-o," said Alberto. "You practice your strokes with the mallets and balls while I set up the hoops."

We had an old croquet set at our house in Torquay, but after Marjorie went away to school, there'd been no one to play with. My skills were still at the level of a six-year-old. Hector, however, proved to be a wonder. He took a particular stance when making a stroke, casting his eye from the ball to the hoop as if measuring a battleship. Right from the start he got extra turns. His blue ball was three hoops ahead by the time I had my first whack at the red one. First and only whack, because I sent the ball right off the court and onto the path. Hector's turn again.

"Did you see Mrs. Shelton's final resting place?" I stepped out of the way as he set up his next shot.

"Yes," he said. "It appears to be an ordinary bench. But it is a bench with *menace*."

"How so?" I was a bit peeved at missing a menacing bench.

"Ssh, while on the court," he said. I shushed and let him play. I kept to myself the many doings in the Wellspring clinic, which, admittedly, were all about bathing rather than unexpected death and not so very menacing. I might have become thoroughly dispirited about my inadequacy as a ball-whacker, but along came George in his rolling wicker chair. I seized the chance to forfeit my mallet to him and squeezed in between Grannie Jane and Nurse Touati on the bench, to watch and cheer. I kept clear of Grannie's elbow, as she *click-clicked* steadily, knitting another little white sweater for my sister's baby-to-be.

"George is good!" I said. "He holds the mallet so deftly that it does not hit the chair."

"He practices for many hours at a time," said Nurse Touati. "I feel about croquet as I suspect you do, Miss Morton. But for George, it is the one athletic game that he can play."

I guessed the same might be said of Hector. Until today I would have said that his skills lay decidedly elsewhere.

"What a pleasure it is," said Grannie Jane, "to excel at a sporting endeavor."

"Winning at croquet might be the best medicine George swallows each week," said Nurse Touati. "He is delighted when a new guest submits to a game, instead of always trouncing me."

"What happens if he doesn't win?" I asked. Hector had just hit a perfect roquet, sending George's yellow ball out of commission.

"I don't think it has ever happened," said Nurse Touati. "Mrs. Shelton came close two or three times, but she always managed to double tap toward the end of a game so that George pulled ahead."

Grannie Jane laughed. "It takes a clever woman to falter at the right moment."

Nurse Touati sighed. "She was clever, all right, but also kind to George without treating him like a pet or a mental defective. She'd bring her paper and brushes and let him paint while they talked."

"And why did she remove herself from the hotel?" said Grannie Jane. "Only to arrive at a mere lodging house?"

"It's a nice enough place," said Nurse Touati. "Near to where I live with George's family. Mrs. Woolsey keeps a clean house. She is overly chummy on occasion, but not one of those landladies with a nose in everyone's pie."

"A quality to be commended," said Grannie Jane. And one that I happened to know she did not possess.

Hector's blue ball hit the center peg with a sharp smack. First one home.

"Mrs. Shelton had digestion troubles." Nurse Touati whispered so that the boys could not hear. "She'd had bad headaches for days. We thought maybe the rich food at the hotel was causing the cramps. Truth is, Nurse McWorthy did not feel kindly toward Mrs. Shelton. There was a friendship, you see, between guest and doctor, that rankled the nurse. She prepared the tonics and happily sent Mrs. Shelton on her way."

A whoop from the lawn interrupted Nurse Touati. George had engineered his ball through two hoops and won an extra shot at a crucial moment.

Nurse Touati and I applauded, disloyal though it was to Hector. But Hector did not require loyalty in order to triumph. He efficiently knocked George's ball out of the way and performed his own double hoop to win. He turned at once to shake George's hand with grave respect.

"It is an honor to play such an opponent," he said.

George may have felt Nurse Touati's eyes on him, for he attempted a gracious reply. "You didn't let the cripple win, that's in your favor . . ."

Nurse Touati produced a bottle of lemonade from the satchel strapped to the handles of the wheelchair. We took turns drinking from two tin cups. Hector hesitated before sharing a cup, but thirst won him over. It seemed for a while that we had strayed far from the interesting topic of Mrs. Shelton's sudden death, until wily Grannie asked whether there had been a funeral?

No, there had not. The poor woman's body remained at the undertaker still, awaiting instructions. The police had come to the hotel trying to discover who her next of kin might be, but Mr. Smythe, the manager, had sent them away unsatisfied.

"He refused to release the information on her card," said George, "saying as it was confidential. But Sidonie knows, from being her friend and having coffee together a few times, that she had no family with whom she was in contact. There is no plan for a funeral."

"Was the coroner involved?" asked Grannie Jane. "Would that not be usual in the case of a death like this?"

"Harrogate shares an old ninny of a coroner with other nearby towns," said Nurse Touati. "It was fortunate that Dr. Baden was here to look after things. Mrs. Shelton had been his patient. Her rotten illness was such that a sudden end was not really a shock. Just, terribly sad for those of us who cared about her."

"I've asked my dad," said George, "couldn't we pay for a funeral? Maybe we will yet." He glanced at his nurse, but she only reminded him that it was nearly time for tea and they must depart.

Grannie Jane needed another ball of wool. She would wait in the lobby while we went upstairs to fetch it for her. Unhappy voices rang out as Hector and I reached the first landing. We stayed where we were. Could there be anything more awkward than interrupting an argument? *Listening* to an argument, however, was usually illuminating.

"My dear Josie," we heard. "Your husband is a perfectly nice chap. Pleasant and respectful, and he dotes on you, anyone can see that."

"He is also a clever inventor!" It was Mrs. Upton's voice, harsh with frustration. "If you would take ten minutes to look at his drawings, you'd see that I'm not just being a proud and silly bride. I would never ask you to hire him if he weren't talented. Please, Uncle Ben? I've put the portfolio of designs in your room."

"You shouldn't have done that, Josie. Every young man needs to start out using his own wits, not relying on the helping hand of an elderly relative. How will he feel if any small achievement is a credit to me and not to him?"

Mrs. Upton gave a cry of exasperation. "You are purposely standing in the way of Eddie's success! I've never known you to behave so hurtfully! If you cannot be more openhearted, I—I—I'll find myself wishing for terrible things!"

CHAPTER 5

A WORRYING TELEPHONE CALL

WE CREPT DOWN THE STAIRS, holding our breath and treading carefully so as not to make a sound. Then we turned around and banged our way back up, chattering noisily, only to find the passage empty. Our room was a bit jumbled when we came in, with my mother on her knees hunting under the bed.

"Mummy! Hello! How did your treatment go?"

"It was sheer pleasure from beginning to end," she said. "Even the nasty-tasting water!" I could see from the warmth in her cheeks that this was no exaggeration. Hurrah for the doctor!

"Madame?" said Hector. "Something is lost?"

"I have looked everywhere for my indigo scarf," she said. "Was I not wearing it this morning?"

"I think you were, Mummy. Don't fret. It will turn up."
She said those very words to me whenever I misplaced
something. "Do you know where Grannie has put her
knitting basket?"

Mummy took out a different scarf to wear, pearl gray
and silky. Hector retrieved the requested ball of wool,
and we descended for an evening of music and delicious food.

Mr. Hart arrived, waving from across the room with
one hand and smoothing down his abundant beard with
the other.

"The young people have gone to hear music at the
bandstand in the park," he told us, "so you have only me
for company this evening."

"I didn't realize they played music in the park," said
Mummy. "Does it happen every night? I'd love to go one
evening, wouldn't you, Aggie?"

I made the forbidden gesture, a shrug, but no one even
noticed because Mr. Hart was drawling on. "Once or
twice a week, I think. We can ask Mr. Bessel, the bell captain. I will be delighted to accompany you," he said, "but
gone are my dancing days, sad to say."

"Have you recovered from your moment this morning?" Mummy said.

"I'm feeling a bit glum," he admitted. "I've put my
niece badly out of sorts. Perhaps it's a good thing she's

gone off for an evening of music and dancing. Give us both a chance to restore our best selves."

"Whatever happened?" said Mummy, in her gentlest voice.

"Did I mention already that I run a family enterprise? Called Hart's Umbrellas. You may have heard of us."

"I *own* an umbrella from Hart's!" said Mummy. "A gift from my late husband some years ago. That's you? How marvelous!"

"I, too, own a Hart's," said Grannie Jane. "Best umbrella I have ever possessed. Snaps up and down as smoothly as the day I bought it."

Mr. Hart chuckled and looked pleased. "Glad to hear it, madam," he said. "My father was the original Hart, and I took over when he died. My brother—Josie's father—became an architect, not interested in business. Josie has been on at me to take a look at young Eddie's designs, trying to find the boy a job since he can't seem to do it for himself. I've brushed her off, thinking he ought to buck up and be a man, now that he's a husband . . ." He took a mouthful of his drink and the ice clicked against his teeth. "Well, I've just had a look, and I'm overdue for a serving of humble pie. The boy is pretty good after all."

"I applaud you," said Mummy. "It is not often that a man will admit to making a hasty decision. Before the night is over, you will make amends with your niece and all will be well."

Mr. Hart leaned over and patted Mummy's arm. "You have cheered me right up, Cora," he said. "I shall endeavor to find a place for young Eddie at Hart's Umbrellas."

The music stopped, and there was a shuffling onstage as the musicians put their instruments away in cases.

"A subtle suggestion to move along to dinner," said Grannie Jane.

"We needn't rush," said Mummy. "It's so pleasant here. And, you see? The quartet is coming to greet the guests."

Indeed, the violinist, Mr. LaValle, approached our table with a warm smile.

"Good evening, Mrs. Morton," he said. "A pleasure to see you here, surrounded by family."

"This is my mother-in-law," Mummy introduced Grannie Jane. "Also Mrs. Morton. You've met my daughter, Aggie, and this is her friend Hector, who is visiting from Belgium. Mr. Hart is another guest of the hotel. How is your shoulder, Mr. LaValle?"

"A little sore, but on the mend," he said. "I hope you did not notice sluggish bowing?"

No, no, we assured him. The music was lovely, his playing divine. He took all the compliments with grace, as if it were his violin who performed, without assistance from him.

"Aggie is a musician also," said Mummy. "She plays the piano and the mandolin."

"Mummy!" I wished to crawl under the table. Mr. LaValle was a real violinist! My plunking hardly qualified as making music!

"Do you have time to sit with us?" said Mummy. "We can delay our dinner a little longer."

"It is part of our job," admitted Mr. LaValle, "to mingle, and to urge you all to attend the Promenade on Mondays and Thursdays." He borrowed a chair from the empty table next to ours and propped his violin case against his knee.

"In French," said Hector, "this word *promenade* means merely to walk."

Mr. LaValle's smile broadened. "And that is exactly what occurs," he said. "Of more interest to those rather older than you, Master Hector. The quartet takes turns with the hotel pianist, to play while our guests walk in graceful circles around the ballroom. It is the social part of a Wellspring health treatment."

"I prefer croquet," said Hector. Then, realizing that such a reply might be considered impolite, he added, "but I will walk in circles simply to hear you perform again, sir."

"And do you play an instrument, Master Hector?" asked Mr. LaValle.

"The recorder," said Hector, "but not very well. I prefer to listen."

"Oh, good evening, Dr. Baden," said Mummy. "Would you care to join us?" Another chair was hastily drawn up to make room at our little table. "We are an odd assortment of new acquaintance." She made another round of introductions.

"Ah, yes," said Dr. Baden, when Mr. Hart's name was offered. "I was meant to see you this morning, was I not? I understand you had a bit of a bad spell?"

Mr. Hart winced, and avoided the doctor's inquiring gaze. "Bad kipper for breakfast, I expect," he said. "I'm tip-top now."

He did not look entirely tip-top. A faint flush had come to his cheeks above the beard, and his hands were clenched around a napkin as if squeezing it for juice. I did not believe his discomfort had anything to do with kippers. Was he still on edge about the argument with Mrs. Upton? Unhappy that the spotlight was on Mr. LaValle instead of on himself? Was he the sort of man to feel uneasy sitting with the dark-skinned musician, as many white English people were? Or was he merely embarrassed at having walked out of the clinic this morning with other patients watching?

And why had he done that?

"It is a pleasure to meet you all," said the doctor. "And you, Mrs. Morton, are the picture of health this evening. Already a new bloom in your cheeks."

Mummy smiled, making her even prettier, as everyone remarked on her rosy serenity. I tried not to care that three of our company were men who eyed her with admiration—and none of them Papa. I particularly ignored Grannie watching me with steady eyes.

"Master Hector," said Mr. LaValle. Hector blinked in surprise. "I have traveled with an orchestra in Europe and had the joy of playing in La Bellone in Brussels. Is this your hometown by any chance?"

"Non, monsieur," said Hector. "I come from a little village north of the city of Spa."

"Spa?" said Mummy.

"Alas, Brussels was our only stop in Belgium," said Mr. LaValle. "Then Luxembourg, and across the Alps to Milan."

"Is there a connection to what we think of as a spa?" said Mummy.

"Like ours here at Wellspring?" asked the doctor. "And those in Europe where I have worked?"

"Indeed, yes," said Hector. "The mineral waters in my region have . . ." He made his fingers dance. "The sparkle! I think you English say, *fizzy*? Our Spa gives the word for your spa."

"Have you traveled much to Europe?" Mr. LaValle asked Mr. Hart. "Belgium? Germany?"

"I have not," said Mr. Hart. He took a gulp of his

drink and then another. "I had a dear cousin who lived in Switzerland," he said. "She traveled there to be the governess for a diplomat in Geneva, two years ago. She remained with the family for many months, but at some point, she fell in love." He withdrew a handkerchief from his breast pocket. "This led directly to her death."

"Oh no!" said Mummy. "Whatever happened?"

"Her brother was my best playmate when we were children," said Mr. Hart, "and Phoebe too, though she was somewhat younger. As the eldest of the cousins, I led the pack and watched out for the little ones. Phoebe was a sweet girl, with a saucy sense of humor."

He went silent for a moment and stared away, at nothing, it seemed, though I fancied he was seeing Phoebe's face. "She fell in love," said Mr. Hart, "with a man she met in Switzerland, or so we think. A Mr. Foster. We never met him. She wrote just days before the wedding, too late for any of us to travel there to celebrate with her. She included a copy of the photograph taken on the occasion of their engagement, which I carry to this day. She looked very happy. Only two weeks later she was dead. Food poisoning, apparently. On the wedding trip, in the south of Spain."

We all gasped with sadness on his behalf. Mummy and the doctor put down their drinks quite clumsily, but Mr. Hart soon collected himself and gave his shoulders a little shake. "Forgive me," he said to the violinist. "Your mention of the Alps stirred up my memories, casting a shadow over the stories of your travels."

"No need to apologize, sir. Your story is a sad one." Mr. LaValle stood and half bowed. "Please excuse me. I must now depart for my engagement at the bandstand in the park, where I shall play dance tunes into the night . . ."

"My niece will be one of your audience," said Mr. Hart. "With her new husband, on *their* honeymoon. A better marriage to celebrate than that of my cousin."

Mr. LaValle clapped a hand on his shoulder, picked up his violin case and made an elegant farewell to each of us before slipping away.

"I, too, must be off," said Dr. Baden. "An early night, I think."

"Do you have quarters in the hotel, Doctor?" said Grannie Jane.

"I have a small suite in the spa wing," said Dr. Baden. "Close to the clinic in case I'm needed—though emergencies are rare in hydrotherapy!" He bowed to Mummy and Grannie and left us.

We were obliged to invite Mr. Hart to join our table for dinner. I believe we all, by then, wished for our own family circle, but his solitude spoke to Mummy's kindness, and we were stuck with his company. I ordered chicken roasted with young carrots, and Hector had

Yorkshire pudding with roast beef, which came rare, thickly sliced and drizzled with gravy.

"I wish Tony were here to help you with that," I said, thinking of how my dog's nose would be twitching.

"Tony misses nothing," said Hector, "as I need no help." And, indeed, he ate the whole meal with gusto. We had ordered our dessert when the buzzardy bell captain appeared at Mr. Hart's shoulder, wringing his hands.

"I beg your pardon, sir," he said, "and madam." He bowed slightly at Mummy, as if she were—*ugh*—the wife of Mr. Hart. Grannie and Hector simultaneously raised one eyebrow.

"You have been summoned to the telephone, Mr. Hart. You may take the call in the hotel office, just off the lobby."

"I beg your pardon?" said Mr. Hart. "I did not expect a call this evening . . ."

"I'm afraid, sir, it seems to be bad news. The caller indicated that your niece has had some sort of accident."

CHAPTER 6

A DISMAL DISCOVERY

THE BLOOD DRAINED from Mr. Hart's face as he took in the meaning of the bell captain's words. He lurched to his feet, made an effort to politely leave our table and was gone before any of us could speak. We watched him leave the dining room, in such a tizzy that he clutched at the doorframe to steady himself.

"Gracious," said Grannie Jane.

"Whatever can have happened?" said Mummy. "They were only going dancing."

"I blame the bell captain for delivering the news with the subtlety of a hammer," said Grannie Jane. "The girl has likely turned an ankle, jiggling about to ragtime music, and only needs a second man to assist her in limping home."

"I do hope it's as simple as that," said Mummy.

"Mr. Hart was nicely contrite about their disagreement, was he not?"

"Quite unlike a man," agreed Grannie Jane.

"And now she'll hear the good news that her uncle has changed his mind about Eddie," I said. "Mr. Upton, I mean. Being talented, after all."

Our desserts arrived, almond pudding with chocolate shavings. The pianist played nocturnes that lulled us, for a while, into believing that all was well.

Mummy ordered chamomile tea. "You two may be excused," she said to Hector and me. She was stretching her evening as long as she could. "Collect the room key at the desk and go on up. We'll be there eventually."

We arrived in the lobby, just as Mr. and Mrs. Upton came through the main entrance. Mrs. Upton's dress was a swirl of parrot green, a curl of her hair coming unpinned as she tossed her head in laughter at something her husband whispered in her ear. Hector and I glanced at each other. Wasn't she meant to have come to some harm? Only half an hour ago, her uncle had been flushed and frantic about a telephone call that told him so.

"Oh, hello." Mrs. Upton noticed us, as her husband requested their key. "We've had an evening I'll remember forever. I can hardly bear for it to end."

"But, madame—" said Hector.

"Your uncle," I said. "He went looking for you."

Her face clouded. "Why would he do that?" I remembered then the scalding words she'd thrown at him before supper. *If you cannot be more openhearted, I'll find myself wishing for terrible things!*

"He receives a telephone call alerting him of an accident," said Hector.

"He left the table," I said. "Before dessert. The Buzz—the bell captain came to fetch him. He said that you'd been hurt . . . or something . . . what did he say, Hector? He rushed away to find you."

Mr. Upton was with us now, hearing our report. "Very odd," he said. "As you can see, she is perfectly fit." He wiggled his eyebrows up and down. "*Perrr*-fectly perfect."

"How could such a mistake be made?" said Mrs. Upton. "Where do you suppose he went?"

"He was going to the bandstand," I said. "He thought he'd find you there."

"We didn't see him," said Mr. Upton.

"We came along the road," his wife reminded him, pointing to the hotel's main door. "The shortcut through the garden seemed too short for such a beautiful evening."

"He is, perhaps, taking the garden route," said Hector. "You miss each other."

"But why would someone telephone to say—" I began.

"I'll nip upstairs and see if he has returned, shall I?" said Mr. Upton, holding up his key. "We have connecting rooms."

"Thank you, darling," said Mrs. Upton. "I might just take a peek into the garden. Even though he was so contrary this afternoon, I wouldn't want the poor dear to be wandering about looking for us when we're already home."

"We'll come with you." I saw that her husband would be concerned if she ventured out alone. "Hector and I will help you look."

"That's kind of you," said Mr. Upton. "We'll meet back here, then, shall we?"

Hector and I followed Mrs. Upton along the passage to the garden.

"Silly uncle," she muttered. "First an angry fuss, then a worried fuss. What fuss will happen next?"

"You might like to know," I said to her back, "that Mr. Hart expressed some admiration for your husband during supper tonight."

She spun around. "What did he say?" All sign of muttering and frustration had flown away, so keen was she to hear this news.

"He said he'd had a chance to look at some drawings, and that the boy—that's what he called him—the boy was pretty good." I left off "after all," as it did not seem necessary.

Mrs. Upton's eyes lit up. "But, that's wonderful!" she said. "I knew he'd see how clever Eddie is, if he'd only take a few minutes to look." She let out a little squeal, which rather took me by surprise. "Let's find him! I can't wait to thank him, and then tell Eddie. Maybe this will mean a job!" She scurried to open the door, letting in a gust of fresh spring air.

The outside world was alive with cricket-song. Light in the garden was cast by lanterns hanging from iron posts, illuminating circles on the path and flashes on tree trunks and benches. I hesitated, suddenly spooked by a place only seen before dappled with sunshine.

"Uncle Ben?" Mrs. Upton's voice would have been normal indoors, perhaps, but now sounded hollow, with all of night surrounding it.

"Monsieur?" Hector whispered, barely heard above the drizzling fountain and the chirping of insects.

"I suppose he is already in the park," I said. But we remained where we were, briefly captivated by shifting shadows that seemed to hint at a sinister enchantment. Then a pony trap went by in the road beyond the gate, the clip-clop of hooves waking us from our moment's hesitation. A few steps farther, we stopped again, for the very worst reason of all. There, awkwardly sprawled on a bench, was Mr. Hart. His eyes stared unseeing at the branches above, and despite our calling, he remained as still as stone.

CHAPTER 7

A WRETCHED INTERVAL

MRS. UPTON SANK TO her knees before her uncle, repeating his name, shaking his shoulders so violently that his head lolled toward her, and she fell back with a horrified gasp.

"Eddie!" she cried out, looking around.

"Hector," I said. "We should summon the doctor!"

A quick thinker and brave as well, Hector slid his fingers beneath the man's collar and held them there for many seconds.

"I do not feel a pulse," he said, "but the skin is warm."

"Warm!" cried Mrs. Upton. "Then he's alive!"

"I do not think so," whispered Hector to me.

"Will you find the doctor?" I said. "And her husband also."

"Go!" said Mrs. Upton. "Please, run!"

"Oui, madame." Hector turned away but had taken no more than two steps when she called out again. "Don't leave me! I cannot be alone with him! Where's Eddie? What has happened to Eddie?"

"I'm staying with you," I said. "Hector will fetch Dr. Baden. And, um, Eddie."

Hector hurried along the path, as close to running as I had ever seen.

"Uncle Ben?" Mrs. Upton's voice was softer now, scarcely a whimper. "Uncle?"

She knelt in the grass by the bench, making me worry for her dress and stockings. I kept one hand on her shoulder as she wept, while I had a good look at Mr. Benedict Hart, soul in transition.

It did not seem that he was sitting with intent, but rather had fallen or been flung upon the seat. One hand lay against his throat, the other arm was thrown wide, resting along the back of the bench. His face was not calm, but nor was it contorted with anguish. It showed more a look of startlement, as if flummoxed by the last thing his living eyes had seen.

A cluster of angels greeting him beside a pearly gate? A critical fellow with a long white beard who sat upon a throne? Or was it something here in the garden that had ended his life with a suddenness he did not expect? *A rabid fox leaping from the underbrush? An attacker demanding his billfold?* Or, merely, *the final clumsy beats of a worn-out heart?*

Mrs. Upton began to mutter words of apology to her uncle. "You are closer to me than my own father," she said, and, "If I could snatch back my angry words!" and, "You've been the best uncle a girl could have; I only wished for you and Eddie to be wonderful friends . . ."

I could not see an injury, though it was dark, and he was awkwardly positioned. No obvious blood or sign of assault. How could it be that this new corpse had been slugging wine only half an hour earlier? Making my mother blush with his banal compliments? Would such a man come outside, sit down on a bench and die? Was his heart so overtaxed with worry for his niece that it simply stopped ticking?

But . . . that call on the telephone! *That* is what caused his worry! What of that? A mistake? A prank? But . . . why? I peered into the darkness, beyond the croquet lawn, to the hulking shadows of the grove of trees. I turned slowly, away from the twinkling shine of the hotel windows, past the trellis and the formal garden, toward the gate. Wait! Had I heard footsteps? Did something move beside the hedge? Or was it only a breeze wobbling a branch? I shivered. Was someone watching us right now? I stared at the spot but could see no one, and heard nothing beyond the lazy trickle of the fountain and Mrs. Upton's urgent murmurs.

"Ohh, uncle!" wailed Mrs. Upton. She had stopped her entreaties and succumbed to sorrow. It would be false to claim that *I* felt sorrow, but I *did* have a moment's remorse for thinking him a toad.

The hotel door banged open and here came Hector, not with Mr. Upton or the doctor, but followed by the officious Mr. Smythe. On reaching us, Mr. Smythe nudged Hector off the path and pushed in front as if trying to win a footrace.

"What's this, what's this?" He leaned over Mr. Hart and then recoiled with a grunt. "What's the matter with him?"

"As I tell you, monsieur—" Hector began.

"He's deaddd!" cried Mrs. Upton. She stared at the hotel, her eyes scanning the bright window squares. "Where's Ed-d-ddie?" She had begun to tremble all over, making her words shake too.

"I cannot find your husband, madame," said Hector. "The doctor also is not answering when I knock at his rooms. I ask a maid, who might be of assistance in a crisis? She tells me Mr. Smythe, but . . ."

But Mr. Smythe was proving not to be a reliable man in a crisis. He'd retreated several paces from the body on the bench and had covered his face with his hands.

"I will find a shawl for Mrs. Upton." Hector was an *excellent* man on such occasions; I knew this from experience. "And perhaps to ask the bell captain to telephone to the police?"

"No!" The word *police* had a powerful effect on Mr. Smythe's ability to focus. "We will *not* be alerting the police!" He glanced at the shivering Mrs. Upton and sighed, pulling off his jacket to throw over her shoulders. He stood with his back toward Mr. Hart, as if the sight were unbearable, and put a hand on Hector's shoulder, preventing him from going anywhere. His voice was cajoling when he began again. "What I mean is, the police can be more an interference than a comfort when you're in the midst of—"

The gate creaked open. Dr. Baden was here!

"At last," said Mr. Smythe.

The doctor took in the situation with a swift look. He calmly assisted Mrs. Upton to her feet and suggested that we move a little away. He put a finger to Mr. Hart's neck, as Hector had done, and then to his wrist. He pushed the eyelids closed, then turned to Mrs. Upton.

"I'm sorry, madam. This must be very shocking to you, though having read your uncle's file only this morning, it is not really a surprise. I believe he has suffered a heart attack, though *suffer* may be too strong a word. It appears to have been a quick death and not painful."

So efficient! Mrs. Upton nodded, and wiped her eyes with one hand while clutching the borrowed jacket closed with the other. The door to the hotel opened, briefly flashing more light into the garden as a man's silhouette stepped through.

"Eddie!"

Mr. Upton halted in shock at the scene, then embraced his wife. The rest of us watched while he kissed her hair and whispered things like, *Oh, Josie, my darling, oh sweetheart.* And then, "Whose jacket is this?"

"Where *were* you?" said Mrs. Upton. "The French boy was hunting for you!"

"Belgian," murmured Hector.

"I went up to the room to see if—" Mr. Upton looked again at the corpse on the bench and winced.

"Excuse me," said Dr. Baden. "I believe we need to take some action here."

"No police," said Mr. Smythe. "Better for all if we avoid the police."

The doctor cleared his throat and spoke in his comforting way. "I would like to make a few practical suggestions," he said. "May I do that, Mr. Upton? Will your wife agree?"

The Uptons nodded, reaching for each other's hand, Mrs. Upton seeming to forgive that her husband had not been at her side for her darkest moment.

"In a matter like this," said Dr. Baden, "with a death fitting to his ill health, there is no reason for involving the coroner or the police." He put up a hand to shush Mr.

Smythe's eager support. "The location of the poor man's death is perhaps out of the ordinary, but the manner is not. As a doctor, I can advise officially. If you concur, Mrs. Upton, I will instead notify the undertaker, who will come to remove the body . . ." Here he paused for Mrs. Upton to whimper. "And to care for it as kindly as any family member. Does this suit?"

The Uptons nodded, looking a bit stupefied.

"But now . . ." The doctor glanced at Mr. Hart, sitting quietly on the bench. "I suggest that Mrs. Upton and the children go inside, while Smythe and I, with your assistance, Mr. Upton? We may put the gentleman in a more comfortable position."

"Oh!" I said. "Rigor mortis!"

Dr. Baden looked at me quite sharply, but kept his voice even. "Yes, indeed, Miss Morton. It will make an immeasurable difference if he lies down before his limbs begin to stiffen." This caused renewed mewling from Mrs. Upton, and I saw my error in speaking the grim words aloud. But if Mr. Hart stayed sitting with his head tipped over and his arm flung out and his hand to his throat . . . rigor mortis would begin to settle in before another hour had passed, and there'd be no hope of changing his position for many more hours after that, when his muscles relaxed once more. A picture came to my mind of black-clad undertakers . . . *The men shuffled into the hotel garden, bearing between them a canvas stretcher. Their feet were wrapped in rags to keep their boot soles from clattering on the stone path and disturbing the departing spirit. "Gone stiff," said one to the other. "I dunno if we'll be able to fit him on . . ." With no more talk, they placed the stretcher as near as they could to the bench and began to wrestle the unwieldy—and unyielding—corpse . . .*

"Aggie," said Hector. "We must assist Mrs. Upton."

Mrs. Upton was reluctant to leave her husband, but the doctor insisted that she did not wish to witness what next would happen to her uncle.

"It is no sight for a lady at the best of times," said Dr. Baden, "but in the case of a loved one, I strongly advise . . ."

"I'll tell you something," said Mr. Smythe, backing away up the path. "I can be more useful if I place the telephone call to the undertaker." He'd finally understood what would be required if he stayed in the garden. "My back has been giving me twinges," he added. "I'll summon old John Napoli to come along with his wagon, and—" Smythe turned about and trotted to the door. He was inside before Hector and I had taken Mrs. Upton's arms for support.

"You two will stay with her until I come?" said Mr. Upton.

Yes, certainly we would. We led her inside, into the shock of the bright lobby with its shiny floors and plush sofas, and the rippling glory of the piano. And Mummy was there, speaking urgently to the Buzzard. Seeing us, her fingers flew to her mouth.

"Aggie! Hector! We thought you'd gone to bed!" she cried, "but when we came upstairs you weren't there! And then the maid said there'd been an incident in the garden, the doctor had been wanted, and I . . . I had a horrible thought . . ."

"Oh, Mummy." I wrapped my arms around her middle and felt her arms slide around me. We hugged for half a minute, each losing a few tears. Not for the dead man in the garden, but for Papa, who we still missed more than ever we said aloud.

Hector gave a small cough, and Mummy finally looked at the woman with us. "Mrs. Upton? Are you ill? Sit down, please, sit." Three of us managed to get Mrs. Upton seated on one of the deep crimson sofas. She sank back and began to cry, silently but enormously. Tears streamed, shoulders shook, mouth gasped.

I explained to Mummy in just a few words. Could she discern upon our faces that we had only just missed meeting a departing spirit? If anyone might understand the forlorn, engulfing sorrow of losing a beloved person, it was Mummy. She told us to please go upstairs to let Grannie Jane know we were not lost, and then turned her full attention to Mrs. Upton. Mr. Smythe approached as we departed, to say that the undertaker would arrive shortly. Mummy brushed him away, scolding him not to bother the poor lady with such matters at a time like this. He lingered, and at last confessed he wanted to reclaim his coat.

Hector and I withheld our laughter until safely on the stairs to the second floor.

Grannie, naturally, was agog to hear the news. "From the beginning until now," she said, tying the cord on her dressing gown. "I want to know every little thing."

We told about meeting the Uptons as they returned from dancing at the bandstand. How they'd walked back along Swan Road, the longer route, instead of coming through the garden gate. How they'd had no injury or illness and were confused by our report of a telephone summons that claimed otherwise. How Mr. Upton had dashed upstairs to see whether Mr. Hart might be in their suite, and how Hector and I followed the garden path with Mrs. Upton to see if her uncle had gone that way. And there he'd been, sitting crookedly on the bench beside the croquet lawn, life extinguished.

"I find it particularly suspicious," I said, "that he died right after a telephone call that required him to rush out into the night for an accident that had not happened! I think we've stumbled across another murder. Do you not agree?"

"You mustn't get your hopes up, Agatha dear," said Grannie Jane.

Too late for that!

"Excuse me, madame," said Hector, from the window. "There is activity in the garden."

We flocked to see what we could from the padded window seat. Though it now was well past twilight and the view partially obscured by leafy trees, the garden lanterns and newly risen moon allowed us to watch two figures gently transfer Mr. Hart from the bench to a stretcher. It was nearly just as I'd imagined, except that he'd been waiting in a suitable, reclining position. The doctor closed the garden gate behind them, stood a moment beside the bench as if in prayer, and came up the path to the hotel.

"Mr. Upton must have gone already to find his wife," I said.

"Meaning that your mother's care will no longer be needed," said Grannie Jane, "and she will arrive to find that no one has brushed teeth or hair."

We scurried to correct this and were in our beds when Mummy appeared, Hector behind his screen and I tucked in next to where Mummy would join me shortly. Grannie inquired if there were any further news.

"Such a sad thing," said Mummy. "The poor girl is dismayed that her last exchange with her uncle was a harsh one. Not an easy sadness to deny, though I did my best to tell her how excited he'd been about her husband's drawings."

"The memory of their quarrel will fade with time," said Grannie. "She will remember only that she was here, a companion to the end for a solitary man. Unlike the other woman who died last week, poor soul. Apparently alone in the world."

"The manager, Mr. Smythe, is somewhat self-serving," said Mummy. "He is determined to avoid any fuss concerning the hotel. Fortunately, the doctor was very calm and took care of removing the body and so on. Such a ghastly coincidence, that there should be two deaths in so short a time."

"I have never held coincidence in much esteem," said Grannie Jane. "It always disappoints as a plot device in a novel and even more so in real life. The notion that two people should die on park benches across the road from each other within a matter of days . . . and have no connection? Pish." She patted my foot, poking up under the quilt. "Good night, my pets. Sweet dreams."

CHAPTER 8

A MORNING IN MOURNING

I AWOKE THE NEXT morning rather hungry, and with a weighty matter on my sleepy mind. It was the first Thursday in nearly five decades that no Mr. Hart had roamed the earth. The earth, I considered, changed its inhabitants every day. Some died, more were born, and the rest of us were passing through, occasionally bumping up against one another in the most unlikely ways. How did it come to be Hector and me who stood on the doorstep at Mr. Hart's departure? Particularly as . . . (I pulled the pillow over my face) I had indulged in unkind thoughts during each of our previous encounters. Could I admit to *relief* that I would no longer see him leering at my mother?

We went for breakfast in the dining room, thinking to divert Mr. and Mrs. Upton from the empty place at their table by inviting them to join ours. Mummy greeted Mrs. Upton with an embrace and took particular care in ordering Earl Grey tea as a restorative beverage.

"The bergamot, you know. It elevates the mood."

Our breakfasts were delivered and devoured with contentment. Mummy had not blinked at my order, this being one of the indirect advantages to finding a dead body. I ate four pieces of toasted bread with honey, always a treat, and infinitely better than porridge.

The newspaper that arrived with breakfast was called *The Yorkshire Daily*. If the Lord Mayor of London were seated next to us, Grannie Jane still would read the news. This morning she skipped past reports of Derby residents recovering from an earthquake, and the bit announcing that the King's favorite bull had won first prize in the spring cattle show. (Would anyone dare to award him third place, if that was what the bull deserved?) Grannie was seeking mention of dead bodies in Harrogate. She saw nothing about Mr. Benedict Hart—thank goodness, with his niece sitting right there!—but found a paragraph about Mrs. Shelton.

THE YORKSHIRE DAILY

APRIL 16, 1903

DEAD LADY
Still Unclaimed!!

by FRANK THOMAS

The BANDSTAND CORPSE has been given a name!! Found in Valley Gardens Park on Saturday last, the dead woman has been identified as Mrs. Lidia Shelton, widow, and thought to be a native of Durham. Police removed the body from the park where boys had mocked her final gasps and, according to witnesses, stolen her handbag. Mrs. Woolsey of Beulah Place informed officers on Saturday evening that her lodger was missing. This led to the discovery that Mrs. Shelton had been a guest in poor health at the Wellspring Hotel for over three weeks before moving to Mrs. Woolsey's lodging house during the Easter weekend. Her remains will reside at Napoli & Son, Undertakers of Harrogate, until the executor of her estate can be notified. Any further information about her background or family should be submitted at the Harrogate office of the Yorkshire Police. The investigation is headed by Detective Inspector "Big Joe" Henry. The Wellspring management expressed regrets at Mrs. Shelton's passing but noted that her health was improved, not harmed, by her treatment at the Wellspring Hotel & Spa.

"The headlines in Yorkshire are even more lurid than in Torquay," said Grannie with a gleam of pleasure. She folded the newspaper and tucked it into her knitting bag.

Mrs. Upton gave a slight shudder. "That is the saddest, loneliest end I can imagine," she said. "People thought it odd that Uncle Benedict joined us on our wedding trip, but thank goodness he was not traveling alone when he passed."

Her husband put down his porridge spoon and reached over to squeeze her hand. "And as he was paying for it, we couldn't say no."

"*Ssh*, Eddie!"

His face was red, from having just shaved I guessed, because a tiny dollop of soap foam shone in one of his big ears. Next to her husband's florid complexion, Mrs. Upton seemed extra pale, betraying a night of little sleep. She wore a dress of soft violet, with a high neckline, making the shadows under her eyes violet also. Mummy had looked just this way for *months* after Papa died, as if she were fading into a spectral being, preparing to meet him graveside.

"Mrs. Upton," said Mummy, "I have been considering your plight of being bereaved far from your home and your own wardrobe. I know there must be a mourning supplier in Harrogate, as everywhere, someone who rents the proper blacks and veils. But I wondered . . . perhaps, would you like to borrow an item or two from me while you're here? I am still in half-mourning for my husband and have plenty of—"

Mrs. Upton clasped her hands together and interrupted Mummy's offer. "Oh, Mrs. Morton!" she cried. "Such kindness! To someone you hardly know! I would be *so* grateful for something to wear while we pass these few days making arrangements. I brought nothing with me but spring colors and feel so very wrong!"

Mummy pressed her arm and looked pleased to be useful. "You'll come up to our room before lunch," she said, "after my hydrotherapy treatment."

"Thank you, Mrs. Morton," said Mr. Upton. "Josie's clothing has been a worry all last evening and this morning. She nearly did not dress or come down to breakfast, except that we need to make so many decisions and arrangements. We find it rather overwhelming."

"It is a difficult time to take on the responsibilities of an adult," agreed Grannie Jane. "Will your father be joining you here?"

"I . . . I . . . don't know." Mrs. Upton looked at her husband. "He is in Egypt. Both my parents are. I haven't thought how to tell him. I . . . I've never had to think about how things work in the world. I put a letter in a box, and a day later it arrives on someone else's breakfast tray. But what happens in between?"

"A letter," said Grannie, "is not the timeliest method under these circumstances. A letter to Egypt might take weeks, as it must travel on a ship. I believe a telegram will be more efficient."

"I've never sent one of those," admitted Mrs. Upton.

"I have," said Mr. Upton, but then, catching a look from his wife, amended his comment. "I have *received* one. About . . . an interview . . . some time ago . . ." He busied himself with putting bits of egg on scraps of toast.

Grannie smiled kindly—quite a feat for her when faced with ignorance. I opened my writing book and made a quick note: *Learn how to send a telegram.*

"This, then, will be your opportunity to enter the world of telegraphic wonders," said Grannie. "After breakfast, we shall speak with the hotel secretary and have the transaction complete within the hour. Are there any other matters for which you would welcome guidance? You have notified your uncle's solicitor, I assume?"

Mrs. Upton's bemused face indicated that she had not.

"Do you know who he might be?" asked Grannie Jane.

"I do," said Mr. Upton, this time very pleased with himself. "Mr. Hart once had occasion to mention the name. He is Mr. Service of Randall and Service, in Nottingham."

"Well, this is happy news," said Grannie. "If he is in Nottingham, Mr. Service may be reached by telephone."

"There is a telephone in the hotel office," said Mr. Upton. "They are quite accommodating when it comes to placing calls."

"Excellent," said Grannie Jane. "We shall have a most efficient morning."

"Very gracious, Mrs. Morton," said Mr. Upton. "May I depend on you to look after Josie?"

"But why can't you—" Mrs. Upton began.

"There is something I must attend to." Was he purposely not looking at his wife?

"You may entrust her to me," said Grannie Jane. "And tomorrow, we will visit the undertaker to make the necessary arrangements."

"The . . . *undertaker*?" Mr. Upton winced. I supposed that moving the body into a position of repose last evening was the last he wished to see of Mr. Hart.

Tears welled in Mrs. Upton's eyes as she looked from Grannie to Mummy and back again. "I do not know how to thank you," she said.

"Coping with bereavement is an art that we are required to learn against our wills," said Grannie Jane, "often under conditions of great anguish. We all must do our part to help those new to the field."

A while later, Hector and I sat upon a sofa tucked neatly in a corner of the lobby, just by the box room. I deduced it was not a spot where people often loitered, as the sofa cushion was still very springy.

"Your grandmother," said Hector, "is formidable!" He used the French pronunciation, but it was just as true in English.

We were ideally situated to oversee the lobby while Mummy departed for a session in the spa and Grannie pursued her instruction of Mrs. Upton in the hotel office. All the little dramas of a hotel morning unfolded before our eyes. I opened my notebook and began to compose a list of the characters I could see around me:

• *Lady with two dogs, who nip at each other and sniff her boots, slowly threading their leads about her ankles while she adjusts the pin holding her hat in place. Will she trip and crack her head on the marble floor?*

• *Dr. Baden sailing across the lobby like a ship out of harbor. (Like a great blue heron rising from the reeds?) (Like a principal dancer through the corps de ballet?) He cheerfully greets every guest by name.*

• *Nurse McWorthy follows doctor like a tugboat (a heron chick?) (a hopeful prima ballerina?), her eyes pinned to his back.*

• *Tall man with pinstriped trousers and bright gold watchchain, clutching a briefcase and extending a hand to Mr. Upton, who smiles like a boy offered a lollipop.*

• *A small, rambunctious child running hither and yon, outwitting his nanny at every turn, ducking behind suitcases and chairs, and laughing with hilarity. Might he escape entirely and have the staff turn somersaults to find him?*

• *Mr. Smythe, officious hotel manager, just behind us inside the box room, telling a story to the buzzardy bell captain about . . .*

"Listen," I whispered to Hector, prodding his toe with mine and tipping my head toward the indiscreetly open door.

"I am already doing so," Hector murmured back.

"There he was," Mr. Smythe was saying, "head thrown sideways and staring like a ghoul. Well, we can't have this, I said to myself, not on hotel property for anyone to come gawping at."

"Who else was there?" asked the Buzzard.

"The newlywed niece, crying like a baby," said Mr. Smythe, "and a couple of kids. That girl with the pretty mother and her little foreign pal."

Hector and I made faces of loathing at each other.

"I sent the boy for the doctor," said Mr. Smythe, "and—"

"I thought you said the boy came to find you?" said the bell captain.

"And so he did, so he did," said Mr. Smythe. "He was clever enough to know I'd be the one to fetch. I'd keep hush about the whole thing. But then I sent him back, to alert Dr. Baden. We'd need a doctor, no question about that."

"He's making it sound as if he was running the show," I said, keeping my voice low.

"In truth, he is running away like a coward when help is needed," said Hector. "Alas."

"A coward? Or someone overcome with guilt?" I said. "If it turns out to be murder."

"Don't you think it's a bit spooky?" said the Buzzard to Mr. Smythe. "Two in five days?"

"Ssh!" The manager hissed. "Keep thoughts like that to yourself. One of the maids up and quit this morning when she heard there'd been a second death, and that is *not* good for business. We're left with Milly, who has the manners of a barmaid!"

Did he have another reason to hide two deaths? He'd been most insistent last evening about not having the police come around.

"Worst thing would be for the Wellspring to be mentioned in the same sentence with the word *deceased*! Rumors and resignations lead to cancellations! It's a nightmare!"

"Well, yes, but—"

"Someone died," said Mr. Smythe. "A perfectly natural event, but not a sight for everyone. We're lucky it happened in the dark of night and not out in the morning sunshine! We have spared our sensitive guests a moment of discomfort."

"Excuse me," said a new voice. I turned discreetly, to see who had joined the conversation. It was the lady with the dogs, hovering at the door of the box room. One of the dogs came over to investigate my stockings and I tugged her silken ear.

"Yes, madam? How may I be of assistance?"

"I've just heard that someone died in the hotel last night. Is it true?"

"Not *in* the hotel, madam. I understand there may have been an incident nearby . . ." Mr. Smythe waved his hand vaguely, as if he hadn't just been bragging about lifting the body. The body he had run away from on his fat little legs.

"This is unpleasant news." The woman's tone was curt.

"A very old man whose health was in miserable decline . . ." said Mr. Smythe. "Perhaps you will be comforted by a complimentary glass of champagne, madam?" He swept his arm toward the lounge, and the lady agreed that champagne might be the necessary elixir for distress.

"An aid, also, for digesting the breakfast," said Hector, "as it is not yet ten o'clock."

"Mr. Smythe won't like it if everyone starts asking for free champagne," I said. "Oh, what's happening over there?"

The doorman, who normally would remain in position outside the main door, had followed a pair of men into the center of the lobby. He wore a smart green tailcoat with gold epaulets on the shoulders, gold braid at the wrists, and two rows of gold buttons adorning the front. He danced around the newcomers in great agitation.

"Allow me to direct you, sir." He addressed the older man, who was also the shorter by nearly a foot, unusually small for a grown-up.

"Police," said Hector.

"Aha!" I said. "The dreaded police!"

Mr. Smythe, returning from his task of dispensing champagne, speedily made the same assessment. He strode across the carpet to greet the new arrivals.

"Th-this is . . . police, Mr. Smythe," said the doorman.

"I am Detective Inspector Henry." The short man's voice was a rumbling bass, making me wonder whether he sang in the church choir. "And this is Sergeant Rook. We wish to speak with the manager."

"*I* am the manager." Mr. Smythe stepped forward with his chest puffed up and his head thrown back so that he gazed at the inspector downward, along the bumpy slope of his nose.

"And your name is?"

"Smythe," said Mr. Smythe. "Wilfred Smythe."

"We are here," boomed the inspector, "to inquire about the dead man removed last evening from your garden."

CHAPTER 9

A CRACK IN THE CASE

A GASP WHISTLED THROUGH the lobby, as those guests who had not already heard the rumor of a corpse were abruptly notified. Hector and I were tempted to stand up on the sofa as gawking adults blocked our view, but quickly found angles suitable for observing everything.

"Dead man?" Mr. Smythe put on the air of someone presented with a preposterous notion.

"The one you had carted away in the dark of night," said Inspector Henry, "witnessed by a night watchman who knew his duty and reported the matter to the constabulary. Chap found on a bench?"

"Oh," said Mr. Smythe. "*That* dead man."

"If Grannie were here," I murmured to Hector, "she'd call him a hopeless ninny. Or cast him such a Withering

Look that even his teeth would curl in shame." Detective Inspector Henry appeared to share Grannie's low tolerance of falsehood and fakery.

"Thank you, Mr. Wilfred Smythe." The inspector put up a hand to stop the nonsense.

"We have taken care of the matter," said Mr. Smythe. "No need for a coroner, as the man was a patient here, and—"

"I will speak with whichever staff and guests had reason to interact with the deceased," said Inspector Henry, ignoring Mr. Smythe's efforts to dissuade. "Was he traveling with a companion or family member?"

"Yes, yes, he was." Remembering that Mrs. Upton, at this moment, was sending a telegram from the hotel office, Mr. Smythe looked sharply over his shoulder at the closed door. "I will inform the niece of your presence," he said.

"And you will direct me to the persons who discovered the body?"

"You're looking at him," said the bell captain. "Mr. Smythe here was first on the scene, along with the young woman, of course."

Mr. Smythe's mouth fell open and snapped shut. He turned abruptly to look at Hector and me, and just as quickly looked away. The inspector, though, had seen his move and now tilted his head to consider us, while we silently considered him in return.

"I shall summon Mrs. Upton," said Mr. Smythe. "I have her in my office, as it happens, knowing you would wish to see her."

"And how did you know I would be wishing that?" Inspector Henry wondered. "As you did not think to alert the police about a dead body on the premises?"

"Oh, well, but . . . it was . . ." Mr. Smythe fidgeted until he recalled the person who might take the blame. "The doctor! As I said before, the *doctor* had the man in treatment, so there is nothing untoward here. Nothing at all."

"Ah, yes," said the inspector. "You are associated with the clinic. I should also like to speak with the doctor, if you would be so kind as to arrange? After I have seen Mrs., *er*, Upton, was it?"

"Certainly, certainly." Mr. Smythe bustled away, followed closely by the sergeant.

The inspector came at once to sit on the chair next to our comfy sofa. The Buzzard lingered in the doorway of the box room, until Inspector Henry waved him away.

"I am Detective Inspector Henry. I'm looking into the unhappy incident last night in the hotel garden. Am I correct in thinking you may have stumbled upon the scene?"

We nodded. Since my first experience in the company of the police, last October in Torquay, I had trained myself—if required to answer questions pertaining to murder—to squelch my usual hesitation when talking to adult strangers. Not that murder was being spoken of just yet, in the case of Mr. Hart . . . but the inspector did not know about the telephone call. That alone might easily transform a *deceased man* into a *victim of homicide* . . .

Inspector Henry pulled out a notebook. My fingers strayed toward my sash. Hector admonished me with a look, that I was not to think of taking notes.

We told the inspector our names, and those of Mummy and Grannie Jane. We explained about the Uptons going to dance at the bandstand. We told him about dining with Mr. Hart, and that he'd eaten the venison with scalloped potatoes and green beans. We told him that just before dessert was served, the bell captain had summoned Mr. Hart to the telephone. His slice of lemon chiffon pie had remained untouched. (A painful waste, in Hector's opinion.) We told him that the bell captain had been so indiscreet as to say, in front of us all, that there was an emergency concerning Mr. Hart's niece.

"And what was this emergency?" said Inspector Henry.

"It is a mystery," said Hector. "No emergency happens."

"We met Mr. and Mrs. Upton coming in from their excursion," I said, "in perfect health. We'd guessed a twisted ankle, or something dance-related, but—" I stopped. The inspector was not interested in what we'd guessed. Nor that we planned to guess plenty more as we pursued our own investigation into the crime. Was it a crime? Every drop of blood dancing in my body, every teeny cell causing friction in my brain, told me that, yes, it was a crime.

"You were with Mrs. Upton when the doctor arrived?" asked Inspector Henry.

"Yes," we said, together.

"And did you watch while he examined the . . . Mr. Hart?"

"We knew already that he was dead," I said. "Hector checked."

Hector tried to look modest, but it was a point of pride that he was not afraid to touch a dead body.

Inspector Henry eyed Hector with a stony face. "You are medically trained?" he asked.

"My mother is at one time a nurse," said Hector, though he must have known the inspector was goading him. "She teaches to me elements of the anatomy."

"Is that so?" said the inspector. "So, there was no need for the *doctor* to arrive on the scene, as you had already surmised the cause of death?"

"The *cause* of death?" said Hector. "This I do not know. Even now we may not be assured of this. The doctor declares an attack of the heart. He has the advantage of reading the file of Mr. Hart, so possibly we need look no further."

"We?" said the inspector.

"The examination is quickly done," said Hector, "out of concern for the distress of the niece. It is possible some clue is missed in the dark." He did not say out loud, *a bullet hole or a stab wound.* Nor did we mention the argument we'd overheard between Mrs. Upton and her uncle.

"Sir?" I said. "There is one thing I'm wondering . . ."

"What is that, Miss Morton?" Inspector Henry stood, and straightened the lines of his coat—not a uniform, of course, but a smart gray herringbone tweed.

"It's about Mrs. Shelton, sir. The lady who died in the park a few days ago?"

The inspector cocked his head, surprised into stillness.

"Did she also die of a heart attack?"

He looked us over, slowly. "The sleuthing game is now over," he said. "Run along back to your mothers."

How dare he! We'd been so helpful! And he, so aggravating!

"Inspector Henry!" Mr. Smythe had arrived, leading Mrs. Upton and Sergeant Rook. The inspector acknowledged Mrs. Upton with an expression of condolence and asked the manager where best he might conduct further interviews in private.

"Allow me to provide coffee in the billiard room," said Mr. Smythe. "Comfortable seating and no fear of interruption at this time of day."

"Miss Morton?" said Mrs. Upton, before she followed the inspector. "Your grandmother asked me to say that she has gone up to your room. She hopes you will tell her what happens next."

Unfortunately, what happened next was the reappearance of Mr. Smythe. He directed the sergeant to the garden, and then arrived on the chair adjacent to ours demanding to know what we had blabbed about—his word, *blabbed*—during our interview with the inspector. We gave a report so dull that he stopped listening.

"You see how many guests are lingering still?" he said. "The Wellspring is known as a very fine hotel, but word creeps out like mold on cheese. Guests will now go away and whisper to their wealthy friends about dead bodies and police and who knows what else?"

"Ghosts?" I said, only halfway joking.

Hector grinned. "Ah, oui!" he said. "You will perhaps be so lucky as to entice a phantom to take up residence. Even people who do not believe in ghosts, they like to be haunted."

"Say that again." Mr. Smythe sat up straight, blinking with excitement.

"You could charge extra money to guests staying in his room," I said, and then put on a quavery spectral voice. "Sleep in the dead man's bed . . . If. You. Dare!"

Mr. Smythe barked a laugh. "That is not a terrible

idea, Miss Morton. Not terrible at all. Not quite the clientele we usually attract, but if the stuffy rich ones are scared off by ghouls and spectres, there may be others who come to seek them out!" He rubbed his chin vigorously, though our suggestions had been made in jest. "I've heard tell of a band of Roman soldiers," he said, "who drag their carts through one of the cellars near York cathedral. Every time there's a sighting, the collection tray on Sunday is that much fuller of coins."

"You see?" I said. "A hotel ghost might be good for business."

We escaped Mr. Smythe and made our way to the garden, only to find Sergeant Rook directing two constables, who poked about in the shrubbery. They followed some sort of system, moving in circles to examine paving stones, rose bushes, daffodil beds and even the water in the fountain.

"Nothing so's you'd notice, Sergeant," said one of them, arriving at the end of his hunt.

"One more circuit," snapped Sergeant Rook. "It'd be a triumph to notice *something*."

Alberto, dressed in his striped games steward waistcoat, walked up the path to greet us, carrying mallets and balls. We must stay on the croquet lawn at all times, he said, and not cross the path to where the police were conducting their search.

"Do you suppose," I muttered to Hector, "that the killer—assuming there is one—was careful not to cross the path when dropping his clue?" But Hector was inspecting the items in Alberto's arms.

"We will, naturellement, stay only on the croquet lawn," he said, "but, if you please, may I use the green-handled mallet? It brings to me the luck."

"Then you'll have bad luck today, sonny," said Alberto, "as the green mallet was not returned to its place on the rack. You'll have to make do with blue or violet." He dropped his load at our feet and went back to the games shed.

"It won't matter a jot what color your mallet is," I said. "You could win against me using a soup ladle."

"This is true," said Hector, "but if George should arrive . . ." He *tsk*ed to express dismay but accepted the mallet with a violet stripe painted on its handle.

"Let us hope that George does not appear for some while," I said. "We need time for a serious Detection Consultation."

"This also is true." Hector prepared to toss a sixpence from his pocket. "The back or the face?" His translations from French were peculiar at times.

"A coin toss is called *heads or tails* in English," I said. "I call heads."

He flipped the coin onto the path and it landed tail side up.

"We needn't really play croquet," I said. "We need only *appear* to be playing."

But Hector decided our consultation could take place while he executed one perfect strike after another, with me trailing along behind, whacking my ball off course and double tapping like a woodpecker. I'd have liked to blame my awkwardness on the presence of the police but that would have been fiddling with the facts. They behaved as if we were not there. Until . . .

"Oi!" called one of the constables. "Miss Morton? Master Parrot? The sergeant wants to speak with you."

"Parrot?" murmured Hector. We laid down our mallets to mark our places and crossed the pathway into police territory.

"You saw the body before it was moved," said Sergeant Rook.

"Yes," we said.

"On which end do you recollect him sitting?"

"He wasn't really sitting," I said, while Hector pointed to the right side of the iron bench. "More as if he'd lost his balance and the bench was lucky to catch him."

"We haven't seen the body yet," said the sergeant, "but I'm wondering, did you notice any marks of violence?"

"It was dark," I said.

"We are concerned with Mrs. Upton," said Hector.

"I didn't see any blood," I said, "but his head was lolling. May I show you?"

I sat as Mr. Hart had been, with one arm flung wide and the other hand to my throat, head tipped back as if drinking raindrops. Hector corrected the position of my legs and one of the constables asked me to stay still while he drew a sketch in his notebook.

It was then, with my arm stretched out and my fingertips resting on the spindles of wrought iron, that I noticed the damage along the backrest.

"Keep still," urged the constable, for I had moved my head to look. I shifted my eyes, instead, and saw the row of filigree quite dented, as if from the blow of a hammer. Hector's gaze followed mine and landed with precision, causing his eyebrows to lift and his eyes to explore further. At last, the artist and his sergeant declared themselves satisfied with the drawing, and I was allowed to stand and shake out my limbs. After those eleven minutes of excitement, the police gathered themselves and left the garden, having done all they could think to do.

"Not really police business," we heard the sergeant say as they departed. "When did it become a crime for an old gent to have his heart stop?"

Hector ran his finger along the damaged section of the bench, coming up with a sprinkling of tiny fragments of black paint. "A fresh injury," he said. "Made since any rainfall, as it is not washed away. But, look also here." He pointed to one of the large stone urns that flanked the bench, each planted with abundant peach and yellow ranunculus. A small, jagged break in the rim of the urn sat like a tulip atop a long, crooked stem—a terrible crack down the side of the vessel.

"Do we see this yesterday?" said Hector.

"I don't remember seeing it," I said. "Grannie Jane sat here for the longest time. Alberto stuffed cushions all around her. We would have noticed bang-ups like these, would we not?" I leaned over to examine the flagstones under the bench. "Do you see a bloodstain anywhere? It would have dried by now, and look like a smear of ink."

"Blood, I think the police would see," said Hector. "And make a much bigger noise."

"True." An obvious—and deflating—point. "But still," I said. "The sudden appearance of dented iron and cracked stone is highly peculiar, is it not? Perhaps we could not see in the dark that Mr. Hart's fingers had been crushed. Or that he'd been conked on the back of the head. In which case . . . all the blood *might* have soaked into his collar and jacket lapels?"

"Many clues point to an end most sinister," agreed Hector.

"The police just searched the whole garden," I said, "and didn't notice what was right under their noses on the very bench where the corpse was found!"

"Also," said Hector, "the inspector seems indifferent when we mention the most important clue . . . a telephone call that summons Mr. Benedict Hart from the dining table to his appointment with death. I wish we do not tell him this."

"'Appointment with death,'" I said. "Nice phrase, Hector. I told him about the call because we can't really keep hush about anything that other people already know. The Buzzard may have reported that he'd answered the telephone and delivered a message."

"This is likely," agreed Hector. "It is better that we cooperate."

"It is better that we *appear* to cooperate," I said, "while we quietly go about deducing on our own, especially as the inspector seems to think we're infants. Our first deduction is that it was not Mrs. or Mr. Upton who made the call. There is no telephone conveniently attached to a tree beside the bandstand."

"In Berlin there is just such a thing," said Hector. "A glass box in a public street, with a telephone inside, to operate with payment of a coin."

"That's a bit silly," I said. "Who has such urgent business that they must conduct it on a street corner?"

"What is more urgent than finding a woman ill upon a bench in a park?" Hector strolled across the croquet lawn to retrieve our mallets from where they lay abandoned.

"We are not talking about Mrs. Shelton," I protested. "We were considering the misleading call to Mr. Hart."

"Mr. or Mrs. Upton cannot place this call from the bandstand," said Hector, "but can we be certain that they do not place it from elsewhere? We have only their word that they ever went to the bandstand on Wednesday evening."

CHAPTER 10

AN UNRELIABLE SUPPOSITION

THIS WAS A PERFECT EXAMPLE of why I admired Hector Perot with all my bursting heart. Inside his head, as he had told me a hundred times, were countless brain cells in constant motion. When he considered a challenging problem, like the matter of whether or not a person had been murdered, his brain cells became frantic with excitement, creating such friction that his deductive abilities were prodigiously increased.

I let Hector's suggestion sink in. "They were dressed for dancing," I said. "That may be a weak objection, but since you are suggesting that we put aside assumptions, I am trying to identify the few facts we have."

"Most methodical," said Hector, with approval. "Let us name the facts."

I pulled my notebook from where it was tucked in my sash. Sitting on Mr. Hart's bench—as I now thought of it—I devised headings for three columns:

Certain Facts. Assumptions. Possible Explanations.

"Certain fact," I said, as I wrote. "They were *dressed* for dancing. And, fact, Mr. Hart said that's where they were."

"Neither of which means they actually danced," said Hector. "Naturally, if they concoct a plan of murder, telling truth to the victim is not of importance. Fact."

"Why would they murder someone she so obviously loved?" I said. "Her joy was real when I told her that Mr. Hart liked Mr. Upton's drawings. She cried and cried when he died."

"Why indeed?" said Hector. We were quiet for a while, considering.

"The usual reasons to kill," I said, "are greed, jealousy or blind rage."

"None of these fit," said Hector, "according to what we know so far."

"Unless," I said, "Mrs. Upton was so hurt and angry with her uncle for scorning her husband that she attacked him."

"And yet there is fine planning," said Hector. "If they dress for dancing *after* they commit murder, this is urgently covering a crime of rage. But putting on dancing clothes *before* the murder? This is a plan."

"Did Mrs. Upton say goodbye to her uncle in person?" But I knew at once that she had not. "She must simply have left a note," I said, "because if she had tapped on his door, she would have found him happily examining Mr. Upton's inventions and the fight would have been over."

"Leaving no reason," said Hector, "for a hot-headed murder. The telephone call, also, does not speak of blind rage. If she hits him over the head with a vase while we listen on the staircase, this is uncontrollable fury . . . but this does not occur."

We swiftly agreed that jealousy was also an unlikely motive.

"Greed, however," I said. "It could be greed. If Mr. Hart is as rich as it appears, and either or both of the Uptons have expectations of inheriting from his will—"

"*Either or both*," repeated Hector. "An excellent point, mon amie. It is possible that one performs the deed without knowledge or assistance from the other."

"Meanwhile," I said, "if one or both of the Uptons—or anyone else—killed Mr. Hart . . . it means that he did not die of a heart attack, despite what the doctor said. The doctor was efficient in his pronouncement, but he could not make a proper examination. It was night, and Mrs. Upton was weeping . . ."

"The weeping of Mrs. Upton is most distracting," agreed Hector. "Is this perhaps intentional?"

Goodness! Had her sorrow been for display? My mind skipped and stuttered. "You think that—" I considered one assumption after another, rather like trying different hair ribbons to see which best suited a dress. "That Mrs. Upton was *pretending* her distress, while Mr. Upton . . . who wasn't there—"

"And is nowhere to be found when I seek for him—"

"You imagine that they might have—"

"Imagination is not practical," said Hector. "I examine the facts and arrange them logically."

"But she loved her uncle," I said, "even if they argued. Mr. Hart will not hire her husband when lying in his coffin."

"Whoever the killer is, this person must use a telephone to lure the prey to a dark place out of doors."

"The Uptons might have gone to a pub," I said, "or a restaurant?"

"Timing matters very much," said Hector. "They must already know where is a telephone to use for this important call."

"Aha!" I said. "Mr. Upton kept asking the waiter, had he received a call? Had his call come through? He knew all along there was a telephone in the office."

"This is where the call is received," said Hector. "It cannot also be where the call is placed."

"You're right. I'm thinking myself into circles. We don't know if it was a man or a woman who telephoned, let alone from where."

Hector nodded at my paper, where I began a new list under the heading

Questions to Pursue

1) Telephone call was made from where?

2) Telephone call made by a man or a woman?

3) Were the Uptons seen at the bandstand where they claimed to be?

4) Was there enough time for one or both Uptons to commit murder?

5) Is there physical evidence that Mr. Hart was murdered?

6) Did Mrs. Upton stand to gain from Mr. Hart's will?

Further questions related to number five: How exactly had the man died? Had Mrs. Upton greeted her uncle while her husband crept up from behind to strangle him with a wire (for example)? Or had the attack occurred face-to-face with bare hands?

"Have you ever looked at Mr. Upton's hands?" I said. "Are they particularly large?" It seemed to me that Mr. Upton was a more likely killer than his wife. Also more likely to have done so without her knowing.

Hector's eyebrows furrowed together as he shook his head no.

I supposed he might have chosen a softer method, one that left no marks? *The spurned inventor retrieved a feather pillow from his hotel room and carried it to this very spot, his knuckles cracking as he flexed his fingers in anticipation. When the victim hurried past, believing his niece to be injured in the park across the road, the wicked young man pounced from behind a tree. He held the pillow over the gentleman's face until, at last, he heard a final, rattling breath . . .*

But surely Mr. Upton could not have appeared in the lobby with such a light heart—praising his wife as *perrrfectly perfect!*—if moments earlier he'd been in a fatal wrestling match? And what would he have done with the pillow afterward? Was the killer's method more inventive, and less intimate, than smothering?

The figure wore his hat pulled down and his coat collar turned up to mask his features, though it was a balmy night. He spotted his prey, who walked briskly despite the cane, unaware that these steps were the last he would ever take. The villain withdrew from his pocket an evil and cunning weapon, a dart stolen from the corner pub, dipped in the lethal poison curare. Now, tossed with deadly accuracy, the dart penetrated the man's chest, just above his faulty heart.

"He could have died from a dozen things," I said. "Gunshot, strangulation, a stabbing, a poisoned dart—"

"A poisoned dart?" said Hector. His eyebrow told me not to be foolish. "Perhaps," he said, "the doctor is concerned for the victim's niece. He tells to us it is a malady of the heart because he does not wish to cause distress by announcing otherwise?"

"What if," I said, "the doctor fibbed to save the Uptons from knowing about a murder that they themselves had committed?"

We quietly pondered that fine example of irony.

"What is the time?" Hector was suddenly alert. "Are we not meant to be meeting—"

"Oh dear, Mummy—"

"Your mother," he said, "expects us to attend the Promenade, which begins at noon, does it not?" He licked his thumb and quickly wiped the dust from the toes of his shoes. I licked my palms and tried to smooth back loose curls.

From the lobby, we followed the guests who seemed— from their elegant swishing skirts and jaunty cravats, and from the purpose of their stride—to be on their way to the Victoria Salon. This long room, lined with tall, leaded windows and painted a pale, mossy green, seemed especially built for a gathering like this. The string quartet, with Mr. LaValle on violin, played music I did not recognize, sprightly and tuneful but not so vigorous as to cause hurry. Indeed, the guests strolled amiably up one side of the hall and back along the other, chatting or listening, with a breeze blowing in through screened doors at the far end.

Mummy was arm-in-arm with the doctor, who leaned in a little too closely to the hair that curled around her ear. The music was not so loud as that, I thought. No whispering was necessary! I took a step in their direction, but here came Nurse McWorthy holding hands with an old woman wearing a fluffy shawl, and she insisted that Hector and I join in the circling flow, while I tried not to crane my neck to spy on Mummy and her partner.

We soon heard our names called aloud, as George urged Nurse Touati to catch us up.

"You may go and get yourself a shandy," the boy said, waving away his nurse. "Nothing for me, thank you." She obligingly disappeared, no doubt content to have a rest from his bossiness.

"And you," George said to us, "will tell me everything! I am vexed beyond words that you found a dead body without me being there!"

"We do not pause to consider that we must request your presence," said Hector.

George laughed. "Just promise to include me in all further escapades concerning corpses."

"I am hoping this is a promise never tested," said Hector.

"But as to this one," I said, "what do you want to know?"

"It was the same gent who threatened me, am I right about that?" said George.

"Yes."

"Keeled over in the garden?"

"Yes."

Guests began to applaud as the quartet completed their time onstage. George pulled over to the windowed side of the room. We lowered our voices as the pianist took his place at the grand piano and flexed his fingers rather showily.

"What killed him?" said George.

"This question does not yet have an answer," I said, "but we think—"

"It's murder?" said George.

"Maybe." I glanced around to ensure that the Uptons were not among our company. Of course, they weren't! They were in mourning! Mrs. Upton could not be seen strolling merrily along in a promenade, no matter how black and dreary her dress might be.

The pianist played the opening notes of the *Moonlight Sonata*, and those waiting began again to walk. We stayed where we were for the moment, as George was eager to hear more. But we were interrupted at once.

"Hello, lovey," said Mummy. "Isn't this a splendid parade of characters for one of your stories?" I nodded full agreement to that.

"Hallo, George," said Dr. Baden, clapping a hand on his shoulder. "Nice to see you making a rare prom appearance! Not usually to your taste, is it, chumming with the regulars?"

"Aggie and Hector aren't regular," said George. "And nor is it usual to have a mystery as a backdrop." He lifted his eyebrows and grinned. The doctor took only a moment to understand and patted George's shoulder, with a sigh.

"Well, young man, if it gives you pleasure to attach mystery to a heart attack, your life is indeed lacking in excitement. But it's good to see you seeking adventure at the Wellspring Promenade." With a bow, he offered his arm to Mummy, and away they went.

"He'll see," said George, "when we catch a killer."

Then along came Mr. LaValle, using his offstage time to mingle with the guests, as usual.

"I hear you young people were the first to come across the gentleman who died," he said.

"Not I," said George. "Worse luck."

"I expect it was a shock," said Mr. LaValle. "Only last evening the man bought us drinks and now . . . well, it is almost past belief."

"He died while you were playing at the bandstand," I said. "Mr. Hart's niece and her husband had gone to hear you, do you remember him telling us that?"

"Ah, yes!" said Mr. LaValle. "That brings it even closer to home!" His head swung back and forth like an unhappy lion. "It is too sad."

"The Uptons dance to your music?" Hector snatched our chance.

"I have never met them," said Mr. LaValle. "I only saw her briefly yesterday morning in the clinic, I think."

"She was wearing a bright green dress last night," I said. "Maybe you noticed her without realizing who she was?"

Mr. LaValle nodded, yes, he'd seen her! She'd looked like a tropical bird darting among trees on the dance floor. "And then, for a while, she stood close to the stage all alone, swaying, and listening with her eyes shut."

George began to wheel his chair forward and back, just a few inches each way, almost as if he were dancing too. "No husband?" he broke in.

"I suppose he'd gone to get her a glass of lemonade or a cream bun," said Mr. LaValle, smiling. "Their last happy moments for a while, I expect. And on their honeymoon!"

He excused himself and moved on to the next group, a couple with American accents.

"You were checking their alibis!" said George. "You think the Uptons did it? That's what you were doing, isn't it? Finding out where they were when the old man died?"

"He wasn't *so* old," I said. "Not much older than my mother." I wasn't *exactly* trying to change the subject, but the Victoria Salon was not the best place to accuse someone of murder.

"She was dancing, though," said George. "Pretty useful of her to wear a bright green dress, don't you think? Did she do that on purpose?"

"Ssh, George," I said. "We're in rather a crowd just now."

He did not have a chance to reply because his nurse came to collect him. He tried to make us promise not to say another word until he saw us again, but such a promise we could not make.

"It does rather clear Mrs. Upton of being the one to attack Mr. Hart in the garden," I said.

"If not the attacker," said Hector, "is she a conspirator? Or an innocent? Does she help him? Or does she, too, wonder, 'Did he do it? Did he not?'"

"That's a grim idea," I said. "How would you feel if your new husband had possibly murdered your uncle in cold blood?"

CHAPTER 11

AN UNUSUAL JOB FOR A WOMAN

WE HAD ONE BURNING question the next morning, as we prepared for our excursion.

Had Mr. Hart been murdered?

Directly after breakfast, Grannie Jane had the Buzzard hire a trap to take us to the undertaker's shop. We might have walked except for Grannie's sixty-seven-year-old legs not liking to do such vigorous exercise. Mrs. Upton seemed quite cheerful, considering our errand. Her husband's duty this morning was to meet Mr. Hart's solicitor at the train station and to keep him occupied until lunch. *If* Mr. Upton had killed Mr. Hart, he would soon learn the contents of the will, and whether the risk had been worthwhile. I tried (but failed) not to watch the Uptons exchange mushy goodbye kisses before we climbed into the trap and set off.

The sun was warm; the gardens along the way were full of daffodils and lily of the valley. Women swept their steps or chatted with neighbors. Occasionally, they waved as we jingled along. What would they think if they knew that the young lady's husband was a suspected murderer? Admittedly, only by children so far.

"Eddie was ever so relieved not to be coming today," Mrs. Upton told Grannie. "Moving my uncle's body the other night was more family obligation than he expected during his first week of marriage. Men can be quite squeamish, as it turns out. Have you ever noticed that?"

"My dear," said my grandmother. "You have done yourself a great service to understand this fact so early on. Though you may want to think twice before informing your husband as to how capable you are. Some facts are not agreeable to men."

I examined Mrs. Upton for telltale signs of conspiracy or greed—until Hector's boot knocked my shin, telling me to shift my gaze. Watching the horse's ears flick flies instead did not stop me from considering her behavior. Was Mrs. Upton cheerful because she and her husband had together devised a dreadful scheme that was as yet undetected? A scheme that relied on a competent woman, rather than a squeamish man, to accomplish?

"I expect it will be a day or two before you hear from your father, Mrs. Upton," said Grannie Jane, as we bounced along. "Do you have relations in Nottingham? Anyone in Britain, rather than Egypt?"

"I'm afraid not," said Mrs. Upton. "We are a very small family. Just my parents, and Uncle Benedict, who was never married. That's why he took an interest in me, I suppose. He and my father had cousins, Gerry and Phoebe. I never met them until Gerry came to my wedding last week. And Phoebe, well, I didn't know her either. She was much younger. She went away, and then died about a year ago."

"Ah, yes," said Grannie Jane. "Your uncle told us about her."

"She'd inherited money," said Mrs. Upton, "but chose to work and travel. She went off to be a governess, or did she nurse a sickly child? No matter. She met a man and was married quite quickly, but then became gravely ill on the honeymoon, some sort of food poisoning. She did not recover and died within a few days. It seems we Harts are cursed when it comes to wedding trips! Even my father or uncle may not know where she was buried."

"A very sad story," said Grannie Jane. "You've had a dreadful time, my dear. I am pleased for you that your husband seems to be a reliable one."

"What a funny word to choose," said Mrs. Upton. "Not very romantic!"

"An underrated quality, as you will learn," said Grannie

Jane. "Kindness and reliability far outshine either handsome or rich."

I hoped this was true, for Mr. Upton was not handsome in the least, being a bit podgy and with those jutting ears . . . but my opinion counted for nothing, as I was not the bride. As to the story of the cousin, it made me wonder if the mysterious Mrs. Shelton might also have suffered from food poisoning? I added the question to the list inside my head. Had she been fond of oysters? Or . . . had cousin Phoebe and Mrs. Shelton both been poisoned by more nefarious means? *On purpose?*

Our carriage pulled to a stop in Old Lane.

The business of Napoli & Son occupied a sturdy brick building with two stories and two wide shop windows shaded by awnings striped in black and gray. A painted sign swung above the door, moaning quietly as it rocked in the hearty breeze that greeted our arrival.

NAPOLI & SON, UNDERTAKER
CABINET AND COFFIN MAKER
NEWEST & MOST APPROVED DESIGNS

A hand-lettered card in the window added further details:

Wreaths, Grave Linens, Shrouds and Plumes
Funerals Performed in Town or Country
Mutes, Horses, Glass or open carriages
by arrangement
on the most reasonable terms
Special lady services

A bell attached to the door dinged as we entered, and a second ding sounded beyond a curtained interior doorway. It was dim inside after the sunny April morning, with whiffs of fresh wood shavings and linseed oil nearly enough to cover an earthier smell, like drains or compost. The entry room was a shop, but small and nearly bare, without colorful merchandise. Here were seven sample funeral wreaths, hanging on coat hooks, some composed of leaves and flowers, dried and woven together, others quilled of dark paper to simulate ornate foliage. A glass-topped case stood against a wall, showing necklaces made of jet, and rings and brooches woven from hair, samples of how a loved one's tresses might become a piece of cherished jewelry. Also available were black mourning bands for hats or sleeves, a variety of gloves, examples of memorial photographs, and other items that one might need to be correctly prepared for mourning.

"We are expected, are we not?" whispered Mrs. Upton.

A hammer striking a nail came as reply, and then a clunk, as if the tool had been set roughly down. The curtain, on large rings, scraped back across a rod, and a man appeared. He was tall with a closely shorn mustache and no whiskers otherwise on his face or chin. Dark eyes, and skin, tough and weathered, that looked to be from a sunnier place than England. He wore his shirt sleeves rolled back, and a carpenter's apron instead of a jacket. His hair and arms and trousers bore a fine layer of sawdust.

"I am Giovanni Napoli," he said, though it was only from having read the sign outdoors that I could guess what he meant. His voice was growly, and the shapes of his words slightly foreign, mixed with the accent of the local people of Yorkshire. Then something like, "What can I do for you?"

Mrs. Upton told the man who she was and introduced Grannie Jane. "My uncle Benedict is in your care," she whispered, "brought in Wednesday night from the Wellspring Hotel."

Mr. Napoli nodded agreeably. "Aye, we've got him." He stepped aside to allow us into his woodshop, pulling shut the curtain behind us. Hector and I were ignored, being children, which meant that we could snoop, discreetly, with our eyes if not with our hands.

Occupying the centre of the room was a large, low table, the height of a man's knee. On it sat a coffin-in-the-making, a man-size box that tapered slightly at one end. Was this to be the vessel of Mr. Hart's final repose? But, no, for Mrs. Upton had yet to be consulted on the particulars of what she wished for her uncle. This room had no window and was dim for the lack. Miniature coffins were displayed on one wall, the perfect size for dolls or rabbits. I thought of the row of pets and birds and strays buried under the tree in our garden at Groveland. How fine to have given them funerals in coffins such as these! Each model was built from a different sort of wood, some plain and others with embellishments like tooled handles or brass hinges or bells or nameplates.

"Oi, girl!" he called, and I jumped, thinking for a moment he meant me. But an answering call came from behind yet another door, which soon opened to reveal a young woman, and a back room where electric lights shone brightly.

"This'ud be me daughter," he said, tipping his head toward her. "Miss Eva Napoli."

Miss Eva Napoli tipped her head toward us. She was tall, with her father's coloring and very dark hair and eyebrows. I inspected her closely, having been told that I would be a tall woman myself, once I'd grown from being a tall girl. Her hair was not especially tidy, which made me like her before she'd said more than hello. She wore a canvas apron with sleeves, covering her dress entirely. Its front was stained with a mosaic of spots and splashes that after a moment I recognized as dried blood.

"We've got her uncle in the back—resting comfortable, eh, Eva?" said Mr. Napoli. "The man we collected from the Wellspring."

"Yes, Papa."

My heart turned over to hear that word from a stranger's mouth, holding a lifetime of love for *my* Papa, and a hundred memories in two little syllables.

"Allow me to . . ." Miss Napoli wiggled gloved hands and disappeared. A moment later she was back, with bare hands and without her bloodied apron. She wore an elaborate chatelaine about her waist, holding a dozen or more items each hanging from its own chain. Scissors, a knife, a needle case, a pillbox, a coin purse, a whistle, a vinaigrette—likely holding smelling salts or a sponge soaked in ammonia, and very useful in her line of work!

Mrs. Upton had been silent this whole time. In the shop, she had peered at the wreaths and looked at the offerings in the case, but without much enthusiasm. The chatty girl who had ridden in the trap was transformed into a woman contemplating mortality. That's the phrase that popped into my head, and I wished I could write it down.

"May I say goodbye to my uncle?" said Mrs. Upton, and allowed Miss Napoli to draw her in to the next room.

The lights dazzled, and we were met with a distasteful aroma of rotting apples and old meat. Grannie put a hand on my shoulder, as if to stop my entering.

"Please?" I whispered. "Please?"

"You needn't tell your mother," she said, and let me go.

"I brought some clothes," said Mrs. Upton, offering the bag she carried. "The suit he wore at my wedding. A week ago." A tear rolled over her cheek.

And there was Mr. Hart, lying on a table, a nearly white sheet pulled up to his neck, the end of his beard resting upon the folded edge. Hector's eyes narrowed as he looked from afar for evidence of a bashed-in skull or bruising on the sides of the neck where the whiskers did not cover. Mr. Hart's skin was the color of oatmeal, but faintly gleaming, like polished china, with a slight pink hue on the cheekbones. His eyes were closed. I could not say that he appeared to be sleeping, but the shock we'd seen in the garden was gone from his features. It would be fair to say that he rested in peace . . . though perhaps his ghost was lurking nearby? Vengeful, and curious to see whether his killer would be captured.

"We don't have many strangers in here," said Mr. Napoli. "Most people like to die at home, not while visiting hotels in Harrogate."

"That is indeed my intention," said Grannie Jane, "if I should have a say in the matter."

"Grannie," I said. "Don't talk about such things." Grannie being old was one of my greatest worries.

"For most men, with a shop like mine, a daughter'ud be a blight on business, but as she's all I've got, she's had to learn it."

"The trade," said Miss Napoli. "I've learned the trade. Been apprentice since I was five."

"And we've turned it, see," said Mr. Napoli, "into a noteworthy attribute." He stretched those two long words even longer, as if he'd been practicing. Note. Wor. Thee. At. Tri. Bute.

"What he means is on the sign," said Miss Eva Napoli. "'Special lady services.' Some customers prefer not to have their dead mothers or aunts touched by a man. That makes me very popular. Most families, they do it themselves. Or their servants look after things. But when that's not possible, I do the washing and preparing, with a woman's delicacy. Keeps them all happy. Some ladies come in ahead, to request that I be the one to perform the rituals when the time comes."

"Very thoughtful," said Grannie Jane.

"Did Mr. Hart belong to a burial club, do you know?" asked Miss Napoli. "The Benevolent Burial Society, for instance? Membership would make a difference to what we can provide."

Mrs. Upton looked uneasy. "I do not know," she said. "I am unfamiliar with . . ." Her voice trailed off as she turned to Grannie Jane for guidance.

"He did not appear to be the sort who subscribes," my grandmother said, full of confidence. "Most club members I know of, they pay their penny-a-week toward the funeral cost because the expense would be a hardship all at once."

"A group of ladies came in a few days ago," said Miss Napoli, "all members of the same club. One of their friends had a cancer in her throat. On her behalf they selected a wreath—the design on the end, you'll see it in the shop there. They carried it over to where she was on her sickbed, and she wept with joy, knowing they'd do her right. Died two days later."

"I believe," said Grannie Jane, "that Mr. Hart had adequate funds to provide for a handsome send-off. Shall we proceed?"

Mrs. Upton was blinking back tears. Grannie took her arm and led her away from her uncle's side. Not everyone could be expected to enjoy the sight of a cadaver in all its scientific glory.

"Papa," said Miss Napoli. "Will you take Mrs. Upton and Mrs. Morton into the shop to choose from among your coffin samples?"

"This way, ladies." Mr. Napoli allowed them to pass, making what he might have thought to be a gracious bow, but looking more as if he'd hurt his back and could not yet stand erect.

Hector and I stayed right where we were.

"I must return to my task." Miss Napoli indicated Mr. Hart. "He will be ready to travel as soon as his niece has settled the details with my father." She wanted to be rid of us.

"We won't detain you," I said. "But—if we promise to be very quiet—may we stay to watch?"

CHAPTER 12

A Dose of Vital News

MISS NAPOLI PAUSED IN the act of pulling on those gloves again.

Before she could refuse, I added, "We've seen dead bodies before. We won't faint or act silly, I swear. We found a murdered corpse on Christmas morning. At my sister's house. Stabbed to death, in the library."

Miss Napoli's face underwent the loveliest of transformations, from vexed and barely polite to eager and curious. "A body in the library? How marvelous!" We knew exactly what she meant. Not marvelous that someone had died so brutally, but, since someone *had*, how marvelous to be the ones to find him!

"The thing is," I said, "we're wondering . . ." I glanced at Hector. How exactly to make this request?

"Mademoiselle," said Hector, with a small bow. "We believe it is possible that the demise of Mr. Hart is not a natural one. We wish to know if your study of his body is revealing any surprise?"

Miss Napoli considered us with gravity. "The poor man has excited much interest," she said. "Why does everyone assume that someone wished him dead?"

"Interest from elsewhere than just us?" I said.

"I had a telephone call from the police this morning," she said. "The sergeant asked the same question. He wanted to be certain that the coroner was not required, as would be usual in a sudden death."

"What do you tell him?" said Hector.

"He wondered whether I'd come across anything—"

"Like a stab wound?" I said, perhaps too eagerly. "Evidence of suffocation, or a thunk to the head? The puncture mark from a Congolese blow dart?"

Hector put a hand over his face, as if I had embarrassed myself with such fancies. But Miss Napoli only laughed, a low, merry gurgle.

"I would have noticed a crushed skull or a stab wound," she said. "Blood usually catches my attention. Even a blow dart with a fine point would cause some bruising upon entry—and where would the dart go after delivering its lethal offering? Unless the killer was bold enough to remove it on site, I would have found it snared in the victim's clothing."

119

"Which methods of killing do *not* leave a trace on the exterior?" said Hector.

One side of Miss Napoli's mouth lifted in a crooked smile. "Such a question would be cause for suspicion if you were any older," she said. "It's a good thing the police are not listening. However, to answer—er . . . I did not hear your name?"

Hector bowed, in that way he had of impressing adults. "I am Hector Perot, mademoiselle. And this is Aggie Morton."

"Well, then, Master Hector," said Miss Napoli, "you wish to know methods of murder that are not immediately obvious?"

"Yes," we said together.

"If force is involved," she said, "there would be signs of that. Bruising where a hand has gripped, a bump hidden by hair, scratch marks perhaps, depending on the assailant. Nothing like that is evident with Mr. Hart."

I sighed. "How did he die, then?"

"The county coroner would probably use a term from the olden days, to explain those times where the cause might be unknown," said Miss Napoli. "*Death due to a visitation from God.* Quite a useful phrase."

"A bit like cheating, if you ask me," I said. "An easy excuse for anything you were too lazy to investigate! Now, what about a needle? Would you have noticed a needle prick if you had no reason to look especially for it?"

"A needle prick . . ." Miss Napoli cast an eye over the sheeted body on the table. "I have not yet examined him closely enough to say yes or no to that," she said. "I needed to have him ready for the niece's visit this morning. We have a few tricks to make him less ghastly for viewing."

"What sort of tricks?" My words coming out in a whisper.

"It was my good fortune," she said, with a bit of a laugh, "that his whiskers easily masquerade the jaw cloth, you see?" She lifted Mr. Hart's beard to show a band of cotton wrapped snugly under his chin and tucked behind his ears, disappearing behind his resting head.

"Mouths often gape after death," explained Miss Napoli, "which can be distressing for the family. The jaw cloth provides a little more dignity. That, plus a cosmetic touch-up . . ." She opened a drawer in the cabinet closest to the table, revealing an array of jars, brushes and sponges, much like those to be seen in an artist's studio.

"Ooh la la," said Hector.

"A bit of rouge does marvelous things," said Miss Napoli. "You see there, on his cheeks? A very little bit, but otherwise . . ."

"Otherwise?" These details were filling a great hole of ignorance, a field of understanding I had not known I lacked. Mummy would be distressed beyond measure to know what I was learning this morning.

Miss Napoli smiled. "Think," she said, "of an old tooth, or of a piano key worn with too many minuets. Think of a splash of cream, soured in the sun. That is the color of a white man's skin when he has died."

"You are a poetess, Miss Napoli!" I said, in admiration.

"A corpse is endlessly fascinating," said Miss Napoli, her cheeks pink. "I often succumb to poetic notions, despite the gripping science."

"But still we wonder," said Hector, "about the manner of his death. Poison, do you think? An injection? Or possibly ingested? Can you know this, yes or no?"

"Ah," said Miss Napoli. "We come again to the question of a needle prick. Or the swallowing of some powder— which often causes external signs as well."

I remembered the body I had discovered under the piano in my dance studio last October. A lady in Torquay had been poisoned. Her face and body had shown obvious evidence of an unnatural death, not at all like Mr. Hart's quiet disarray.

"Sometimes, though," Miss Napoli went on, "sometimes the end comes gently, whether by natural or poisonous means. The gentleman shall receive my utmost concentration over the weekend. You have sparked my interest, particularly in the light of—" Her voice broke off as she glanced over her shoulder to where an elegant screen shielded a portion of the room. What might be hidden there? Or—considering where we were—who?

"Is that . . . Have you . . . Is she?" I had not yet brought forth the words, but Miss Napoli was nodding. She glanced toward the door to the workroom and shop, then back at us, holding a secret too big, it seemed, for her arms alone. I was atremble with curiosity. I felt Hector beside me, as ready as a bird dog before a hunt. Miss Napoli pressed her ear against the door, to listen before hurrying on.

"I have not told Papa what I've done," she said. "His disapproval of my curiosity can be fierce. He thinks himself a carpenter and . . . a disposer. Nothing to do with science. But I . . ." Her voice trailed off. And then she smiled, a bright, excited gleam. "I do so want to tell someone . . ."

She waited, watching us.

"We're ever so good at keeping vows of silence," I said. "If only you knew! We cannot explain, because that would be breaking the pledge, but we swear—"

"A blood oath," said Hector.

"I do hope such a valiant offer will not be necessary," said Miss Napoli. She laughed and then clapped a hand to her mouth and pressed her ear against the door again. "Already our livelihood is peculiar, no matter that everyone needs us. If I take a wrong step, we are severely judged. For being foreign, you see? Well, Papa is foreign, and I am cursed with the same name."

"This I understand," said Hector—who only this morning had been called Parrot.

"I was quite a disappointment to my father," said Miss Napoli, "being a girl . . . and one whose birth killed my mother."

A whole life without a mother! Could anything be sadder?

"But here, the mortuary and the woodshop, these were my nursery. It was only as I grew older that I realized one benefit to having no mother. She was not here to hinder my curiosity or object to my learning the trade."

I had never imagined that a mother might be a hindrance. It was terrible enough to have lost Papa, but what if I no longer—or had never had—Mummy? Surely Miss Napoli did not mean she was *happier* without a mother . . . but . . . my gaze fell again upon the bulky form of Mr. Hart beneath the sheet. If I were to report to Mummy the details of this room, of this visit? I do believe she'd faint. And here, Miss Napoli, a motherless daughter, had turned a Morbid Preoccupation into a lifelong pursuit!

"Well, then," whispered Miss Napoli. "I shall confess my crime." She led us across the room and pushed aside one panel of a folding screen to reveal another body, lying under a sheet like Mr. Hart, on what seemed to be a flat-topped chest rather than a table. The face was covered as well as the rest of her, but we could see it was a woman, because chestnut-colored hair tumbled over one end of the chest.

"Goodness," I breathed. The peculiar smell was stronger here. "Mrs. Shelton? Mrs. Lidia Shelton?"

"The very same," said Miss Napoli. "She's on a cooling table. The chest is full of ice, with holes drilled through to allow cold air to pass. Directly beneath her is a mat lined with charcoal, to absorb the moisture and the smell. But it is nearly a week since she died, so . . ."

I felt as if I'd like to sit down, preferably at the seashore with a salty breeze. I dared not look at Hector, as he could be a bit fussy when it came to unpleasantness. Seeking a pulse was one thing, smelling a week-old cadaver was another.

Hector stepped back. "I will check on our companions," he said, "so as not to be disturbed?" He hurried to the door and leaned against it with his eyes shut, recovering himself while pretending to listen to what went on in the other room.

Miss Napoli smiled at me, sealing a conspiracy between ghoulish girls.

"Such pretty hair," I said, almost tempted to touch it.

"I never had a doll," she said. "My earliest task for Napoli and Son was to comb out the hair of the deceased.

I learned to braid my own hair by practicing on corpses. Not having a mother to teach me."

Whatever could I say to that? Instead, I chased the mystery. "But what crime have you committed?"

"I could not help but wonder why she died. The coroner—who normally might investigate—was away for Easter. Dr. Baden said Mrs. Shelton had been quite ill. I have been instructing myself in forensic procedures," said Miss Napoli. "As there is no family to express further concern . . . When someone dies, the body has ways of telling what happened. That is what my studies are leading me to understand." She gazed steadily into my eyes to be assured that I followed.

"It was Mrs. Shelton's fingernails that put me on alert. They show white marks that are common when . . . I took it upon myself to . . . It was her hair, after all, that revealed the secret of her fate." She reached out to touch it, letting her fingertips ruffle a curl for the briefest moment, just as I had wished to do a moment earlier.

"I performed a test that I've been reading about, using strands of her hair," said Miss Napoli. "I will not recite the steps, which may be incomprehensible to those who have not made a study of chemistry, but the result is certain, as the hair shaft reveals that Mrs. Shelton had been consuming small quantities of poison quite steadily for an extended time, with a large dose just hours before she died."

"Mon Dieu," said Hector by the door.

"God's breath," I said, in the same instant.

"As I had guessed," said Miss Napoli, "that poison was arsenic."

CHAPTER 13

A LONG LIST OF SUSPECTS

ARSENIC! MISS EVA NAPOLI could have told us no better secret.

We were rapidly schooled on the subject of arsenic in the mortuary room of Napoli & Son. We were surprised to learn how common it was in the world around us, not always as a weapon but as an ingredient in medicines and face creams, wallpaper and fabric dyes. It was also an ideal killer—inexpensive, easy to come by and easy to stir into food or drink, with a taste not difficult to disguise.

"Stronger flavors work best," said Miss Napoli. "Something sugary, like cake. Or coffee rather than tea."

It could be administered in small doses over a period of time, causing a variety of disorders, including stomach troubles or headaches or blurred vision. A fatal dose, only a few grains, could take effect within an hour, causing a period of agony before a person died. The useful part—not for the victim, obviously, but for the coroner or investigator—was that the corpse had multiple ways of exposing the means of its own demise. A look inside the stomach would show bright red inflammation if arsenic were the cause of death. In Mrs. Shelton's case, however, because Miss Napoli had no permission from a family member to cut into her, the examination was limited to hair and fingernails. They, too, told clearly how the story ended.

My neck tingled with joy—until I remembered that Lidia Shelton had been a living woman, presumably beloved by friends and even family . . . though none had yet been found. News of arsenic poisoning would not likely be greeted with tingles of joy by all. I glanced at Hector, beside me in the rattling trap as we headed home. His lips were clamped together to suppress the smile that pushed from within, and I was swept again with an unbecoming giddiness.

"Have I been asleep without knowing?" Grannie Jane looked back and forth between us.

"Why, no, Mrs. Morton, I don't think—" said Mrs. Upton, startled out of a reverie.

"I only meant," said my grandmother, "that the children seem to be in a particularly elevated mood. Surely it cannot be that visiting the undertaker is so stimulating as that?"

"It was quite educational, Grannie." I did not accept the challenge to meet her eye. The toe of Hector's boot pressed into my ankle. "Though I am deeply sorry that your distress was the cause of our instruction," I added, to Mrs. Upton. *Not that you display distress*, I thought. *Which is alarming, if you have assassinated your uncle.* Why *was* she so content just now? Because her uncle would soon be inside a coffin and laid to rest beyond the reach of suspicion?

Grannie cast me her Withering Look, which I possibly deserved for my not-quite-fib.

"Your mother and I will have lunch brought to the room," she said. "You may join us—or fend for yourselves in the dining room."

"We may sit at a table all alone?" I said. "And order whatever we'd like?"

"No lobster and no sherry," said Grannie.

Mrs. Upton laughed aloud at this instruction, and so we arrived to the hotel in high spirits.

Grannie Jane and Mrs. Upton departed for their rooms. Hector and I were unusually buoyed by the prospect of lunch.

But, "Wait!" I stopped Hector with a hand on his arm. "The Buzzard is right there, in his kiosk. We must ask about the telephone call."

Hector dutifully approached him, while I followed a small distance behind.

"Excuse me, Mr. . . . uh . . . Bessel?"

"What is it, Master Perroot?" The bell captain tapped gloved fingers together.

"You bring to Mr. Hart a message Wednesday evening, at our table in the dining room?"

"And if I did?"

Hector ignored the rudeness. "We are wondering, it is a man or a woman who tells you of an accident with the niece?"

"Are you now a member of the police force, Master Perroot?"

"Not yet," said Hector.

"Or you, Miss Morton? Am I now to address you as Detective Sergeant Morton?"

What a ninny. I was twelve and a girl. Two reasons why I could not—nor ever would—be a police officer. But we needed the answer, so I acted the way he expected a twelve-year-old girl to act.

I giggled.

"That's silly," I said, feeling very silly. "Just that we're curious. Mrs. Upton wants to clear up any misunderstanding." Was that vague enough? It wasn't exactly a fib.

"I cannot really help," said the Buzzard.

My shoulders slumped.

"Because the person whispered," he said. "It might have been a woman with a cold, or it could have been a man out of breath. More air than voice, when I think back to it."

An answer that answered nothing.

Alberto did not seem to think it odd that Hector and I were unaccompanied, allowing us to feel very grand. We ordered something called A Tasting Lunch. Smoked fish, cucumber sandwiches, liver paste (which I detested), sausage rolls (which Hector found too flaky because the crumbs littered his jacket), Battenberg cake, jam tarts and lady fingers. I drank peppermint tea, and Hector, as always, had chocolat.

We tasted everything and finished nearly all of it. We did not consult while chewing, but instead had the benefit of overseeing the Uptons sitting by the window with a man we guessed to be the solicitor from Nottingham. His face was engulfed in a rusty-colored beard, while the top of his head was as smooth and shiny as a croquet ball. What was he telling them? I tried to discern from their expressions whether or not they had received news of an inheritance. They were disappointingly polite and friendly, revealing no sign of elation or despair.

Alberto delivered a plate of cheddar cheese and purple grapes, with a tiny pair of scissors to cut the fruit from the stems. "Will that be all?" he said (I think in awe of our appetites). Yes, that would be all, and thank you. Alberto sailed away to tend to a family with a teething baby who had requested a dish of ice chips.

"Mr. Alberto has an occupation ideal for a poisoner," said Hector, as casually as if he'd said *The English climate is ideal for growing heather*. "What a simple matter it is for him to poison us—or anyone else in the room. He knows precisely which plate is prepared for whom and puts that plate before each diner. We eat with contentment."

"And then," I said, "one of us becomes so ill that she ends up on an ice chest at the undertaker's shop."

We turned to stare at the waiter. He carried every meal from the kitchen, along the narrow service passage, pausing perhaps to collect a fresh napkin or a segment of lemon before arriving at the table, after two minutes alone with every dish.

"*And* he knew Mrs. Shelton," I said. "The guests come and go, but he is always here."

"The motive, however . . ." said Hector. "Why does he do such a thing?"

"Perhaps he is *Mr.* Shelton in disguise," I said. "We already know he's not really Italian. What if he's not really dead and she wasn't a widow, as Mr. Hart suggested. He ran away to Italy and worked in a vineyard or a tomato farm and learned through hard labor to be more responsible. He came back to England to seek the wife that he—"

Hector put up a hand to stop me. "This, I do not believe," he said.

"He might be a master jewel thief," I said. "Like someone else we've met recently."

Hector squeezed shut his eyes, not liking to think about our encounter with that villain.

"He eyes the jewels worn by the ladies he serves and counts the watches in all the men's pockets," I said. "He sneaks into their rooms at night to take what he likes."

"Such a high rate of robbery at the Wellspring Hotel must logically cause trouble," said Hector, "and yet we hear of no such thing."

"Not a very clever idea, I suppose," I said.

"It is possible that Alberto has a hidden reason to despise Mrs. Shelton," said Hector. "This we must discover. Perhaps she is the cause of great harm to him, as you fancy. A wicked stepsister or a trickster who steals his savings. Who knows why a man may murder? We can only say that Alberto, better than anyone, is in a position to feed her poison every day . . ."

"Better than anyone . . ." I was struck by a sudden thought. "*Except . . . the chambermaid. She* might have delivered breakfast to Mrs. Shelton's room every morning and administered poison with no trouble at all."

"Which of the maids takes care of Mrs. Shelton?" said Hector.

"Milly?" I said, "or . . . the one who resigned the morning after the murder!?"

Hector's eyebrows lifted in excitement. "Ah, oui! Does she resign overcome with guilt? What is the name of this maid? Where do we find her?"

I opened my notebook and added these to my list under Questions to Pursue.

"Et voilà!" said Hector. "Here is someone who may have the answer."

The hotel manager was making his way through the dining room, pausing to chat with guests here and there.

"He's on the suspect list as well." I closed my notebook. "Just for being oily. That makes four potential murderers in the dining room this very minute, between the Uptons and the staff. Plus, the nameless maid."

"Well, well," said Mr. Smythe, arriving at our table. "Where is your esteemed mother and grandmother, Miss Morton? You appear to be unchaperoned for a sizeable piece of each day."

My shoulders prickled. Why did certain people feel they had anything helpful to say about other people's families? One might *think* whatever one pleased, but making a remark in a pretend-jolly voice while stinking of criticism? I vowed to perfect Grannie Jane's Withering Look. I found myself unable to say a word.

"We are permitting the honorable ladies a time of rest," said Hector, saving me. "And enjoying a delicious lunch."

Mr. Smythe eyed our crumb-littered plates. "*Heartily* enjoying, I'd say."

"Indeed," said Hector. "Also, we chat about your wonderful staff. The efficient Mr. Alberto, the ever-eager Mr. Bessel, the kindly maids . . ."

Mr. Smythe's eyebrows drew closer together.

"One maid in particular," Hector carried on, "is most helpful when I break the bootlace on our first morning." He stuck out his foot, to prove that he had a new lace.

Mr. Smythe's gaze had begun to wander, planning an escape route, I guessed.

"I do not know her name but wish to thank her." Hector spoke more quickly. "And then I am told she is no longer working at the hotel. Alas! She is departed—"

Hector's careful approach was too slow, for Mr. Smythe was nodding to a gentleman two tables away and would leave us any second.

"She left the morning after the murder," I said.

"The what?" said Mr. Smythe.

Hector sighed. I shrugged an apology at him, even while

repeating myself. "I said, we are looking for the maid who quit her position on the morning after the murder."

"THERE WAS NO MURDER!" said Mr. Smythe, rather more loudly than he intended, for he winced as the tearoom chatter fell to silence. He put on a broad, false smile and waved to his guests. Then he leaned on our table, put his face much too close to ours, and whispered a tirade. "I will not have children making up stories and shouting them out while people are having their lunch!"

The shouting had been his, not ours. I bit the tip of my tongue to avoid saying there had likely been *two* murders and not just one.

"If a chambermaid ups and leaves at the sad passing of a guest, she's not the sort of girl we want working at Wellspring, is she? And Flo proved that she was not. She is better off working at the button shop, where nobody ever dies. That is the end of the story." Mr. Smythe straightened up. "I do not have time to stand about talking to children. I have other guests, important guests. I will suggest to your mother that diners under eighteen years of age are not permitted in the—"

A noise, something like the honk of a young goose, came from the table where Mrs. and Mr. Upton sat with their solicitor. The noise was quickly smothered by Mrs. Upton clapping her hands over her face. Mr. Upton had an arm about his wife's shoulders, but also a hand over his own mouth. Had it been a joyful honk or one of dismay? The solicitor was shuffling through a sheaf of papers as if to allow his clients time to absorb some piece of news.

News, such as the contents of a rich man's will . . .

CHAPTER 14

A BUTTON AND A SUBVERSIVE ENCOUNTER

SADLY, WE WERE TOO MANY tables distant to hear the cause of Mrs. Upton's outburst. We were also nervous of Mr. Smythe's return and wished to remove ourselves from sight.

"We may not hover like buzzards beside the Uptons," said Hector.

"That would be rude," I agreed. "The news can wait. Where will we go?"

"Mr. Smythe tells to us that Miss Flo, the former chambermaid, now works in a button shop."

"An excellent suggestion, Master Perot!"

"Thank you, Miss Morton. It is permissible without a guardian?"

I next did something terribly mean but necessary.

"Close your eyes," I said. "I have a plan, but you may not watch the first step."

Obediently, he closed his eyes. I picked up the scissors that accompanied the grapes and leaned as near to him as I dared.

"Keep them closed," I said. With a precise pounce, I took hold of the middle button on his sailor jacket and snipped through the threads that held it in place. His horror, as expected, was fierce. His pale face blanched, and then burned with two spots of scarlet on his cheeks. I pretended not to know that the noises escaping from his mouth were French curse words. I needed only to wait for the affronted tidy boy to subside and the cunning detective to emerge once more—and the wait was not long.

"I dislike your method," he said, "but . . . I admire the result."

"You know that if I'd simply asked, you would have said no."

"This is absolutely true." He stood, and flicked a stray crumb from his jacket. "And now we tell to your grandmother our errand on a matter of urgency?"

Grannie Jane sighed in empathy with Hector's plight of having lost (into his pocket) one of his buttons and agreed that we could walk to the button shop by ourselves to see if a replacement might be found.

"It is a small village, and I trust that no harm will come to you in the brightness of day," she said. "You say the waiter gave you instructions?"

"The shop is called Dainty Notions," I said, "and is only three streets away."

Despite being in an unfamiliar town, we set off with confidence using Alberto's directions to the button shop. One street later we were faced with a change of plan when we spied Mr. Eddie Upton darting furtively into a lane ahead of us. We had merely to exchange a look before darting after him. What secret had drawn him away from his wife and solicitor within the very hour of some kind of big news?

Our quarry turned left at the other end of the narrow lane as we slid into the shadows and hurried after him. I was well ahead of Hector—running is not one of his strengths—but pulled up short before swinging around the corner.

"Do not appear to be watching," said Hector, panting slightly. "If he is able to see us, we will claim an accidental encounter." We strolled into the new street, glancing casually this way and that, just in time to see Mr. Upton go through a doorway several buildings along. These were not houses or hotels but business establishments. Some had shops on the street level, while others had gold lettering on windows that showed the names of companies within. We sidled toward the place where Mr. Upton had entered. What next? Trailing him inside could lead to folly, and not be easy to explain. But how would we know what he did, unless we followed? Just as we came closer, the door swung open and there he was. It would remain my shame that I squeaked but, with Hector, dove behind a letter box and then peeked out again—to see Mr. Upton shaking the hand of a man who had emerged through the door behind him. A man I recognized.

"He was in the Wellspring lobby," I whispered to Hector. "I have a note in my writing book. He's wearing the same pinstriped trousers."

Mr. Upton took an envelope from the inside pocket of his jacket and passed it over. The other man clapped a hand on Mr. Upton's shoulder and put the envelope into his own pocket.

Spying done for now, Hector and I leaned our backs against the letter box to consider what we'd seen.

"So much smiling!" said Hector. "What agreement do they make?"

"And what is in that envelope? Money, do you suppose? Did Mr. Upton hire someone else to commit the murder of Mr. Hart? Was that pay, for a job well done?"

"Hey!"

I flinched. Mr. Upton loomed over us, wearing a furious scowl. "Are you following me?"

"A game," said Hector. We climbed awkwardly to our feet. "Just a game, monsieur."

"It's no kind of game when you pry into people's business!" Mr. Upton's face reddened further with every word. "You get away from here! Snooping around like a pair of ill-mannered mutts! And do not say a word to my wife about what you've seen. Do you hear me? You'll ruin everything!" The jovial big-eared Eddie had transformed into a barking mastiff.

I bowed my head and so did Hector. I was unable to apologize, for it would not have been sincere.

"Pah!" he growled, and stormed away. We looked up to find that curious passersby were loitering, but no one thought to interrupt a man shouting at children in the street. They must have thought we deserved the scolding.

"He does not want his wife to know," I said, trying to swallow my jitters. It was not pleasant, being snarled at. "That means she was not part of the plan."

"Does bad temper at being followed presume guilt of being a murderer?" Hector said. "I do not think so."

I stared at him. "You don't think his behavior means he's guilty?"

"Guilty of something? Yes," he said. "But guilty most definitely of murder? Non. Also, it is possible that we try too hard to connect two unconnected deaths. We may be chasing two killers, not just one."

"But Grannie Jane said—"

"She is most wise, your grandmother. I concur with her, almost always. A coincidence is not likely. But what if . . . by assuming one killer only, a second killer is unnoticed and runs free?"

That would indeed be careless. But how to untangle the knotted mess before us?

"Shall we begin with the most obvious suspect?" I said. "The man who just gave us a wigging and who also stands to gain from the victim's will?"

"From *one* of the victims' wills," said Hector, in the most aggravating and reasonable tone. "Shall we begin with logic and method instead of wild guessing? Let us look at the directory on the building to discover who the pinstripe man might be, and why Mr. Eddie Upton is meeting him in secret. Better for us to act than to slouch like ruffians on a street corner."

"You have never slouched in your life," I said. "Your back would snap if you tried." We set off to have a closer look at the building in question, and at the sign displaying the businesses within.

"Are we expecting to find an office of Killers for Hire?" I said.

But no. Instead there was a Mr. Stuart Klein, Dental Surgeon; the West Riding Toy & Novelty Company; a company of glaziers called See-Through Windows; and the Furbank Finance & Accounting firm.

"Does he have a sore tooth?" said Hector.

"He was not inside long enough for a dental examination," I said. "And why should that be a secret?"

"As yet, he has no children needing toys," said Hector. "Nor any broken window to fix."

"Was he consulting the financial people?" I said. "About the wealth that his wife may be about to inherit?" Mr. Upton was becoming more suspicious every hour, in my opinion.

"This is possible," said Hector. "But still, I am missing the button."

"Goodness, I nearly forgot! Let's find Dainty Notions and investigate the *other* murder. The one where the means is confirmed to be poison, and the motive is still a dark mystery. Where we have no suspect at all."

"We have Alberto, one of the maids, or anyone else who Mrs. Shelton sees often in Harrogate," Hector corrected me. "The poison is consumed each day for more than three weeks."

Pursuing Mr. Upton down a lane had altered our position. We asked a fruit vendor for directions, and soon arrived at the button shop.

Flo was Flo Higginson, a skinny girl no taller than I was, but probably ten years older. She had a pointy chin and wide brown eyes, giving the impression that she stared in wonder, or fear, at whatever was being said. Her sister was the shop owner's wife, and Flo was not at all happy to be working for her brother-in-law, a fact she shared in our first few minutes inside Dainty Notions.

"His breath smells," she whispered, "and he leans in too close when he talks. It's not nice, especially as our customers are looking for pretty and delicate items. Ladies selecting ribbons don't want to be plagued with puffing blasts of cabbage and beer. I don't know how my sister puts up with it." Flo had liked being a chambermaid, "except for the dirty bits." Having a dead man on the premises definitely qualified as dirty.

"Now, though, I wonder if my decision might have been a bit hasty," she said. "I do miss being with my chums at the Wellspring. But the dead gent come along when I'd hardly recovered from that lady who up and died in the park. Her, what I'd served breakfast for a month nearabouts, and they're saying she got sick from the food? That was a blow. I took it personal. I didn't dare sleep for fear her spirit'ud turn up to point an accusing finger."

"What did she like to eat for breakfast?" I said.

"A bit of sliced fruit and a boiled egg," said Flo. "Nothing to upset the tummy, like they said happened."

"She prefers the coffee or the tea?" said Hector.

"Ooh, a full pot of coffee," said Flo, "and not a grain of sugar. Horrible!"

Coffee!

"Did you lay out the trays yourself?" I said.

"Not likely," said Flo. "Kitchen did that. All the trays lined up along the table and set up by different girls. One's boiling eggs; one's brewing coffee; one's toasting bread. Milly and me, we just fetched and carried."

"Many hands contribute to each breakfast!" said Hector. Any of those hands might have contributed poison as well.

"Did you happen to meet Mrs. or Mr. Upton?" I said. "In room 209? They'd just got married. Her uncle was the one who died."

"Yeah, they were very, er, *affectionate*," said Flo. "I was sad for them about the uncle. May he rest in peace. Even if he was a bit pompous. Did you say you needed a button?"

We realized at once that our ruse was flawed. The "lost" button in Hector's pocket had worked to deceive Grannie Jane, but we did not need to replace it at Dainty Notions as we already possessed the perfect match. Again,

Hector had the solution. He showed the button to Flo and began his confession.

"My button is torn off, but I do not wish to embarrass my hostess by appearing so . . . disarranged," he said. "I have not the needle and thread to correct—"

"I'll do it for you," said Flo, more cheerfully than we deserved. "You can even keep your jacket on." She deftly threaded a needle from a sewing kit that sat upon the counter. "We're always doing bits of mending for useless men," she said. "You'd be surprised the number of fellows don't want their wives to know how that button popped off or where that tear came from.

"See? All done!" She clipped the thread with a pair of scissors that dangled from her neck on a ribbon. "Have they got a new girl yet?" she said. "I keep thinking I should just go back, even if being a shop girl is simple as sewing on a button."

"Well," I said, as we headed home to the hotel. "All she really told us was that breakfast was fixed by too many people to be a reliable method of murder. Unless Milly or Flo dumped arsenic into the coffee. Every day."

"Alberto also must do this, if he is the killer," said Hector. "The deft administration of the poison into the food, many days in a row, where he might be noticed at any time."

"While juggling plates," I said, "and for no reason that we can see."

"No reason that we can see, *yet*," said Hector.

"Yet," I agreed. "But we do keep hopping back and forth between motive and opportunity."

"Also, between Mr. Hart and Mrs. Shelton," said Hector.

"Because I really do believe they are connected," I said. "Even while trying to keep an open mind."

We were nearly back at the hotel, near enough to see the tubby doorman assisting a lady from a motorcar. But something was tugging at my memory, a picture in my mind's eye of Mr. Hart. I paused to lean against the fence of the Valley Gardens Park.

"Let's not go inside just yet," I said. "I'm trying to remember—"

Hector wasn't listening to me. He was thinking out loud. "The manager, the waiters, the maids . . . All the staff has many chances to meet both the victims," he said, "but *meeting* and *wishing to kill*, these are separate activities."

"Mr. Smythe," I said. "The bell captain. Mr. LaValle, the violinist . . ."

"The doctor also knows both," said Hector.

"And Nurse McWorthy . . ." I said. "Oh! Wait! I've remembered! I began to tell you days ago, but never finished. An odd thing happened in the clinic our first morning here. I went with Mummy, remember? Most of the people we know were there, except we didn't know them yet . . . Alberto was with the doctor. George, Nurse Sidonie Touati, of course, and Mr. LaValle, for his sore shoulder. It was crowded. Also Dr. Baden and Nurse McWorthy. Then Mrs. Upton came in, with Mr. Hart behind her, and Mr. Hart looked across the room . . ." I summoned his anguished face from my memory.

"And?" said Hector.

"From where I stood, it was unclear what he saw. Did one of those people cause him to . . . *freeze*? It may also have been from seeing George and recalling his alarm the evening before. His face turned a peculiar color and he wanted to leave at once. Mrs. Upton was worried but embarrassed too. She told the nurse she would reschedule and hurried after her uncle."

"Nobody is staring back at him," said Hector, "with a murderous glint?"

"Apart from Mr. Hart, no one behaved in the least bit oddly. Mrs. Upton mentioned that she'd misplaced a brooch, and the nurse said she'd watch for it. The nurses exchanged barbed words, but that seemed to refer to some past grudge. The rest of us were patiently waiting our turns."

"Later in the day, we hear Mr. Hart arguing with his niece," said Hector. "But, in the Champagne Lounge after this, he appears content, does he not?"

"He felt miserable about the row with Mrs. Upton," I said, "but only said 'kippers' when the doctor asked what had upset him in the clinic."

"And yet he dies the same night," said Hector, "and still we have two mysteries."

"Did you get the sense that Mr. Hart was rather a lonely person?" I said. "That spending a few days with Mrs. Upton was an unusual pleasure?"

Hector nodded. "Most certainly. Also, Mrs. Shelton is solitary," he said. "She takes her treatments. She is pleasant to the staff. She makes sketching of the little birds. Occasionally she plays croquet with George or has supper with Dr. Baden or takes coffee with Nurse Touati."

"Coffee with Nurse Touati," I repeated. "Are we being especially thick-headed because we know that George loves his nurse? Might we be saying, *After washing each morning, Mrs. Shelton's habit was to put her head into a crocodile's mouth?*"

Hector laughed his squeaky laugh. "Nurse Touati will be dismayed to be a crocodile, I think. But it appears she is the only confidante of Mrs. Shelton. I propose that we learn more about this friendship."

"Also," I said, "in the realm of mysterious friends, we should uncover the identity of the gentleman wearing pinstriped trousers."

CHAPTER 15

AN EXPLORATORY EXCURSION

"I AM AT SIXES and sevens this morning," said Mummy, brushing out her beautiful hair.

"What question are you weighing?" I asked from the window, where I looked out on spitting rain.

She laid her brush upon the dressing table and took up the first of many hairpins. "It does not seem right that we are enjoying our holiday in a place where someone . . . two someones have died. Poor Mrs. Upton is having the saddest week of her young life, while I am looking forward with much eagerness to lolling about in a room full of steam! I wonder whether we should consider leaving early?"

"No!" I cried. "No, no!" It was a dreadful thought, that we might be dragged away before the murderer was caught. And while Mummy was happy, of course.

"Your cheeks have not bloomed with such color since before Fletcher got ill, my dear." Grannie patted Mummy's hand. "I should be very sorry to cut short a treatment that is doing you so much good."

Thank you, Grannie Jane! "If there is to be a vote," I said, "and females permitted to participate—" I waited while they all laughed at this idea. "I stand firmly on the side of staying. I believe that Hector stands with me."

Hector agreed that, yes, this was his ardent wish.

Mummy's smile showed that she'd hoped we felt this way, though if she'd known our delight was inspired by anatomy lessons and the pursuit of a poisoner, she might not have been so cheerful.

"Well, then," she said. "Who will walk with me to the clinic and be brave enough to taste the waters?"

Hector and I eagerly agreed, anticipating the morning's entertainment to include an encounter with George, a polite interrogation of his nurse, and possibly the identification of a killer.

But, "You've just missed your friend," said Nurse McWorthy. "He came early today."

And still, we were obliged to taste the waters. Which were *disgusting*. Mummy claimed that she had acclimatized her palate, so the taste to her was not so foul, but I cannot think why a second try was ever taken. The sulphur water was bright and clear with a carbonated sparkle that tingled the tongue, but the flavor! *Ugh!* Like drinking the contents of an eggshell left for hours in the sun. Another cup, this time called saline chalybeate, made me think of licking an iron railing and having a mouth full of metallic, salty rain. No matter that Nurse McWorthy helpfully listed the marvelous ways our health might improve, Hector and I were not eager to partake again.

"More appealing, I confess," said Mummy, "is sinking into the warm saltwater pool. There is simply nothing like it for lifting away one's cares. Even the cold pool is not entirely dreadful. You might like it, Aggie, accustomed as you are to swimming in the sea."

"With a temperature close to that of lemon ice," I said.

"We have liniments for rubbing into aching joints," said the nurse, "and a variety of tonics to refresh the spirits or to calm the nerves, the doctor's own recipe, especially customized depending on your needs. My old mother takes a teaspoon—the blend we call Sweet Dreams—every evening after she says her prayers, and she sleeps as peacefully as an old dog." I glanced at Mummy. How would she like it if I should ever compare her to an old dog?

"How *is* your mother today, Nurse?" Mummy asked. They'd become quite friendly, it seemed, likely thanks to Mummy being such a good listener. Nurse McWorthy was of the opposite breed, who liked to talk and rarely heard what anyone else had to offer.

"One of her good mornings, thank you for asking, Mrs. Morton. It's such a comfort when she wakes up and knows her own name. Makes me sad to leave her, on a good day, with only a neighbor to check in now and then. I'd like to be right beside my mother every minute, but I've the bacon to put on the table, haven't I?"

Mummy agreed that, alas, the bacon must get to the table, and then a noisy gust of wind rattled the window and fierce rain spattered the glass.

"Goodness!" said Nurse McWorthy. "That was sudden!"

"Oh dear," said Mummy, hugging me. "If only you'd left five minutes ago!"

"Don't worry, Mummy. The walkway is covered."

"I would offer my umbrella," said the nurse, looking to where it hung on the coat stand beside the door, "but two spokes are broken. I've been meaning to have it repaired."

"Not a Hart's," I murmured, and Mummy cast me a look of caution.

"We will not melt," said Hector.

We successfully dodged the raindrops and arrived back in the lobby to find—hurrah!—George and his nurse waiting out the rain before walking home. Nurse Touati held a bagful of buns that smelled fresh from a warm bakery oven. She must have nipped out to the shops while George had his treatment. She gave us each a bun to nibble, and before we finished, it wasn't raining anymore.

The front doors began to swing open and shut with guests released from their rooms after the downpour.

The nurse glanced at the sky, where gray clouds were scudding past, leaving a field of soft blue. "I think it's safe to head home, George."

"Mademoiselle will accept help carrying the package?" said Hector. "We are having a walk after the rain and happy to escort you."

"How very kind, Hector, thank you." Nurse Touati handed him the bag from the baker, while I silently applauded his cunning. A chance not to be missed, strolling with a witness in our investigation! Witness? Or suspect? I needn't have worried about how to direct the conversation because George was keen to direct it himself.

"Sidonie?" He tipped his head back when he addressed her, so that he was really speaking to the brightening sky. "In all your nursing days, did you ever meet a murderer?"

The nurse stopped so suddenly that George was jolted. "Why do you ask that question in particular?"

"I only meant . . . Here we are, at a hotel where two people have died," said George, "and one of them we knew pretty well. Is it possible . . . that one of our acquaintance is living a wicked secret life?"

"Mmm," said Nurse Touati. She wiggled the wheelchair to avoid a bump in the pavement. The wicker creaked, and the chair moved clumsily forward. "It seems a rare chance, that one has a murderous villain for a friend. But neither are friends always who we understand them to be."

We greeted this remark in silence. Was she warning George that she might let him down? Was she confessing she had not been the friend that Mrs. Shelton believed her to be?

"Are you acquainted with Mr. and Mrs. Upton?" I said. "The newlyweds? She is the niece of Mr. Hart, who died."

"Does nearly bashing into their uncle count?" said George.

His nurse shushed him. "I have not met them," she said. "They've only been here a few days. So many people come and go."

"Did Mrs. Shelton have any reason to meet them?" Or to have a clandestine meeting with Mr. Upton and rile him up so much that he wanted to kill her?

"The Uptons?" said Nurse Touati. "I don't think so. She kept mostly to herself, except for the occasional coffee time with me."

And how often had they met for coffee time? I could not bring myself to ask.

"Why does Mrs. Shelton tire of the hotel?" said Hector. We'd heard an answer before, but one could never anticipate when a new flicker of light might shine.

Nurse Touati pursed her lips and spoke—I fancied—reluctantly. "She was getting sicker instead of better. It worried me. I suggested that she move out, and she complied."

Aha! A tiny new fact. It had been George's nurse who'd urged Mrs. Shelton's move! For a more nefarious purpose than worry?

"The lodging house is just ahead," said George. "The landlady, Mrs. Woolsey, is a friend of Sidonie."

"Will you show us?" I said.

It was an ordinary house, not so big as Groveland, where I lived, but two stories high and made of brown bricks. Similar houses sat on either side, with a patch of garden out front marked by a white-painted fence as high as my waist. Nurse Touati leaned on the gate.

"Let me see if Mrs. Woolsey is in," she said. "George's chair does not fit through the gate, so she'll come outside to say hello if she has a few minutes."

"The first time we tried to visit . . ." George pointed to scrapes on the gatepost. "The wheels got wedged. Now we usually just wave." His nurse headed up the walk and knocked on the door, quickly opened by a thin, white-faced maid.

"That's Gretchen," said George. "She speaks only German, and she doesn't like snakes. Care to hear how I know that?"

"I, also, am not fond of snakes," said Hector, quickly. I hoped this wouldn't give George the notion of finding a snake to wave about in Hector's face. Snakes were not *my* favorite animal either, but I think for Hector they were at the bottom of the list. How would George go about catching a snake? Could he even touch the ground unless he was on it? How frustrating not being able to simply crouch and snatch up a snake if one felt the need!

Mrs. Woolsey had appeared on the stoop with Nurse Touati and cheerfully ambled closer. She was very round with a smiling, pock-marked face and graying hair as curly as new ferns.

"Hello, duckies. Lovely to see you, lovely to see young George with friends."

George scowled. "What makes you think I don't have friends? I have dozens of friends. All members of the Love-a-Cripple Society."

"Hush, George," said Nurse Touati.

"A pleasure to meet you, madame." Hector bowed, causing Mrs. Woolsey to shake with laughter.

"These young ones found the man dead on Wednesday night," Nurse Touati told the landlady. "In the hotel garden. We're all in a tizzy, as you may imagine."

"It takes no imagination whatsoever!" said Mrs. Woolsey. "I'm still feeling the shock over poor Mrs. Shelton, may she rest in peace."

A vision of Lidia Shelton's luxurious hair flashed through my mind, along with a whiff of the perfumed air in the Napoli mortuary.

"We took to each other like ants to a jam pot." Mrs. Woolsey was still talking. "Though she was only here a few days. She arrived very poorly, didn't she, Nurse? But two days of good plain food, you could see she was improving by the minute. There's nothing porridge won't fix, and fix her I did." She shook her head sadly, making those curls jiggle all over. "Until the last day."

"What happened then?" I said.

"She went out for a walk, poorly as she was. She was a great one for fresh air, always wanting to sit out, to feel the sun on her face, she said. She'd had her lunch. She'd had her tonic. It was a bright day and she'd take a turn about the park and do some sketching. She did love her sketching. Little birds and such. The afternoon went by. I was baking, it being Saturday. Bread, and game pie. Some of my tenants like that, thruppence extra."

Mrs. Woolsey sighed a great sigh, her bosom heaving with the weight of her tale. "I got the last loaves out of the oven, and she still weren't back. That were not right, as the light dimmed and she'd be needing her tea. I asked the newsboy had he seen her. I asked the fishmonger. He said there'd been a woman took sick in the park, a lady artist. He said the patrol constable had come along to look after her. Well, that word 'artist' chilled my bones. I pulled on my shawl and hurried to where he said, near the bandstand, but she'd been taken away by then. By the police, said the dawdling boys. She was dead, they said, but that was just boys talking, I told myself. Down I go to the station, fretting, did anyone call the doctor?" Mrs. Woolsey's voice sounded as if she were being shaken by a fierce set of hands.

"My dear," said Nurse Touati. She laid her palm on the woman's back and patted gently.

"You needn't keep telling us—"

"I'll tell anyone who asks. She was as dead as a dustrag," said Mrs. Woolsey, "and been collected already. Not by the coroner, as he was away, but, 'Gone to Napoli,' the coppers said. Her handbag was missing, so they didn't have a name. I might know who it was, I said, so they took me over in a buggy, giving my swollen feet a rest. Old Napoli was banging away on a coffin, and his peculiar daughter led us in to have a look, me and the sergeant. When that sheet got pulled back, there was poor Mrs. Shelton, God rest her soul, blood drained out of her face like a vampire's breakfast."

George laughed. "I like that, Mrs. Woolsey! Very descriptive. Have you read a book named *Dracula* by Mr. Bram Stoker?"

161

"Twice," said Mrs. Woolsey.

"An excellent story!" said George. "Maybe Miss Napoli is a vampire!"

"What father lets his girl fiddle about with corpses, I ask you?" said Mrs. Woolsey. "She'll be a spinster for life, you mark my words."

"But so much better for the ladies," said Nurse Touati. "I mean to put my name in with her, when the time comes."

"Not for some time yet, Nurse!" said Mrs. Woolsey. "Please God. I told the reporter who come by this morning, I said to him—"

"A reporter?" said Nurse Touati. "Oh, my dear, you shouldn't speak with men like that."

"He was very polite," said Mrs. Woolsey. "Skinny fellow with spectacles. Wanted to know all about poor Mrs. Shelton. How long had she been living here, who found her body, who was her next of kin, that sort of thing. It perked me right up, knowing someone cares."

Had we learned anything today? Our encounter with a querulous Mr. Upton put him at the top of my list of suspects in the death of Mr. Hart. Spending a pleasant hour with George and Nurse Touati had done nothing to suggest that the nurse had killed anyone. Except for an odd hesitation when we asked about the move from hotel to lodging house. Was that discretion about something other than homicide? Or a poisoner covering her tracks?

Kind people had fooled me before.

Walking back to the hotel, Hector and I went over every word we'd heard, determined to spot a new clue to gnaw on.

"Mrs. Woolsey describes the last day of Mrs. Shelton," said Hector. "She says, 'She liked to feel the sun on her face. She'd had her lunch . . .'"

We stopped and stared at each other, before saying the next words together.

"She'd had her tonic . . ."

CHAPTER 16

A Vanishing Motive

WHAT SIMPLER WAY could there be to kill someone than to put poison in the bottle she thought held medicine? Had Mrs. Shelton brought the tonic with her from the hotel? Was it a fresh bottle already containing poison when it left the Wellspring dispensary? Or partly used, and tampered with along the way? Where was the bottle now? Sitting on a shelf in Mrs. Woolsey's bathroom? Or disappeared along with the handbag?

We arrived back at the hotel with many questions, and not an answer in sight!

"Aggie?" Mrs. Upton waved at me inside the big front doors. She stood with the rusty-bearded visitor. "Come and meet Mr. Service before he leaves."

She displayed no sign that she knew of our recent

scrape with her husband. My cheeks burned with the awkwardness of knowing something I was not meant to know, but Hector and I obeyed the summons and were introduced to the solicitor. He had remained in the hotel last night and now was returning to Nottingham.

"These are the young pups who rallied in your hour of need?" said Mr. Service.

"I cannot think what I should have done without them," said Mrs. Upton. "Eddie had gone upstairs to look for Uncle Ben—"

Or so he said, I thought.

"—and if not for these two I would have been alone . . ."

That hour of need, I did not remind her, had been thrust upon her by us waylaying the Uptons on their return from the bandstand. If we had not told them about the telephone call, with its report of a fraudulent emergency, someone else would have discovered the body—and we would have missed out on our good fortune!

"I commend your courage," said Mr. Service. "I am not confident I could have done the same."

Hector answered for us both. "It cannot be called courage when there is no choice," he said. "We are with Mrs. Upton seeking the location of her uncle. Et voilà! We find him! Suddenly we face a much bigger task!"

Everyone laughed, the sort of surprised laughter that includes sadness.

"Mr. Service has been a wonderful support," said Mrs. Upton, "just as your grandmother said he would be, Aggie. He has explained everything we need to know and to do."

"Grannie Jane will be happy when I tell her." I wished I could ask whether she now was rich. Had her motive— or that of her husband—been strengthened or erased by news delivered by the solicitor? We did not wait long to hear answers!

"Mr. Service read us the will." Mrs. Upton spoke in a husky whisper with tears in her eyes. "My uncle has bequeathed to me the family business. I am now the owner and director of Hart's Umbrellas!"

"Goodness!" I said. "That's . . . that's . . ."

"Our felicitations, madame," said Hector. "This is honor indeed."

"It *is* an honor. I believe Uncle Ben meant to honor me . . . but . . ." She looked at Mr. Service. "Did he choose the wrong Upton?" she said. "Perhaps my husband's ingenuity and his design experience would be better . . . Eddie thinks it's tough for a girl to be a leader. He's a bit miffed that it was forced upon me without warning."

Had Mr. Upton expected Mr. Hart to assign the factory to him, being the man, and now was disappointed? Is that why he was so fractious yesterday afternoon? It seemed ever more likely that Mr. Pinstripe was an advisor on financial matters.

"From what I've seen, you'll do very well," said Mr. Service. "Asking questions is what matters when you're learning. Never pretend to know what you do not know." He shifted his briefcase from one hand to the other.

"And here I am babbling!" said Mrs. Upton, "while you need a hansom cab, Mr. Service, to get to the station on time."

They hurried toward the door, passing Dr. Baden as he came in, trailed by four or five men in flapping coats, waving notebooks and shouting questions. Reporters! The doorman darted this way and that, unable to corral the intruders.

"Doctor? Doctor!" Like a flock of noisy starlings, pencils pecking at the air.

"How can I help?" said Dr. Baden, not quite friendly, but not unfriendly either. "I have precisely . . ." He pulled the watch from his vest pocket. "Three minutes to answer your questions."

"What did the man die of?"

"Mr. Benedict Hart was a new arrival at the Wellspring clinic, suffering from a heart ailment. Sadly, he succumbed to his malady when alone and help came too late to revive him."

"What about the lady last week?" shouted a fellow in the back with wiry black whiskers. "You've had two patients die this month."

Dr. Baden put a hand on his chest, where his heart must beat beneath the jacket lapel. "The lady was no longer a patient, but she was a friend. Her loss was a heavy blow. Though she had left our care, and I was not present post-mortem, I can only say that she, too, was ailing before this lamentable end."

"What about medicine?" one of the men asked. "Everyone knows you hand out potions and elixirs like a quack at the county fair."

"*Everyone* knows something so untrue?" said Dr. Baden, with a genial smile. "Our curative elixirs and balms are carefully developed, and I trust my staff to follow the recipes precisely. I think that will be all. Good day, gentlemen." He slipped into the hotel office, where they dared not follow.

Instead, the newspapermen loitered by the potted tree near the entrance to the tearoom, chatting and looking about with interest at the fancy lobby. The front doors opened, bringing Mrs. Upton back from bidding farewell to the solicitor. She was now accompanied by her husband. Had he been out pursuing further clandestine encounters?

"Sorry to rush off like that," Mrs. Upton said to us. "I'd lost track of the time. And look who I found climbing out of a taxi!" She nuzzled against her husband, who turned his face away from Hector and me, as far as it could go without cracking his neck.

"Eddie?" Mrs. Upton reached a hand to touch his cheek. Did she see that he was behaving oddly? "After no luck yesterday, I hope today was more fruitful? Did you find the drafting tool you so urgently needed?"

Tool shopping? Hector's toe pressed my own seemingly by accident.

But then, Mr. Upton's eyes swung around to meet mine. My heart skipped. Would he scold us again? Or would that mean exposure of his nefarious actions? He blushed and his ears almost glowed.

"Josie, my darling," he said. "I have been less than truthful."

"Oh dear," she said. "That sounds serious." But her voice was light, as if she trusted utterly that he would not deceive her. Let alone kill her Uncle Benedict.

"I was only trying to impress your uncle because it meant so much to *you*," he blurted. "I never wanted to work for him. I don't care about umbrellas. It's *your* family business, not mine. You *should* be the one looking after it!"

Mrs. Upton stared at him.

"We came to Harrogate for our honeymoon because I wanted to surprise you. That telephone call I was waiting for? I met with the chief designer yesterday and delivered my signed contract. Just now, I had a quick tour of the offices. I . . . I wasn't trying to replace a tool. I have a new job. I lied to you and these children know it. I just wanted it to be a lovely surprise, to show you—and your uncle—that I can be a proper husband and take care of my wife, the way a man ought."

"Oh, Eddie," said Mrs. Upton again, "and here I am, suddenly not a wife but a factory boss!"

(Oh, Eddie. And here we were, thinking you were a murderer!)

"Are you ready for the news?" said Mr. Upton. "I am officially the new junior designer at the West Riding Toy and Novelty Company!"

Mrs. Upton flung her arms around him and squealed more like an excited child than a factory boss. "But that's wonderful, Eddie! I'm so proud of you!"

Mr. Upton's arms were cozily embracing her. He vowed to never, ever tell another fib.

"Must we watch?" murmured Hector—feeling the same *blech* that swept over me.

"Oi," called one of the reporters. "You, madam? You're the niece?"

"That's her!" said one of the others. "Name of Upton, am I right?"

Mrs. Upton turned away, face blanching. Her husband's protective arm pulled even more tightly around her shoulders. He tried to lead her to the stairs, but no arm could shield her ears.

"How did your uncle really die?" shouted someone.

"Are you going to inherit anything?" another one asked.

"Was this part of your plan?" said the whiskered man. "Take him on a holiday and kill him off? Or did you just get lucky?"

"How's that for a headline? 'The Lucky Heiress!'"

"How dare you!" said Mr. Upton.

"Was it murder?"

"Will you be arrested?"

"Have you got *any*thing to tell us?" came one plaintive voice.

Mr. Smythe sprang through his office door like a fox into a chicken coop, making no effort to be calm or polite. "Tabloid muckrakers!" he shouted. "If any of you comes inside my hotel . . . Ever. Again." He brandished his finger as if it were a sword. "I will kick you into the street with my own expensive boots. I will have you dragged out in handcuffs by the agreeable constabulary. I will have you locked in stocks in the public gardens, and I'll supply the rotten eggs for passersby to throw at your heads! Do you hear me? Do not let me see you again!"

The reporters snickered and snorted with general disrespect, but they shuffled toward the doors. Mr. Smythe moved right behind them like a sheepdog, still barking threats.

"Hector," I said. "Do you see that fellow? The reporter just putting on his gray cap?"

Hector stood on tiptoes. "Oh my!" he said. "Do my eyes deceive?"

"No, your eyes are seeing quite clearly." My heart sank with the inevitability of trouble. At the same time, it expanded with a burst of anticipation, almost glee. "What do you suppose Mr. Augustus Fibbley of the *Torquay Voice* is doing here in Yorkshire, so far from home?" His presence seemed to promise that our instincts were correct.

"And just when Mr. Eddie turns out not to have a motive after all," Hector said, "but wants only to surprise his wife. Suggesting that the killer is someone else."

CHAPTER 17

A LONG, DULL SUNDAY

THE NEXT MORNING BEGAN with grumbling thunder and windows slashed with rain. Mummy and Grannie allowed that we children might remain cozy in our beds while they prepared to attend a church service, as they were accustomed to do on Sundays. Perhaps they did not wish to be bothered with damp, reluctant companions during their hour of spiritual gratification. We were *not* glum about being left behind.

A tap on the door announced Milly with breakfast. Seeing that Hector and I were alone, she did not bother saying good morning. She plunked down the tray so roughly that some of Hector's chocolat splashed from its pitcher.

"Sorry," she muttered, wiping the spill with a napkin. "I'm hurrying so, I'm making extra work for myself.

Usually on Sundays, I only do breakfast and then I'm off, but today I'm to train the new girl. Hired yesterday, since Flo up and quit when she heard the gent had died. She's ever so scared of ghosts, is Flo, and that made two in one week. Do you need any fresh towels?"

"Has Flo ever seen a ghost?" I asked.

"Don't be daft," said Milly, which she would never have said if Mummy were there to hear.

The breakfast porridge was hot and creamy, the toast crisp and buttery, the jam made of raspberries and full of pips that caught between my teeth. We were in no hurry to leave the room simply to arrive in the lobby, domain of the tiresome Mr. Smythe. I sat on the window seat and surveyed the rainy garden, while Hector buffed the tips of his boots with a cloth provided especially for that purpose. I opened my notebook and began a new list.

"One," I said. "Discover where precisely Mrs. Shelton's probably lethal tonic came from." I jotted that down. "Do you suppose Nurse Touati might know?" Without waiting for his answer, I kept writing.

2) What happened to Mrs. Shelton's handbag? Would Nurse Touati remember what it looked like or what she carried?

3) Visit the bandstand.

4) Talk to—

"Oh, there goes Nurse McWorthy," I said. "Is she on her way to church? Look how windy it is out there. She is fighting with her umbrella. She'd know more than anyone about the tonic, but dare we ask? Would she answer us or think we were accusing her?"

"Write down all the questions." Hector sighed. "We will not be playing croquet today, I think."

"Boo-hoo," I said. No use pretending anything but relief.

"We can perhaps assemble the jigsaw puzzle?" said Hector.

"While we're thinking," I said, "about all the other people we've met this week who might be murderers."

We adjourned to the table and opened the box that Mummy had brought with us. The puzzle was named Events from English History, each piece hand cut and painted. It featured pictures of such memorable moments as the construction of Hadrian's Wall, the beheading of Anne Boleyn, and Wellington's triumph at the Battle of Waterloo.

"Waterloo is in Belgium," said Hector, "less than one hundred miles from my home."

"One hundred miles away, and nearly ninety years ago," I said. "Your life was not in peril."

"I only comment as a matter of interest," snipped Hector. "You tell me many times that Queen Victoria visits Torquay when she is young."

"Torquay itself," I said, "not one hundred miles away."

"I believe the rain, it is making us testy," said Hector.

He meant me, making *me* testy, but I fit in the piece with the tip of the sword that took off Anne Boleyn's head, and decided to stop provoking him.

"I am not familiar with this historic episode," said Hector, pointing. "The Duke of Clarence drowning in a butt of wine. It is significant because . . . ?"

"Something to do with the succession of the Crown," I said. "I've never been to school, remember? My knowledge of history is missing a number of chapters."

The puzzle was not difficult and we soon were done. "Mummy and Grannie will be back at any moment," I said, "and then we will be four people trapped in a room because of rain, instead of only two." I stood up. "We may *not* be bored! There have been two murders nearly within spitting distance of this room. The police have made no progress on learning who the killer might be. They're not certain there even *is* a killer! We should be taking advantage of a useful resource lurking uncomfortably close at hand!"

Hector's eyebrow went up, inviting me to explain.

"Mr. Augustus Fibbley, bloodhound reporter for the *Torquay Voice!*" I said. "We know the police are not so clever as he is. Has he traveled all this way on a whim? He must know something, don't you think?"

Hector reached the door before I did. "I am what you English call *all set.*"

Only two reporters stood inside the carriage port, where the doorman had grudgingly allowed them to huddle out of the rain, now that they had been banished from within the hotel. But no Mr. Fibbley. Why were these ones nosing around? Were they hoping for another glimpse of the Uptons, hoping, like us, that Dr. Baden's verdict of a heart attack was a mistake? The glorious truth that Mrs. Shelton had been a victim of arsenic poisoning was not yet known, so why were these men staying behind? And where was Mr. Fibbley?

"You mean the skinny little fellow with the slippy spectacles?" said the shorter man, in answer to Hector's question. He wore his hat pushed way back on his head, showing a broad freckled forehead. "He was scribbling notes like a courtroom scribe, but then he disappeared. Gave up, like the rest of them, I guess. We're about to pack it in ourselves, as nothing has turned up."

It hadn't occurred to me when Mrs. Woolsey mentioned a skinny fellow with spectacles that her visitor might have been Mr. Fibbley. But now I had seen him with my own eyes.

"Do you know where he lodges?" Hector asked.

"Why would he be lodging anywhere?" said the freckled reporter. "How far is he from home?"

"He writes for the *Torquay Voice*," Hector said. "In Devon."

And, being Mr. Fibbley, he had absolutely *not* given up. He must be snooping somewhere else. What new tidbit had taken him away from the hotel?

"I thought I knew that face!" said the taller man. "What is that little blighter doing in Harrogate?" His jaunty blond mustache matched eyebrows that hung low over bright hazel eyes.

"Torquay?" said the other one, with great surprise. "What does he want here?"

"We, also, are from Torquay," said Hector.

"*You're* from Torquay, with that foreign talking?" said the freckled man. "That makes me a monkey from Zanzibar. What do a couple of kids want with a roaming reporter?"

"Don't mind my colleague's manner," said Mr. Blond Man. He was looking more closely at us, with something I'd often seen in Mr. Fibbley's eyes—real curiosity. "I am Frank Thomas, *Yorkshire Daily*." He extended a hand and

Hector shook it. "And this is Douglas Dunham of the *Ripon Times*." Mr. Thomas tipped his head toward his colleague. "But everyone calls him Dotty." He tapped his fingers on his own cheeks, in case we'd missed the freckles dotting those of Mr. Dunham.

"Hector Perot," said Hector, with his usual half bow.

Mr. Thomas turned to me. The way he'd called Mr. Fibbley a little blighter made me think they were not strangers. I had not yet spoken, as my mouth seemed full of chalk dust, but I said my name in as clear a voice as the dust permitted.

"Fibbley being here rings an alarm bell inside my head," he said. "He's always first to pick up the scent of blood, if you catch my meaning."

We did indeed catch his meaning. We knew Mr. Fibbley's tracking abilities were admirably accurate.

"But I'll bet you've noticed a thing or two," Mr. Thomas was saying. "Kids snooping around . . . What do *you* know about the man who died on Wednesday night?"

I evaded the question by remembering something about Frank Thomas.

"'Dead Lady Still Unclaimed,'" I said. His headline from the *Yorkshire Daily* story we'd read on our first morning. Mr. Thomas threw back his head and laughed. The other man looked back and forth between us, trying to see the joke.

"A reader of the news!" said Mr. Thomas, and I liked him for that. "So, what are you chasing after Fibbley for?"

"We used to know him," I said, "and we thought—"

"I used to know him too." Mr. Thomas laughed again. "We both were assigned to a big story, five or six years ago, in London. Maybe you heard about the actor who was stabbed at the stage door of the Adelphi Theatre?" We shook our heads no. "I suppose not, you'd have been scarcely more than infants. The killer was declared insane. Fibbley somehow got an interview with the actor's daughter, Ellaline Terriss, and wrote a story to break your heart."

Hector and I exchanged a look, recalling just how tricky Mr. Fibbley could be when in search of a good angle on a story. It did not surprise me one single smithereen that he'd won over a grieving daughter.

"I'm thinking if Fibbley's here . . . I'd better sharpen myself up," said Mr. Thomas. "Clever weasel, I tell you. Proof of that, he's using kids to spy for him."

"We're not spying *for* him," I said. "We're spying *on* him, and—"

But there, Hector clapped a hand on my arm and hauled me out of the carriage port into the drizzling rain.

"Hush, Aggie," he said. "Never tell a reporter more than he needs to know! This lesson we learn through much trouble!" He opened the door of the hotel before the doorman thought of it. We were children, after all, and rarely deserved the same service offered to grown-ups. Hector wanted to get inside before his clothing had soaked up any more rain. Too late. Even a few drops were too many for him. We headed upstairs so that he could change his shirt.

On our way along the passage to room 201, we skirted the chambermaid, Milly, earnestly explaining to another girl how to tap properly before entering a room.

"One soft knock, then one a bit louder. Count to seven. Another soft one, then use your key if you don't get an answer."

"Have you ever wished you'd counted to ten?" said the new girl.

"Plenty of times." Milly giggled. They wore long black dresses covered by white aprons adorned with a frill at the shoulders.

"Next room we come to, you try on your own," said Milly. "No! Not that one! The gent who was staying there—" Her voice dropped to a whisper to explain about the dead resident of room 207. I peeked back over my shoulder, hoping, for Milly's sake, that the new girl was not rushing in horror to the stairwell to make an exit. But no, she merely nodded and moved on to the connecting room, number 209, where the Uptons stayed.

Where was Mr. Fibbley? It put a different light on things to think of him trailing after a lead. The sort of light that comes from a candle with an untrimmed wick—wobbly and spitting. What had brought him to Harrogate? What had he learned before we had?

Dry, and back downstairs, we met Mummy and Grannie Jane for lunch in the dining room. Mummy perfectly illustrated the phrase "in the pink," as a way of saying a person was blooming with health. Her face actually glowed, her cheeks and the tip of her nose a warm, shining rose color. After lunch, she and Grannie excused themselves, with naps in mind. The sky was in our favor and had stopped pelting rain. A shaft of sunlight broke through gray clouds and beckoned us outside.

"The lawn is too wet still for croquet." Hector nudged wet grass with a toe and pouted, as if whacking a wooden ball with a wooden stick were the only reason to venture out of doors.

"The perfect spring outing awaits us," I said. "I believe there is a crime scene at the bandstand demanding to be scrutinized."

Hector's green eyes sparkled as if the sunbeam had hit him directly. "Allow me to guide you," he said, "to the place of Mrs. Shelton's final breath."

It took only six or seven minutes to walk to the bandstand, down the hotel garden path to the gate, across Swan Road, and into Valley Gardens Park through an ornate iron stile. Daffodils and crocuses lined a wide path. Tree branches spotted with bright green buds dripped leftover rain with every gentle sway. Hopping robins trilled to each other.

Three small children were kicking a ball back and forth, two boys and a girl, with a puppy who was going mad for the ball, not knowing which way to scamper through grass still wet from the rain.

"Don't let Brutus get the ball!"

Their nursemaid sat placidly on a bench, with a folded towel under her bottom, patching a pair of red rompers.

"Grandmother, grandmother, tell me true! How many years till death have you?"

And then the chorus, "One! Two! Three! Four!" counting all together, as the children kicked the ball to and fro, trying to keep the rhythm going to extend their grandmother's life. "Five! Six! Ohhhh, bad luck!" The kick had gone awry, and they would need to begin again. The puppy was delirious with barking.

"You miss Tony," said Hector, watching.

"I do miss Tony," I said, "but also, I miss him being a puppy. He has grown to be a tubby old gent."

Around the next bend in the path stood the octagonal bandstand, with a high peaked roof topped by a pretty spire and adorned with filigree ironwork.

"We should discover when the next evening of music is scheduled," I said. "Mummy and Grannie Jane would like that, I think."

"The Buzzard will know the schedule," said Hector. "Or the pleasant Mr. Smythe."

I gave his shoulder a friendly punch. "Which bench?"

"There is not, as yet, a plaque," said Hector. "But I deduce that she expires on the seat nearest to the drinking fountain, over there, you see?" A cast-iron bench, like all the others, sat at the edge of the wide stone path that circled the bandstand, well-placed to see the musicians and the dancing.

"Why do you think—?" I said.

Hector pointed at the flowerbed behind the bench. "There," he said. Stems had been broken and blossoms scattered, as if accidentally, or unavoidably, crushed by heavy feet.

"Very observant, Sherlock! I suppose the police did that, when they found her?"

We stood for a while, just looking at the bench. I tried not to think about how her corpse must have appeared, possibly contorted with the agony of arsenic poisoning. Contorted and discolored? I pushed away that thought

184

and imagined instead that her spiritual essence had been transformed into a chickadee and sat on a branch of the tree above.

"Aggie?" Hector poked me, and we turned back along the path. I did appreciate having a chum. I opened my mouth to say so aloud when a small furry animal galloped past my feet, putting me off-balance for half a moment.

"Brutus!" cried the little girl. "Brutus, come baaa-ack!" But the puppy had discovered the new game of chase, and could run much faster than the child. He bounded over the low, sturdy fence that bordered the path, scampered pell-mell through violets and forget-me-nots, and veered off to sniff around the base of a tree. The nursemaid and two boys sat on their bench, utterly uncaring, nibbling on cut sandwiches and watching as if this were their usual lunchtime entertainment.

"Brutus!" She was a very little girl, not more than three or four. A puppy might hop over a fence but not she. I, however, was twelve and a half, and tall for my age— quite able to step with ease wherever I liked. Hector was not the sort of boy who liked to venture off a path. The transgression would be mine alone. I soon was treading lightly through the flowers and whistling softly for Brutus, now rooting about on the far side of the tree. I crouched low to the ground and called the puppy's name.

"Catch him!" called the girl. "Catch him, will you?"

"Brutus?" I leaned forward, poking my head as far around the tree as I could manage without tipping over and landing my knees in the dirt. He was nestled in a bed of myrtle, readying himself for a nap. I gently scooped him up, his velvet ears flapping against my neck and his tongue licking my chin.

As I turned to crow with triumph, I spotted something else tucked out of sight of anyone on the path. Leaning against the tree was the croquet mallet with the green-striped handle.

CHAPTER 18

AN UNSETTLING ARTICLE

HECTOR AND I DEVISED a game on Monday morning, as Mummy and Grannie Jane wandered about (too close to us) in the hotel room. We pretended to write a poem together, but were instead trading urgent notes on pages of my writing book. Much of our discourse was a repetition of last evening's efforts to puzzle out the matter of the green-striped mallet. We'd examined the cracked urn and the dented bench upon our return to the garden, whooping with joy at the discovery of minuscule flecks of black paint embedded in the round, flat end of the mallet. We then put the mallet into hiding—not in its place on the rack in the games shed, but tucked under a pile of blankets, where it would likely remain out of sight until midsummer, when picnics on the lawn became a wished-for activity.

We now alert police? wrote Hector.

Not until we learn whether Hart was coshed, I wrote.

There is no blood on his head.

We didn't have a weapon before! Now Miss Napoli can look for evidence of a mallet.

A light tap on the door announced breakfast delivered by the chambermaid who was not Milly. We were obliged to tuck our notes away. The maid looked for somewhere to put the tray, and Hector slid our jigsaw puzzle back into its box to make room on the table.

"Hello," said Mummy. "You're new. What's your name?"

The girl bobbed a curtsy. "I am Verity, madam." Her voice was breathy and high, like the notes of a flute. Her skin was burnished with gold freckles and wisps of taffy-colored hair peeked out from under her cap. "I brought the post as well as breakfast," she said. "And the local newspaper."

"Thank you, Verity," said Grannie Jane. "I am a great appreciator of the news."

"Yes, ma'am." Verity arranged dishes on the table and leaned the tray against a wall to be used later for removing things. She began to pour the tea.

Mummy turned an envelope to show that it bore my sister's handwriting.

"Read it aloud, Mummy."

"Dear Family," she began. "Thank you, Mummy, for

letting us know that you have arrived safely and find the hotel to your liking—"

"Excuse me for interrupting," said Grannie Jane. "There is not quite enough milk for my tea. Verity? Would you please . . . ?"

"Yes, madam. I will return at once." She picked up the little pitcher and slid out of the room.

"Keep going, Cora. What else does Marjorie say?" Mummy continued:

Your Turkish baths sound splendid and I am relieved to hear that you like the doctor and nurse in charge. It makes all the difference to trust one's physician, as I have learned from my undignified position as a pregnant lady. I resemble a snake who has eaten an ostrich egg for tea, but dear Dr. Musselman, as creaky as he is, assures me that this is perfectly normal.

I hope there are walks or activities to keep Aggie and Hector amused as well?

James sends love.

Fondly,
your loving Marjorie

"There's a postscript," said Mummy, "to explain the enclosure. She says, 'Goodness! James has just brought in today's copy of the newspaper! Imagine my shock at finding this article' . . ."

Mummy unfolded the newspaper clipping and scanned its contents.

"Mummy!" I said. "What is it?"

"From the Saturday edition of the *Torquay Voice*," said Mummy, "written by your old friend, Augustus C. Fibbley. He's writing about the recent deaths here in Harrogate, stirring up scandal, as usual. Does that mean he's here? Have you children seen him about?"

"He is not precisely a friend, Mummy," I said. "We did think that we might have seen him with the other reporters, but it seemed so unlikely."

I felt Grannie Jane scrutinizing my face. "Another not-coincidence, I expect," she said. "They do seem to multiply in the wake of suspicious death."

We hadn't told them that Mr. Fibbley was in Harrogate, for why would they ever need to know? And yet, here he was, blundering his way into the room as if assuming he'd be welcome.

"Recent curious events," read Mummy, "have induced this reporter to investigate the death of a woman in the town of Harrogate, in Yorkshire. The body was identified by her landlady, Mrs. Woolsey, but has yet to be claimed by a family member. Mrs. Shelton's demise, so far from Torquay, might not normally inspire interest in readers of the *Voice*, and even a second death, five days later and 400 yards from the first, would not have shrieked for attention, if not for—"

The door opened to interrupt. The chambermaid slipped back in holding two small pitchers of milk.

"—if not for the identity of the young girl who found the still-warm corpse."

Mummy turned the clipping over in her lap, as if to hide it from her own eyes. "Still-warm corpse!" she said. "Need it be so *very* specific? *Was* he still warm, darling?"

"I didn't touch him. Hector did."

The maid clinked the china pitchers, perhaps alarmed at the topic of conversation.

"How does Mr. Fibbley know the temperature of the body?" said Hector. "Though he is correct in using the word *warm*."

"It is a vivid detail," said Grannie Jane. "The reporter's guess allows us to feel that the death has only just occurred."

"It only just had!" I said.

"Oh dear." Mummy sighed. "Here is Aggie's name, and yours, Hector. I despair of ever holding up my head again." She kept reading.

"Miss Agatha Morton, a 12-year-old native of Torquay, accompanied by her friend, Master Hector Perot from

Belgium, and Mrs. Josephine Upton, niece to the victim, discovered the body of 46-year-old Mr. Benedict Hart—"

"Was he so young as that? He looked much older, did he not?"

"It was the cane," said Grannie Jane. "A cane does age a person."

"And the silver in his beard," I said. "His beard alone! *Ugh!* So much *beard*."

"And his illness, I suppose," said Mummy. "Poor man."

"And the bad temper we witness when he accosts George in his wheelchair," said Hector.

"That was not admirable," agreed Grannie.

"Where was I?" said Mummy. "Ah, yes. '. . . discovered the body of 46-year-old Mr. Benedict Hart during the evening of April 15th under circumstances not entirely above suspicion.'"

"'Circumstances not entirely above suspicion,'" said Hector. "With this we concur, do we not, Aggie?" I shot him a look, warning him against saying detecting things with Mummy listening.

Verity used the moment to deliver the milk pitchers to Grannie, and then went into the bathroom to collect the dampened towels.

"The victim's niece, Mrs. Josephine Upton," Mummy continued, "confirmed that she is her uncle's sole heir. It is of note that Mrs. Upton is already in suitable mourning, as if she came on holiday prepared to wear it."

"The implication being that she expected her uncle to die?" said Grannie Jane. "What nonsense."

Mummy was laughing. "They aren't even her clothes," she said. "I loaned her the skirt and jacket, as I am very well supplied."

The maid departed with a bundle of towels, saying she'd be back momentarily with fresh ones.

"Finish reading, please, Mummy?"

"Although Mr. Hart's abrupt end was assumed to have been the result of heart failure, it would be prudent of the constabulary to examine the situation closely. Two unexplained deaths are cause for concern in any small community, but when they both occur so near to the same location—the Wellspring Hotel—the concern must escalate to alarm. The presence of Miss Morton, renowned for having discovered two other corpses during these past six months, adds an extra element of suspicion to the situation. Let us hope that the authorities do not shirk from conducting an official investigation."

Verity had returned, and quietly folded the stack of towels onto their shelf, then set to clearing away the breakfast things.

"Is he accusing *me* of being some sort of jinx?" Outrage tasted like charcoal in my mouth, quite overwhelming the sweetness of honey on toast. "Or is he calling me a killer?"

"It does rather hint at some sort of involvement, does it not?" Grannie Jane stood to get out of Verity's way and sat on the window seat. "It seems to me that Mr. Fibbley is struggling to make news where no news yet exists. Two bodies are not news unless someone is responsible. Until he has an identity for a killer, all he can do is make news from thin air."

"Mr. Fibbley doesn't know about the telephone call," I said.

"*That* is not thin air," said Hector. "Someone calls Mr. Hart away from the table before he eats his dessert! Mr. Hart is lured into the dark of night for no reason."

"The reason," I said, "was murder."

"It is surprising," said Grannie Jane, "that the loitering bell captain has not yet sold the story of that mysterious telephone call to an eager reporter."

"Oh dear," said Mummy. "Could we change the subject to something less grim? I must gather myself for this morning's treatment. What will you do today, Aggie?"

"Hector and I are meeting George," I said, fumbling with my sash and letting Grannie fix it. "His nurse is visiting the dentist, so we offered to go for a walk with him."

"That's kind of you," said Mummy. "Pay attention

wheeling the boy over the cobbles, won't you? I will see you both at lunch." And off she went.

The maid was loading her tray, the china rattling gently as she gathered teacups and jammy knives. Hector and I waited just long enough for Mummy to be well ahead of us, and then opened the door to depart.

"Another moment, Agatha?" Grannie Jane beckoned us back. "It would please me to know where your walk with George will take you."

We'd so nearly made our escape without confessing the plan! But now, as Grannie's nose for fibbing was well-developed, we must state the truth.

"We are returning to Napoli and Son," I explained. "George was vexed, you see, to miss the first excursion, especially as he knew Mrs. Shelton and liked her." My mind's eye saw her hair tumbling out from beneath the mortuary sheet. Would her dead body alarm or comfort him?

Grannie cupped my face in her hands. "He may not be so bold as he thinks," she said. "Nor as bold as you are. Take care, will you?"

"Yes, Grannie."

We slipped out in front of the maid, with her fully laden tray.

"In less than one hour," said Hector, as we careened along the passage, "we hear the cause of Mr. Hart's demise and what part is played by the croquet mallet!"

CHAPTER 19

A CROWDED ROOM

THE BELL RANG ABOVE the door as we entered the undertaker's shop, and jangled again in the back room. Miss Napoli came to answer, wearing her apron.

"Papa's not here," she said.

Was that her way of saying that someone had died? Did every ding of the doorbell, every ring of the telephone, announce bad news? The beginning of a year like the one that my own family had just traveled through? Or perhaps Mr. Napoli had simply gone to the tobacconist for a new pipe cleaner. The important thing was that we were alone, and that Miss Napoli soon would be telling us about Mr. Hart's murder! George was so excited that he bounced in his chair, looking about like a child in a sweet shop.

"So many wreaths!" he said. "It never occurred to me what choice there'd be!"

He caught sight of something I had not noticed on our previous visit, on a shelf tucked below the window. It was a miniature procession, like a set of tin soldiers, except this one had eight carved ponies painted white pulling a gun-carriage that carried a tiny coffin, bedecked with flowers.

"Queen Victoria's funeral cortege!" breathed George. "Who made this?"

"My father and I," said Miss Napoli. "As a tribute. We worked on it together."

"Miss Napoli?" I said. "This is George. George, this is Miss Eva Napoli, Special Lady Services—and more."

George slipped off his driving gloves and made a sharp salute. "George Bellamere, miss."

She smiled. "I have seen you rolling around town, Master Bellamere. It is a pleasure to meet you. Come in, come in."

George blushed to the roots of his floppy brown hair, and got his chair as far as the woodshop, where it collided with the worktable holding a coffin-in-the-making, different from the one we'd seen on Friday. Was this to be for Mr. Hart? Poor George could not pass any farther. His disappointment was pitiable.

"Mostly, I make the best of my lot," he said, "but on occasion, having noodles for legs is a terrible impediment."

I didn't like to leave him there but was longing to speak quietly with Miss Napoli, to hear the verdict on how Mr. Hart had died. I took a half-step into the back-room mortuary. Hector signaled that he would keep George company, that I should—

But then the doorbell rang, with its speedy echo in the woodshop.

"Who now?" Miss Napoli sighed and squeezed past Hector and George to make her way into the shop up front.

"She is splendid!" George whispered. "Just as you said, Hector. Think what she must know about how a body works! She'd likely be a better doctor than old Baden at the spa. He thinks that every ailment can be cured with a hot bath."

But I was listening to the conversation in the next room.

"Good afternoon, miss."

That husky voice was only too familiar. I glanced at Hector.

"My name is Gus Fibbley. I am a reporter from the *Torquay Voice*. Would you consider speaking with me for a few minutes? I understand you are a brilliant scientist. I have some questions about recent clients of yours."

Mr. Fibbley, up to his flattering tricks! Miss Napoli spoke quickly. "I am busy today, sir, and have no time for repor—"

"I am content to wait," he said. "For hours if need be. Your reputation is well worth waiting for. I am here to investigate the deaths of Mrs. Lidia Shelton and Mr. Benedict—" He broke off. I had stepped into his line of vision, with Hector beside me.

Augustus Fibbley pulled off his cap and stuffed it into the pocket of his coat.

"Miss Morton," he said. "Master Perot. Fancy meeting you here."

"Mr. Fibbley." I jumped right in. "I wish you hadn't written what you did! It wasn't fair to suggest that wherever I go, someone surely dies!"

"Is that what I said? And hello to you too."

The door to the street banged open and the bell made its double jingle. Miss Napoli looked beyond Mr. Fibbley and let out a small moan of exasperation. "You again?" she said.

"Oi!" said another man's voice. "Don't you go talking to him!"

"Move aside!" George tapped my arm. "You're blocking my view!"

I made room for him to see, as Frank Thomas of the *Yorkshire Daily* pulled out his notebook and pencil.

"Anything you say, Eva, you say it to both of us." Mr. Thomas flipped to a fresh page.

Eva? They were well-known to each other, then. I supposed that a reporter and an undertaker must have cause to meet quite frequently. Certainly when a murder came along.

"This fellow is from Torquay," said Mr. Thomas, "a million miles away. Shouldn't you be loyal to the *Yorkshire Daily* instead?"

"Shouldn't *you* be loyal to the truth?" barked Miss Napoli, "and not to whomever happens to be paying you on the sly this week? Which I expect is the Wellspring just now, since you're letting them slip out of any responsibility for two deaths!"

"Bribes, Frank?" said Mr. Fibbley. "You've sunk that low?"

"I don't see it's any of your business," said Mr. Thomas, turning his back. But a flush crept up his neck that confessed embarrassment. "What are these children doing here? Snooping? Or do you run a nursery now, Eva?"

"I've been warned not to say anything to anyone," said Miss Napoli, "by the police."

"The police?" said the two reporters in the same instant.

Again, the street door opened. Again, the bell rang, this time announcing Inspector Big Joe Henry. He could not cross the threshold, for the shop was already crowded to its limit. Sergeant Rook peered over the inspector's shoulder, with no hope of pushing in just now.

"What's all this?" said the inspector.

"What are reporters doing here?" said Sergeant Rook. "Didn't we tell you—"

"We've got every right!" blustered Mr. Thomas.

"Reporters and policemen," said Mr. Fibbley, "are like salt and pepper. Always together."

"And who brought children to a place like this?" Big Joe Henry wanted to know.

"Nobody brought us," said George. "We're here on our own to investigate a—"

Hector clapped a hand on George's shoulder to end his comment there.

"You showing up, Inspector Henry, confirms that there's a story," said Mr. Fibbley. "You may have read my article in the—"

"His article was full of guesswork," said Mr. Thomas. "But you know my work, Inspector, and you can trust—"

"Would you care to make a statement, Inspector?" said Mr. Fibbley. "To confirm or deny the rumor that two people have been murdered while you stand by—"

"Move off and leave him alone!" said Sergeant Rook, stepping closer to the reporters, one hand on the truncheon in his belt.

"Are you threatening me?" Mr. Fibbley tipped up his chin in defiance. Offering it as a punching target, maybe?

A shrill note pierced the clamor. Miss Napoli held a whistle to her lips, one that usually hung from her waist among the other essential tools on her chatelaine. An echo of the whistle's cry seemed to vibrate in the air.

"Enough," she said. "Indeed, too many. I wish you all to leave."

At once the questions and grumbles began again. A second whistle echoed the first, this time wielded by the detective inspector.

"You heard the lady!" he called, in his booming bass. "Step outside. Police business comes first." He wriggled his way between the reporters, allowing his sergeant to enter also. The shop now held six living humans, the woodshop two more—as well as the wheelchair—and in the mortuary were two dead bodies and countless hovering souls. A busy day at Napoli & Son.

"We're here," said Inspector Henry, "to confirm arrangements for the bodies currently in your custody. The county has received an application to have Mrs. . . . uh, Mrs. Shelton! buried at the expense of a private donor."

George pinched my wrist. "My dad," he mouthed, and then beamed.

"Naturally," said the inspector, "this raises new questions." He caught sight of Mr. Fibbley taking notes.

"Oi! Clear off!" said the inspector again. "This is police business! I'll burn your notebook if you write another word!"

Mr. Fibbley and Mr. Thomas exchanged a look and made a big show of tucking pencils behind their ears.

Inspector Henry tried to squeeze past George's wheelchair. One by one we traded places, eventually allowing the policemen inside the mortuary with Miss Napoli while the rest of us lurked in the outer shop. The curtain had been pulled shut to prohibit our entry, with all of the woodshop lying empty between us and the conversation we wished to hear. The reporters quickly contrived a bit of theater, whereby Mr. Fibbley stood at the street exit while Mr. Thomas kept a hand on the curtain.

"I'm off!" called Mr. Fibbley. "I have a deadline!" He opened the door, activating the bells, as Mr. Thomas slid the curtain aside on its noisy rings. They grinned at each other like schoolboys and slipped into the woodshop together. None of us would consider snitching, as we sneaked through to eavesdrop too, inching George as close as we could get his chair.

Happily, Inspector Henry's booming bass reverberated nicely. And nor could Miss Napoli be described as soft-spoken, having nearly a man's timbre to her voice. We held our breaths and stretched our ears.

"Well, Miss Napoli? We're waiting," said the inspector. "Sergeant, try to take notes, will you? Even if what she says is beyond your ability as a speller."

Miss Napoli laughed. "I'll keep it simple." I imagined her long neck straightening, her shoulders rolling back.

She must be nearly a foot taller than Big Joe Henry. Who would find that more discomfiting?

"I will confide on both cadavers currently in my care," said Miss Napoli, "as you have insisted. But you must prepare for a surprise. After careful analysis—"

We could hear the sergeant repeating, "Ann. Al. Iss. Iss," while he presumably wrote it down.

"I will remind you that I am not a coroner," said Miss Napoli. "I cannot perform an autopsy or make any cuts without permission from a family member. My comments are merely observations and not official statements. I did nothing invasive to the woman's body." She took a deep breath. "But I did conduct a test, using a few hairs from her head and the trimmings from her fingernails."

"You've guarded yourself nicely, Miss Napoli, against any challenges of protocol," said the inspector. "Get on with it and tell me the truth."

"As a faithful scientist," she said, "I conducted the test twice. The results prove that Mrs. Shelton's death was due to poisoning by arsenic—"

George, beside me, gasped and threw his arms into the air. Was it horror or rapture? He dislodged one of the miniature coffins by accident, pulling it clear off its hook. Hector's hands shot out to catch it in midair, avoiding the calamity of a noisy landing. Mr. Thomas and Mr. Fibbley were scribbling faster than I thought possible.

But Miss Napoli was not finished. "According to the evidence, Inspector, which I considered as fully as any coroner would have—"

"More fully than the one we've got," interjected the inspector.

"The quantity of arsenic in the victim's hair shows more poison than mere traces from sources around the home," said Miss Napoli. "Without question, a homicide."

"I'll be jiggered!" Sergeant Rook's eagerness made us miss the next few words.

We re-joined in the middle of a sentence. ". . . will examine your notes in detail, Miss Napoli. Those become police property in a case like this, and I expect I'll have to alert that fool of a coroner. Now, for the sake of Sergeant Rook's dubious abilities, could you tell us the main points of your testing procedure?"

"What does *dubious* mean?" said Sergeant Rook.

Miss Napoli gave a quick synopsis of her experiment, as she had done for us, focusing on the amazing fact that due to the poison adhering to the keratin within a shaft of hair, even the finest of strands displayed the full timeframe of the deceased's ingestion of arsenic. A scientific wonder!

"As to the other body in your care," said the inspector. "Did you perform some form of examination on him as well? Authorized or otherwise?"

"I did," said Miss Napoli.

"Have you determined the cause of his death?"

"I have."

Hector's hand found mine.

"Well, let's hear it!"

"Mr. Hart's death was entirely natural," said the undertaker. "The result of sudden and massive cardiac arrest."

The groans were mine and Hector's. We had wished so urgently for evidence of murder. Mr. Fibbley and Mr. Thomas scuffled in a run for the exit. Propelled by astonishment, I turned the other way and pushed open the door to the mortuary.

"Whoa." I heard Mr. Fibbley stop dead behind me. "Miss Morton! What are you—"

"Are you absolutely, positively certain," I said to Miss Napoli, "there was no sign of him being hit? No bruising anywhere? In the shape of a circle? About the size of an orange?"

"Hey!" The sergeant herded me backward. I stepped on Mr. Thomas, who had crept back in after Mr. Fibbley to hear the answer to my question. Neither reporter could abandon a story that might have another chapter.

"I'm very sorry, Miss Morton," said Miss Napoli. "No sign of violence at all."

The inspector put up a hand. "Wait. How is this girl part of—"

"Why did you ask her that?" Mr. Fibbley said to me. "What do you know?"

"Why do you care what *she* knows?" said Mr. Thomas. "Am I missing something?"

"Hey!" said George. "Stop banging into my chair!"

A whistle pierced the clamor. Inspector Henry, this time.

Boom. Boom. Boom. My heart drummed in the moment of silence, while nobody moved.

"Oh, hello, Inspector," said Mr. Fibbley, as cheeky as ever.

I expected a bellow, but the inspector spoke only one syllable, with steely calm.

"Out."

CHAPTER 20

A PUBLIC COMBAT

MR. FIBBLEY WAS POLITE enough to help us maneuver the wheelchair onto the street, but he'd galloped away on Mr. Thomas's heels by the time we'd got to the corner. The road was now slightly uphill, and the cobbles seemed to have doubled in size, while George bumped and jounced without noticing, excited by Miss Napoli's announcement that Mrs. Shelton had been poisoned. Hector and I, taking turns as chair-pushers, were feeling dismal, however. The arsenic news was not news to us. What mattered was the apparent fact of Mr. Hart's normal death.

If he was not the victim of murder, we must rearrange our deductions! The Uptons could not be considered suspects for either crime—and, in fact, there was only one crime! Despite a worm of disbelief still crawling around in my chest, I must turn my thoughts and sleuthing skills to Mrs. Shelton. The police would now vigorously be doing the same.

"Arsenic!" George repeated the word every other minute, as if it were something delicious, like butterscotch pudding. "I cannot wait to tell Sidonie," he said. "She will be dismayed to tears." He squeezed his eyes briefly shut. "This is not the reason for my pleasure in making a report, you understand. Only that my nurse has a particular curiosity about poison, which goes back to her days at nursing school. I will tell you sometime. It's an excellent tale, full of subterfuge and horror, but I expect that with a friend being the victim this time, her interest will be tempered with frustration."

"Why frustration?" I said.

"For not preventing it!" said George. "Mrs. Shelton suspected that poison might be the reason for her ailments. She sought Sidonie's counsel during one of their coffee times, about whether she might improve away from the fancy food and the mineral waters."

"The waters!" said Hector. "These foul-smelling, awful-tasting . . . Why do we not consider the waters before now?"

"Nothing wrong with the waters," said George. "They've been tested twice this month, because of Sidonie insisting on Mrs. Shelton's behalf. McWorthy was mighty peeved by the bother. Especially as no one else had suffered similar symptoms."

Nurse Touati had suggested to Nurse McWorthy that the Wellspring pumps might carry poison? Nurse Touati had a particular curiosity about poison? And for weeks she had met regularly with Mrs. Shelton to drink coffee, which Eva Napoli said was a fine masquerade for the taste of arsenic. Nurse Touati rose quickly to the top of the suspect list.

"George?" I said. "Did Mrs. Woolsey say something about Mrs. Shelton taking tonic on her last day?"

"Yes," said George.

"What tonic was that? Where did it come from?"

"From Wellspring. Made of flower petals and gingerroot and who knows what? McWorthy mixes them up according to individual recipes, whatever the patient needs. We carried three bottles to Mrs. Shelton, the day before. Sidonie and I picked up the package from McWorthy, because Mrs. Shelton had paid but forgot to take it with her."

"What happened to the bottles? Shouldn't they be tested?"

George's face brightened. "Is that what killed her, do you think?" And then darkened. "It was us who brought what killed her? I'll ask Mrs. Woolsey next time we go by," he said. "She may still have Mrs. Shelton's belongings, waiting to be claimed."

"Here you are!" We'd arrived at the hotel and Nurse Touati was waiting outside the front doors. Frank Thomas leaned against one of the columns, writing in his little notebook, his eyes mere inches from the page. Mr. Fibbley was nowhere in sight. "I nearly came looking," said the nurse, "but did not know which way you'd gone."

"Just wait until you hear," said George. He took his nurse's hand and told her gently about the murder of her friend. She closed her eyes and kept George's hand in hers. As it seemed weird to stand there watching, Hector and I silently agreed to move inside. Grannie Jane had chosen a sofa in the middle of the room and was madly knitting a baby's bootie. Hector and I, no longer bound by secrecy, now could tell her one piece of the truth about Mrs. Shelton's death. Arsenic! We added what George had said about his nurse being familiar with poison.

"I should think that any good nurse can recognize the symptoms of various poisons," said Grannie Jane, "and their treatments too. Perhaps young George has glamorized a perfectly mundane fact of Nurse Touati's experience." She tugged on her wool to let it unwind more easily, and began a new row.

"He *is* fond of all things gruesome," I admitted.

"One might say," Hector added, "that he has a Morbid Preoccupation."

My laughter was interrupted by a kerfuffle at the front door. The burly doorman helped Nurse Touati get George's chair inside, but she had taken only two steps when Detective Inspector Henry and his sergeant came in as well. Mr. Smythe appeared and slid over to the policemen as if drawn by a powerful magnet.

"Sergeant Rook and I will speak with the kitchen staff, the medical staff and the service staff," said the inspector. "In the most convenient order, the sooner the better."

"May I inquire as to the reason—" said Mr. Smythe.

"It has been confirmed that your former guest, Lidia Shelton, died as the result of poison," boomed Inspector Henry.

"Inspector, please!" The manager's hands were balled in fists that cranked up and down at his sides. "Will you listen to reason! Every minute you spend in the Wellspring lobby is another minute of wrongly informing my guests that we are not to be trusted!" He attempted to smile at guests who lingered, but he looked rather as if he'd eaten a beetle when he was expecting a peppermint. Nurse Touati had settled herself on the sofa next to ours, with George at her side. I watched her watching the exchange with police, *as unruffled as a peahen. As smooth as a pane of glass. As calm as a summer lake.*

"The woman was not even a guest when she died!" Mr. Smythe protested. "No one else here has been sick, have they? Plain as day, whatever she ate to cause indisposition was at the lodging house!"

"Thank you for your opinion, Mr. Smythe," said the inspector. "Do you consider yourself more capable than I, to perform my job? Would you like to trade for a day? I believe I would excel at adjusting flower arrangements and pretending to notice rich people's dogs."

Mr. Smythe flinched at the insult, but had no sassy reply at the ready.

"The sooner you assemble the staff," said Inspector Henry, "the sooner we can leave you to your important work."

"Better than a music hall," murmured Grannie Jane.

"I dare not breathe," said Hector, "in case I miss a word."

Within a few minutes, the two chambermaids faced the sergeant, scarcely an arm's length from where we sat. Milly looked vexed as she adjusted a hairpin. Verity was perspiring and breathing rapidly while retying her apron strings. The sergeant appeared to be puffed up with the duty of interviewing two pretty girls and did not notice us, the avid onlookers.

"Do you understand why we want to talk to you?" said Sergeant Rook. "You've heard the rumors?"

"You think we've been poisoning people," said Milly, "but we haven't. *I* haven't, anyway. I can't speak for *her*."

She did not look at Verity, but tipped her head disdainfully in the other girl's direction. On Sunday they'd been giggling together! What had they quarreled about?

"We're not saying you did the poisoning yourselves," said the sergeant, "but you might have noticed something odd and could tell us. You're in a special position, carrying food to people in their rooms."

"Chambermaids *do* see everything," said Milly. "You wouldn't believe what people put in their wastebaskets!"

"Today is only my second day here," said Verity. "I wasn't hired yet when the gentleman died in the garden, and I was not here when the lady died in the park. I don't know nuthin' about nuthin'." Her cap was awry, and one apron strap slipped off her shoulder. She was not as tidy as the Wellspring management expected.

"You know enough about something to have a man visiting our room!" said Milly, crossly. "I saw him sneaking out when I came back upstairs earlier, looking to see where you'd got to. That is strictly against the rules and I'm not getting sacked on your account!"

"It was my brother! I told you that! He only come to tell me our dad is sick!" Verity's pleas were tinged with desperation. Something in her voice was poking at my memory.

"Didn't look like a brother to me!" said Milly. "And you gone missing since then until now."

"Miss . . . uh . . ." stumbled Sergeant Rook, "both of you, misses. Whatever rules you break or don't break, that's not my business. I'm here about bigger things than sweethearts."

"He is *not* my sweetheart!" Verity protested.

The officer clapped his hands smartly together. "I'm here about *murder!*" Milly and Verity looked properly chastened. "You say you're new here?" he asked Verity.

"Yes, sir. I got trained yesterday, today being my first full day."

"You are free to get on with your duties, then," he said. "Doesn't mean I won't need to speak with you later, mind!"

She bobbed her head and backed away, leaving Milly to roll her eyes and scowl.

Verity paused near to where Hector and I were sitting. She straightened her cap and retied the lace on her boot. When she stood again, she looked directly into my eyes, as she had not done when serving us in our room. My heart jumped. She strolled away, making the bow on the back of her apron jiggle a little more than was polite. I was so mad at myself I wanted to pinch my own arm till I squeaked.

"Ooh la la," said Hector.

"Very saucy," said Grannie Jane—just in time to stop me from blurting out what I was thinking. Verity was not the novice chambermaid she had pretended to be.

The incorrigible Mr. Fibbley had tricked us again!

Reporters had been banished from the lobby on Saturday afternoon. But Gus Fibbley had been secretly operating inside the hotel ever since! He'd been—*she'd* been—creeping around getting extra milk and changing towels in our very room! Eavesdropping! She'd listened to us read aloud from her own article for the *Torquay Voice*! What else had she heard us say that might end up in the newspaper?

"I wonder," said Grannie Jane, "whether someone might deliver a pot of tea? Will you join me, Nurse Touati? I am reluctant to leave this ideal seating arrangement."

Hector and I hopped eagerly to our feet to do her bidding.

"Bring biscuits!" called George.

"The nerve of that conniving fiend!" I whispered, as we hurried to place Grannie's order.

Hector was laughing his rare, weird laugh that sounded like a creaky gate. "But so clever!" he said. "I admire this strategy most ardently. Mr. Fibbley does not see a bump in the path without seeing also how to hop over it, or slide around it, or dig under it, or—"

"Yes, yes," I said. "His tactics are resourceful to the highest degree. But, *grrr*, so sneaky!"

"This only irks," said Hector, "because he is even more sneaky than you!"

I narrowed my eyes and willed myself to look fierce, because he was right, of course.

"*Humph*," I said.

Alberto delivered tea and a plate of ladyfingers just as Dr. Baden and Nurse McWorthy arrived in the lobby and were hearing the news from Inspector Henry.

"Poor Mrs. Shelton! Poison, after all," the nurse was repeating. "Poor, poor lady. Poison! And after we tested the waters!"

"*Ssh*, Nurse." The doctor's face was grave. He cast his eyes about the lobby at the circle of spectators, including us. "I wonder, Inspector, whether we might speak with more privacy?"

The inspector summoned Mr. Smythe again, to request a more secluded spot for conducting his interviews.

"The Smoking Room is available," said Mr. Smythe. "If you'll follow me?"

"Rotten luck," I said, passing the plate of biscuits to George.

"The advantage of our location could not last forever," said Grannie Jane.

Oh, but she spoke seconds too soon!

Mr. Smythe led the inspector and the medical team past us toward the Smoking Room. Nurse McWorthy jerked to a stop upon seeing George and his nurse.

"You!" she cried. "Here's your culprit, Inspector! Look no further! She claimed to be a *friend* of the deceased, and now look! She knows all about how to kill with poison, and here she is in our midst! *And* she's one to turn against friends. I know what I'm talking about. Why aren't you questioning *her*?"

Nurse Touati stood up, dark eyes blazing. "Stop it, Lizzie," she said. "You're being very foolish."

"Nurse?" said Sergeant Rook.

Nurse McWorthy took a breath and spoke in a much lower tone, but as fierce as a wasp. "I won't let you get away with it," she said. "One corpse in the tub is one too many, but two? You've done it again."

"You know that's unfair, Lizzie," said Nurse Touati.

"Is it? And what about afterward? When you blamed me?"

"Not for that, I didn't."

Their voices had got even more quiet, enticing onlookers to creep closer. Inspector Henry and Sergeant Rook were frozen, straining to hear. George's gaze clicked back and forth between the two fuming women.

"You were guilty as accused," said Nurse Touati. "You needed counsel, as I've told you countless times. I expect you still do."

Nurse McWorthy seemed near to crying. There had been occasions when I, too, had been so angry that my eyes spilled tears—which made me angrier still. I believed that's what we were witnessing here. When George reached out a hand to each nurse, Lizzie McWorthy slapped it away, while Sidonie Touati held on.

"You be careful, son," Nurse McWorthy told George. "Those in her care—"

"Don't you tell me anything bad," said George. "She has saved my life just being my friend." His knuckles whitened as he squeezed his nurse's hand more tightly.

Inspector Henry cleared his throat. "Miss?" he said. "Nurse McWorthy? We'll conduct our conversation in a room at the clinic instead of the Smoking Room. Please come along."

"Why aren't you questioning *her*?" said Nurse McWorthy. But she followed obediently when the doctor took her arm and led her away, with the inspector alongside.

"And you, miss?" said Sergeant Rook to Nurse Touati. "We'd like to ask you a few questions as well." Grannie Jane agreed that George might stay with us, while his nurse was directed to the Smoking Room.

"Sidonie," said George. She withdrew her hand from his and patted his shoulder. But she looked flummoxed and even alarmed.

"In Algeria, where I come from," she said to Grannie, "a summons from the police can be an invitation to great disquiet."

"We shall wait for you here," Grannie Jane told her. "We'll have another cup of tea when you're done."

Grannie was kind, I knew, but I suspected that the phrase "one corpse in the tub" had piqued her ravenous interest, as it had mine. Sharing that cup of tea would be a second interrogation for Nurse Touati, whether she realized it or not.

The lobby had come back to chattering life, now that the entertainment had subsided. Mr. Smythe took a mauve handkerchief out of his waistcoat pocket and vigorously dabbed his neck and forehead.

"What do you suppose," I said to my fellow sleuths, "caused those nurses to spar so bitterly?"

"I can answer that," said George. "They harbor an age-old grudge against each other."

Grannie's needles rested for a moment.

"Please tell," said Hector.

"I know some but not all." George amended his claim. "Sidonie is a bit cagey about the details."

"Whose corpse was in the tub?" No reason to pretend that was not the top question on my mind.

George flashed what could only be called an Evil Grin. "Its name," he said, "was Honey."

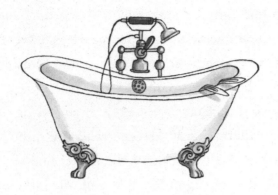

CHAPTER 21

A DISTURBING SECRET

"IT?" SAID HECTOR. "The corpse is an *it*?"

"Sidonie and Miss Lizzie McWorthy were at nursing school together," said George, teasing us by stretching out the story, reveling in being Mr. Know-All. "They shared rooms in the dormitory at The General Infirmary in Leeds for their second year of training."

Grannie Jane had begun to knit again, but without the usual clatter.

"Sidonie always scored top marks in chemistry," said George, "but I suspect that she was rather like Miss Eva Napoli, too curious for other people's comfort."

Grannie Jane made a noise that might have been a snort.

"Go on," I said. "God's wig, you're slow!"

"Agatha!" Grannie looked truly shocked. "Language!"

"She experimented," said George quickly, "on animals. She tested her concoctions on shrews and birds and anything else she could catch."

Oh dear. *Please not dogs.*

"Not cats or dogs!" George read my mind. "Little creatures from the woods or the dales. She set snares. Lizzie McWorthy didn't like that, not one little bit."

"That does sound horrible," I said.

"Sidonie says it was for science," said George, "that sometimes progress comes through disobedience to rules. Which suits me just fine. But, they were meant to be learning things from books, according to Lizzie McWorthy, not feeding dubious powders to harmless animals. Lizzie woke up one morning to find a dead rabbit in the bathtub. That was it. She went mad, Sidonie says. She threatened to have the police in. She threatened to have Sidonie carted away to the bin, or, at the very least, expelled from school."

"Is this what happens?" said Hector.

George sighed. "I've asked a million times and still don't know the whole story. My guess is that Sidonie knew a secret about Lizzie McWorthy, some dark transgression that she didn't want reported. And Sidonie won't tell me, due to being so honorable. But they each had something to hide."

"Nurse McWorthy referred to being accused." I tried to remember the exact sequence of the angry words they'd hurled at each other. "And Nurse Touati said, 'Not for that,' meaning the corpse, I suppose? The corpse that was Honey?"

"Honey Bunny," said George. "The second one was only a vole and didn't have a name."

Grannie Jane rolled her eyes, quite amusing for an old lady wearing gold spectacles on a fine linked chain.

"But Nurse McWorthy's crime was so dark that it kept her silent when blackmailed?"

"But she *didn't* stay silent," said George. "She blabbed, and Sidonie was expelled before they graduated. Sidonie blabbed back, and Nurse McWorthy was expelled too. Even though they were nearly done their training and knew everything about nursing, neither of them ever officially qualified. That's why they're not in a hospital. Sidonie looks after me, and Nurse McWorthy hands out towels at a hotel clinic."

"But each lady is called Nurse," said Hector.

"That's because they both—"

"Hello." Nurse Touati appeared, glancing over her shoulder as if trying to shake a pursuer. "Here I am, back from the inquisition." Her fingertips touched the top of George's head to gently ruffle his hair. Her hands appeared to be trembling ever so slightly. Had dull-witted Sergeant Rook managed to rattle her? *What was she hiding?*

223

"Hullo." George studied his gloves. He must be worried that the nurse had overheard him revealing her secrets. "How did it go," he asked, "with the sergeant? How many tries did it take before he could spell your name correctly?"

Nurse Touati managed a laugh. "I took his pencil and wrote it for him. He's really pretty dim." She turned the wheelchair around and gave us a little wave. "We'll find you later, or tomorrow."

"I don't like to agree with Sergeant Rook," I said, watching as Nurse Touati skilfully skied through the lobby behind the rolling chair. "But, of all the candidates, she knew Mrs. Shelton better than anyone. Does that not make her the most likely suspect?"

"Pish," said Grannie. She finished a row and held up the little bootie to see how it was taking shape. "Convincing me of that will take some effort."

"The poison was being administered for weeks. Nurse Touati is the only one who had steady contact with the victim during that time. They often drank coffee together. *Coffee*, Grannie. An excellent disguise for arsenic."

"Just now we hear that she is expert in the chemistry of medicines and poisonous substances," said Hector.

"Not such an expert if she killed her subjects in the bathtub," said Grannie Jane. "I do feel sympathy for Nurse McWorthy on that score."

I fell into a reverie . . . *Tousled by sleep and chilled by walking barefoot down the passage this wintry morning, the girl hugged her flannel robe more tightly around herself. A warm bath in the soft gray light of morning would soothe rumpled spirits. Leaning over to turn the faucet, her bleary eyes were shocked to see the body of a hare stretched out along the bottom of the bathtub. Its fur seemed to have stiffened in a bristle of fear; its one visible pink-rimmed eye stared up in anguish . . . She turned with a jolt of panic to splash her face in the basin—but found it full of black feathers. A crow lay in its porcelain grave, glossy wings spread and beak uplifted as if to catch a drop of rain. A tidy row of mice, tied by their tails to the towel bar, swayed in a gentle gust of air.*

"It *would* make a disturbing start to the morning," I said.

"We struggle, however," said Hector, "with finding a motive."

"I am not surprised," said Grannie Jane. "The woman appears to be blameless apart from a long-ago affection for chemistry. Perhaps you will tell me your thoughts thus far?"

"She might be a lunatic who plays with poison," said Hector, "but this hypothesis does not bear close inspection."

"Nurse McWorthy might have told Mrs. Shelton about the rabbit in the bathtub," I said. "And Mrs. Shelton started to blackmail Nurse Touati—"

Grannie Jane had stopped knitting and was listening with a steady little shake of her head.

"She chooses not to stab her with a hat pin," said Grannie Jane, "but to poison her slowly over an extended period of time, so that Mrs. Shelton might have as much opportunity as she needed to tell the police that she was the victim of a prolonged assault by the same person who sneaked about rummaging for voles in the bean fields?"

"It does sound foolish when you put it like that," I admitted.

"I cannot help but think," said Grannie, "as you have noted, that there is a second nurse on the premises, whose acquaintance with Mrs. Shelton was just as long as that of Nurse Touati."

I looked at her. I looked at Hector. Hector looked at me—a different sort of look from the one that said my imagination bordered on insanity.

Nurse McWorthy!

"Speaking of whom . . ." Grannie glanced at the watch pinned to her bodice. "Were you not meant to meet your mother in the clinic, Agatha?"

Off I flew to find Mummy, and arrived to find her in conversation with our newest suspect!

Mummy, rosy and happy, slid an arm around my shoulder to say hello. The nurse winced at the sight of me. I had just witnessed her vicious accusation of Nurse Touati.

"Here I am, jackling on, but I was rattled by the inspector being here, *while we had patients in the waters*! I'm only thankful you weren't disturbed, Mrs. Morton. He did keep asking questions. When was the last time we'd seen Mrs. Shelton? How long had she been poorly? The doctor kept his temper, but I could see his patience draining fast. Which pumps did she drink the waters from? They'd be taking samples to be tested in their laboratories, no please or thank you, not caring it had been done already. What was Dr. Baden treating her for? What sort of medicines was she using and who mixed them? Well, it was *me* who mixed them! *I'm* not the one who mixes up the wrong ingredients for medicines. I told them that as plain as day."

She glanced at me and flushed. "And even if I was, does that make me a murderess?"

THE YORKSHIRE DAILY

LATE EDITION

APRIL 20, 1903

LADY MORTICIAN CLAIMS
ARSENIC
IN BANDSTAND CORPSE!!!

by FRANK THOMAS

The lady found dead in Valley Gardens Park a week ago Saturday was poisoned!! So says Miss Eva Napoli, daughter of our Harrogate undertaker. No one requested a test for toxic substances, including the police, but Miss Napoli took it upon herself to perform experiments on a decomposing corpse. She wished to prove that widow Lidia Shelton [33 yrs.] ingested the poison over a period of weeks, leading to a fatal dose 10 days ago. And the police believe her! The finger of blame is being pointed at the Wellspring Hotel & Spa where Mrs. Shelton was resident for an extended time. Miss Napoli declares that hair cut from the dead woman's head indicates an intentional dosage, not the mild levels we all exhibit through contact with arsenic in our daily lives. Consider the list of well-known sources of arsenic that might easily have contaminated Mrs. Shelton: Her own face powder! The green dye in her dress fabric or wallpaper! The candle burning on her bedside table! The stuffed bird that ornaments her hat! The bottle of liver pills in her medicine cabinet! Are any of these related to a stay at the Wellspring Hotel & Spa? Not at all! It is irresponsible to spread faulty rumors about a revered local establishment. Is this ploy part of a plot to oust the current County Coroner and take over the position herself? A Conniving Female! Is that what voting men in West Riding want? A "lady" self-taught on matters of death and disposal? Allow the police to investigate and decide if wrong has been done.

TORQUAY VOICE

APRIL 20, 1903

THE HARROGATE BENCH KILLER
ONE VICTIM OR TWO?
SUSPICIOUS DEATHS UNCOVERED
BY TORQUAY RESIDENT

by Augustus C. Fibbley

Two people died outdoors in Harrogate last week and the townspeople have many questions. The first of these unfortunates, Mrs. Lidia Shelton, was certainly a victim of murder. She expired on the afternoon before Easter Sunday, alone on a bench in a public park. Prompted by intuition (a valuable quality often possessed by women), Miss Eva Napoli, notable undertaker and ambitious forensic scientist, made a methodical analysis of the dead woman's hair to expose a grim truth. Mrs. Shelton's illness and, finally, her death were the result of systematic arsenic poisoning by a cruel, unknown hand, during the more than three weeks that she was a guest at the Wellspring

Hotel & Spa. Her worsening symptoms of headaches and wretched internal distress led her to move into a lodging house on Beulah St. An interview with the landlady there has shed further light on the last few hours of Mrs. Shelton's too-short life. The window of her room overlooked Valley Gardens Park, with a view of the very bench upon which she met her Maker. Mrs. Woolsey reports that Mrs. Shelton swallowed a dose of her usual tonic—from a fresh bottle— just hours before she died. Have other bottles in the Wellspring clinic been tested for a fatal ingredient?

A second death occurred a mere three days later, also alone on a bench, and this time right inside the Wellspring grounds. The death of Mr. Benedict Hart (46) has been deemed the result of natural causes—though some find this difficult to believe. The corpse was discovered by his niece, Mrs. Josephine Upton, who was accompanied by Torquay native Miss Agatha Morton (12) and Belgian native Master Hector Perot (also 12). The fearless Master Perot ascertained that Mr. Hart was dead by feeling his neck for a pulse. One puzzling incident, not reported elsewhere, was a "mysterious telephone call" placed to the victim less than an hour before his stricken body was discovered. An unidentified caller lured him to the dark and lonely place where he met his end.

Though police are not pursuing inquiries, one can only wonder who placed the fatal telephone call?

Wellspring Hotel & Spa, Harrogate

April 20, 1903

Dear Marjorie,

I have much to tell you about the hotel and the murders, and our new friend, George. But I am writing all that in a note inside the envelope from Grannie Jane. This letter is private, just between sisters. My innards are roiling, and I do not quite know what to think about something that is very hard to think about. It's Mummy, you see, and how our time here at the Wellspring has turned her, in only a few days, into a different person. That may be inaccurate. It may be that she has begun to be herself again, pretty and calm and even laughing at times. She loves the spa, with its warm mineral water pools and steam and icy dips, and she comes to meals with rosy cheeks and shining eyes. But I am not the only one to notice these things. There are men here, who seem to think it acceptable behavior to flock around our mother like vultures around a freshly killed zebra. It is a most uncomfortable feeling! More than that, it makes me ache for Papa to stride into the room and banish them all. Grannie shoots me warning looks as if to say that admiration is part of Mummy's recovery, but what if she stops remembering Papa? Will that make it harder for me to keep my memories too?

Please tell me what to do.

Love,

Aggie

PS Pat your tummy for me xo

CHAPTER 22

A FEARSOME CONSIDERATION

"GOOD AFTERNOON." Mrs. Upton stood beside our table on Tuesday, looking elegant in Mummy's black silk jacket and skirt. She wore a necklace of jet beads at her throat and an ebony comb in her hair.

"Excuse me for interrupting," she said. "I wanted only to tell you . . ." She lifted her hand to show a yellow paper. "I've had a telegram from my father in Cairo. He cannot make the long journey from Egypt, so the decisions are all mine. He has agreed that I should transport the bod—er, Uncle Ben, by train, to be buried near my grandparents. Eddie has conferred with Mr. Napoli, and we will accompany the coffin to Nottingham on Thursday morning."

"Such a sad ordeal for you," said Mummy.

"I will return your dresses before I go," said Mrs. Upton. "I am so grateful that you were here to help me."

I looked at Hector. With Mr. Hart's death officially named a natural one, the police had no reason to insist that the Uptons stay in Harrogate. They were no longer under suspicion—and even Hector and I must admit that if there had been no murder, there could be no murderer. The Uptons had no reason to kill Mrs. Shelton—they'd barely met her—and Nurse McWorthy seemed a much more likely suspect for that crime than they did. So why was I still uneasy about Mr. Hart?

"Let me go up with you," said Mummy, rising. "We're finished here. Will you come too, Jane?"

"Not just yet," said Grannie.

I watched Mrs. Upton take Mummy's arm as they strolled away. Was this Happily Ever After for the Uptons? I briefly considered a different ending to the story.

The newlyweds arrived at the railway station in high spirits. They watched her uncle's coffin being loaded into the baggage car—did deceased passengers ride in the baggage car?—*with something akin to joy. Josie had purchased a First-Class Salon compartment and requested that champagne be waiting on ice. They had something to celebrate, now that she was an heiress!*

Was she also a murderess? I did not think so anymore. And . . . her husband? After days of observation, he seemed to me not likely capable of great deceit. Those ears turned pink so easily with every surge of emotion . . . And yet, he had managed to have secret meetings and achieve new employment without anyone the wiser. I sighed, long and hard. Hector had been watching Mrs. Upton as well. He lifted his shoulders and allowed them to drop.

"Do explain the long faces," said Grannie, "before your chins fall off with drooping."

"Let's find a corner of the lobby," I said. "It is too tricky a topic for the dining room."

After the usual fuss with Grannie's knitting, we were ensconced on the sofa by the box room, ready for a Detection Consultation.

"As much as we want to learn who killed Mrs. Shelton . . ." I said. "And I know this will sound odd, Grannie, even *macabre*, but we are disappointed that Mr. Hart's death has been deemed not suspicious. We were rather depending on *both* deaths being murder!"

"Ah," said Grannie Jane. "I thought it might be something like that." She nudged soft creamy wool into place for the next row. The booties were finished, and this was to be a blanket for the cradle. "One sticking point with your theory is that murderers are usually loyal to their methods. By which I mean, when a poisoner uses poison successfully, he sees no need to start shooting people. A stabber is likely to stab again. And so on."

"Well, yes," I said. "But we thought maybe just this once . . . There mightn't have been enough time to dispose of Mr. Hart so carefully."

"And while you were considering Mr. Hart's fate," said Grannie, "had you decided who might be capable of such a deed?"

Neither of us spoke. It seemed a grave matter to name a name.

"At first . . ." I began, in almost a whisper, "we considered Mrs. Upton as the most likely suspect. She has the best motive, since she inherits the factory and the money, but she was at the bandstand during the time that he died, and she seemed truly distraught to find him dead."

"Go on," said Grannie Jane.

"Remember the telephone call? Telling Mr. Hart about an emergency? We believe someone lured him outside. Mr. LaValle told us that during the same time period when Mr. Hart was dying, Mrs. Upton stood beside the bandstand in her green dress, listening to music all alone, with no sign of her husband."

"We think possibly Mr. Eddie leaves his wife for a few minutes—" said Hector.

"And placed a telephone call, from . . . well, we don't know where from," I said, "but he sneaked out of Valley Gardens Park, across the road and into the hotel garden to wait for the chance to kill Mr. Hart."

"This is what we think until yesterday," said Hector, "when we hear the reason for death is an attack of the heart."

"Until yesterday, we thought that Mr. Upton killed Mr. Hart," I said, "and hurried back to the park to dance another dance with his new wife. Then he steered her to the main door of the hotel, purposely avoiding the garden because he is not so mean as to make poor Josie be the person to find her dead uncle."

"But Miss Napoli, she cannot find evidence of murder. And so, we are puzzled."

"That telephone call does seem to insist that wicked intentions were at play," agreed Grannie Jane, "but perhaps not where you expected to find them." She peered for a moment at her knitting and then kept going. "This all brings to mind Mrs. Trumble's unfortunate son."

"Mrs. Who?" I said.

"Evan Trumble's mother, who worked in the draper's shop. I'm afraid she was the dithering sort," said Grannie Jane. "Evan was a boy who liked to read and play jokes and sprinkle sugar on cake. He'd been born with one leg shorter than the other, so it was a matter of the stairs, you see?"

I did not see, and Hector's eyebrows told me that he did not see either. But we were used to Grannie's occasional bouts of odd reminiscence, and simply waited.

"Both the leg and the books left him open to teasing by the other boys, even in his own family. It was a birthday supper for one of his cousins, when a prized engine disappeared from a railway set upstairs. Evan was blamed because he'd disappeared from the party for half a dozen minutes. His mother believed he'd never touch what wasn't his, but the other boys gave him quite a roughing-up." She'd come to the end of a row and adjusted her knitting needles.

"I've always wondered, why didn't they simply ask Evan?" said Grannie Jane. "No one bothered to ask because they assumed he'd lie, as they would have done in his place. No one thought how he'd never have got up those stairs and down again in just those few moments, or had time to hide the train. It turned out he'd been inflating a rubber balloon as a surprise for the birthday girl."

"The stairs!" I said. "The distance from the bandstand to the bench . . ."

"Might it be useful," said Grannie Jane, "to know the piece of music being played while Mrs. Upton swayed in her green dress beside the stage? Just how many minutes was Mr. Upton out of sight?"

Hector and I were silent for a moment. It was a practical suggestion to prove or disprove a supposition. But the length of the music playing was only part of the puzzle.

"And how long might it take," I said, "for someone to dash from the bandstand to a telephone to the bench in the garden and back again to the bandstand?"

"Much of this we know already," said Hector. "Walking to the bandstand from the hotel, it takes six minutes? Seven? In each direction."

"It would be less if he were running," I said.

"He cannot run with so many witnesses," said Hector. "Nor does this time account for finding or speaking on a telephone."

"Shall we say eighteen or twenty minutes at most, but perhaps as few as fourteen?" I said. "If he'd planned ahead where to find a telephone."

"I concur," said Hector.

"Well, then," said Grannie Jane. "What next?"

"Now, we find out which piece was playing at the crucial moment," I said, "and see whether the times add up. It still could be that Eddie Upton killed his wife's Uncle Ben, hoping for the inheritance. Or, it still could be that there are two murderers. It even still could be . . ." An idea had seeped into my head like a splash of ink. "What if these two murders are not in the least bit connected except by the hand that performed them? What if the killer wanted Mrs. Shelton to die, and poisoned her, quite efficiently? But then . . . he—or she—hunted about to find a random stranger to be the decoy victim. It didn't matter how the next one died—probably better to strangle or suffocate, just to be different. Attention would turn away from the real victim and focus on the new one! The police would be utterly baffled! *What could the motive be??* The perpetrator would never be caught!"

Hector was giving me that look, where one eyebrow went higher than seemed possible and his eyes held more than a touch of exasperation. "You are admirable for many reasons, mon amie," he said, gently, "but not always for the invention of plausible reasons for homicide."

"You did not give it much consideration." I tried not to pout. "If ever I need to devise a murder, you'll see how diabolical I can be."

"Dear Agatha," said Grannie. "Of this there is no doubt." She hauled herself up from the plump cushions of the sofa, ready to retire for her nap. Hector tucked away her knitting and I pulled straight her shawl. Turning to depart, Grannie found herself nose to nose with the Buzzard.

She lurched back, grasping my arm in her shock. "Announce yourself, man, if there's a reason to be here! You scared me witless!"

The bell captain flushed and bowed and reversed a few fumbling steps. Grannie Jane's wits returned with no trouble, and scorn burned from her eyes as he attempted an apology. He'd had no reason to lurk, but pretended an urgent need to know what time we'd be dining this evening. Grannie's scorn escalated, and she swept away to Room 201. All the while, my brain friction had been fizzing, like kernels of popping corn over a fire.

I took hold of Hector's sleeve and led him out to the garden. "I am in the middle of having a big idea."

He was wise enough to stay quiet and wait for me to burst. The birds did not cooperate, but chirped and cawed and twittered. The fountain burbled and spat. I made Hector sit on Mr. Hart's bench exactly where we'd found the corpse. I trailed my fingers along the scarred bump on the back of the bench, and then to the broken line in the stone urn.

Scared witless, Grannie had said. It was one of those phrases people used to exaggerate a fright. *Scared stiff, paralyzed with fear, panic-stricken* . . . And yet, could it be?

Strike fear into . . .

The murder that was not really a murder.

The natural death that did not seem entirely natural.

I closed my eyes and thought back to our first encounter with Mr. Hart, when George had nearly knocked him over in the passage. It hadn't been so near as that, the knocking-over part. Now that we knew George, it was clear that he was in complete control of his wheelchair.

But Mr. Hart had been afraid.

"Mr. Hart was afraid," I said, opening my eyes. "Remember the first day, when George thundered toward him? Mr. Hart put a hand to his chest, and you had to help him sit."

Hector nodded. "He has the weak heart and does not like surprises."

"And!" I sat up straighter. "In the clinic that morning, the odd way he behaved . . . Something made his color go ashen. Was that fear?"

"Something?" Hector was nodding steadily. "Or some*one*?"

"And when he got a message that his niece was hurt—"

"Once more, he is afraid."

"What if someone chose that moment to threaten him further? To *strike fear into him*?"

"This fear," said Hector, "is fatal."

"What we need to know," I said, "is whether it is truly possible to scare someone to death?"

CHAPTER 23

A STARTLING REVELATION—AND THEN ANOTHER

WE BOTH WERE ON our feet, not going anywhere, but too prickly with the new idea to stay seated.

"Can a bad fright actually cause a fatal attack if a person has a faulty heart?"

"I think yes," said Hector, "but who imagines this to be a reliable method of murder?"

"Do you suppose that the killer intended to bash him over the head with the croquet mallet? But Mr. Hart was so unnerved that he fell down dead!"

"Maybe the aim of the killer is not accurate, because of the dark," said Hector.

"And that's how the urn was cracked and the bench got dented."

"My lucky mallet," said Hector, with profound sadness.

"Does this bring us back to the Uptons?" I said. "They knew better than anyone the fragility of Mr. Hart's health."

"The Uptons, or the medical personnel," said Hector. "Two nurses and a doctor."

"Was *fear* the actual murder weapon?" I said.

The gate squeaked. Mr. Fibbley came up the garden path, removing his cap and jacket as he hurried along. Hector and I stopped talking. I practically stopped breathing. Had the reporter heard our deductions?

"Don't let me interrupt." He tucked the jacket neatly under his arm and smoothed his hair. "I'm just passing through."

"Mr. Fibbley," I said. "Have you learned yet who placed the telephone call to Mr. Hart on the night of his death? The call you learned about by eavesdropping in our hotel room?"

"Not yet!" He went past us, but then tossed a comment over his shoulder. "Interesting theory," he said. "Fear, as a weapon." He trotted up the path to the hotel. "I am obliged to be elsewhere. Good afternoon."

"Reporters have been banned," I called out. "You're not allowed inside, dressed that way . . . you know, as Mr. Fibbley."

"Am I not?" And in he went.

"I'd like to know pre*cise*ly what he's looking for," I said.

"Suspicion still lurks in his brain as it does in ours," said Hector. "Perhaps suspicion lurks in him *because* it lurks in us?"

"Did he hear us say that the doctor or one of the nurses would have known about Mr. Hart's weak heart?" I said. "All three of them were present in the clinic on the morning of his alarm."

We watched, for half a minute, as a cheerful robin bobbed its way along the rim of the fountain. "However," said Hector, "I wish to suggest that we complete the task we have begun."

"The music?" I said.

"The Eddie Upton alibi," said Hector. "We must not abandon this possibility before it is disproved."

"Good thinking," I said. "Let's go to the tearoom and listen to music."

"And eat cake," said Hector.

By chance, we met Mummy in the lobby.

"Goodness," she said, her eyes sweeping over me, head to toe. "You'd best come to the room and wash up before tea, don't you think?"

Hector made a small effort to hide his smile, but I

knew she meant that my hair was escaping, my hands were grubby, and my dress could do with a fresh collar. Once clean and polished, we all stepped out and were confronted by an episode down the passage.

"It's only my third day, Mrs. Upton, I didn't realize!" pleaded Verity, the chambermaid. "If you tell Mr. Smythe, I'll lose the position! Me dad's off sick, and we need my wages terrible bad. Please, madam, I won't come in there again, I promise, unless you ask me." She seemed to be fighting back tears, head bowed, cap trembling. Mummy moved closer, spurred to action by the sound of distress. We followed close behind, though for different reasons.

"Very well," said Mrs. Upton. "I'm touchy, I expect. It seems you meant no harm. But my uncle just died, and . . . here you are, touching his belongings . . ." Her voice cracked.

"Oh, thank you, ma'am, with all my heart. I meant no harm, not ever. I will not bother you again." Verity bobbed her head and turned to flee, but there we stood, accidentally blocking her path. How had she changed her clothes in the few minutes since we'd seen her in the garden? She bobbed her head to Mummy and dodged around us to escape down the stairs.

"I do not believe the girl is a thief," said Mrs. Upton, "but since my pretty brooch went missing . . . I know she can't be blamed—she wasn't even working here a week ago—but I do think she's a bit stupid not to understand."

Stupid is the last word in the dictionary I would have chosen.

"She's still learning," said Mummy. "Perhaps she is overwhelmed and found herself in the wrong room."

"Thank you," said Mrs. Upton. "I do not wish to make her job more difficult."

"We are expected downstairs for tea," said Mummy. "Please excuse us for running off."

"Goodness!" said Mrs. Upton. "As am I, and have not yet changed my dress!" She disappeared into her room so quickly that she shut the door on her own skirt and had to open up to free herself.

Our arrival in the tearoom exactly coincided with one of the interludes when members of the Wellspring string quartet loitered among the tables in the audience. We easily could approach Mr. LaValle to make our request.

"Please, sir? Mrs. Upton told us that you played something so entrancing the other night at the bandstand that she stopped still to listen. Do you recall which piece that might have been?"

"The lady in the green dress?" said Mr. LaValle. "Is she here?"

"She will be, in a few minutes. She's the one whose uncle died, so she's wearing black this evening. Perhaps you could play it again? Especially for her?"

"I would be happy to put it on the program," he said. "It is a piece by Eduard Strauss, the lesser-known brother of Johann. His opus 90. We'll play it as soon as she gets here."

We thanked him profusely and returned to our seats.

"Grannie Jane? May we borrow your watch?"

"Certainly not." Grannie's fingers flew to the sturdy silver watch pinned to her bodice. It had been a gift from my Papa's father, Laddie, the grandfather I'd never known.

"Unless," she said, "it remains attached to me."

Alberto arrived to offer a slice of coconut pie, and we succumbed.

After one bite, I composed a poem.

"Why, oh, why,
Can't I have pie,
Every day,
Until I die?"

Finally, Mrs. Upton—and her husband—joined our table. Grannie coughed a small cough. Hector and I bugged eyes at each other. An elegant tearoom, a lovely string ensemble, a glimmering chandelier, a wedge of pie sprinkled with slivers of shaved coconut . . . and a possible murderer watching us time his alibi!

Mr. LaValle caught my eye and raised his bow. Opus 90 began.

Grannie's fingers stroked the glass face of her watch throughout the piece by Mr. Eduard Strauss. The moment that Mr. LaValle's bow made its final swipe across the strings, she peered down to see the time. Hector and I applauded the musicians but gazed at Grannie, yearning for the verdict as surely as if we were in a court of law and waiting for a judge to speak. But how would she tell us, with Mr. Upton sitting right there?

"That was enchanting," she said. "Eight minutes and seven seconds of heavenly music."

Only eight minutes? Goodness. Far short of fourteen, let alone twenty! Across the table Mr. Upton's hand rested on his wife's shoulder, head tilted to listen to the next musical selection with those impressive ears. Probably not a murderer after all. I waved a hand to Mr. LaValle to thank him—for eliminating another suspect on the shrinking list. Now we could concentrate on our medical contenders.

Nurse McWorthy led the pack. She knew both the victims. She probably had access to arsenic. She was a bit unhinged, if her fury at Nurse Touati was any indication. Though she might be pretending to be unhinged. She might have accused Nurse Touati in public on purpose, to divert attention from herself! Or, possibly . . . the two not-nurses were cohorts? Had they invented a public feud to cover a dangerous and criminal partnership?

I imagined the look on Hector's face if I made that suggestion out loud.

Grannie would say *pish*.

And what would Mr. Augustus Fibbley say?

I signaled Hector with shifting eyes and a tipping head. *Meet-me-in-the-lobby-for-an-emergency-consultation!* Mummy and Grannie both looked faintly askance at our excusing ourselves, but did not stop us.

"What do you suppose Mr. Fibbley was doing inside room 207?" I began. "He heard Miss Napoli say perfectly clearly that Mr. Hart was not murdered, so why is he sniffing around and sneaking into his room? Why did he go to all the trouble of getting a job as a chambermaid?"

"This I do not know," said Hector.

"Time to find out," I said. "Please tell Grannie and Mummy that I . . . Oh, I don't know! What might I be doing? Use your imagination!"

Hector looked stricken. "But I do not have—"

"All right, tell them I went to find my notebook. They accept all manner of peculiar behavior when it comes to my notebook. And it might even be true."

I knew exactly what I needed to do. In our room, I went into the bathroom. I took two neatly folded towels from the shelf and put them on the floor. I trod on them, catching up the edges with my toes and crunching them into wrinkles. Then I put them in the bathtub and splashed them with a little water. I bundled the sodden lump into my arms and walked the corridors of the Wellspring Hotel until I found the person I was seeking.

"Hello," I said.

"Hello." She glanced behind her and then behind me.

"Our towels are damp," I said. "I wonder if you might replace them for us?"

"Clever girl," she murmured, and, in a louder voice, "Come with me, miss. I will fetch fresh towels for you."

Moments later, we were tucked inside the linen cupboard, which luckily was a linen *room* rather than a cupboard, with enough space for us to stand between the shelves stacked with bedding and other linens. We traded my armful of damp towels for a tidy stack of dry ones, while I asked her questions.

"Why are you in Harrogate?"

"Would I miss a chance to share another murder with you?" she said.

"But really," I said. "Why?"

"I ran into your friend Constable Beck, at the pub," she said. "He mentioned that your family was visiting Harrogate. The very next day came the report of a suspicious death in the same town. The *Voice* editor said I could write the story, if I paid my own expenses. So here I am."

"What did you find in room 207?"

"What makes you think that I found anything?" she said.

"Because you always do."

"Do I?"

I glared at her. "I had forgotten until now your most irksome habit!"

"And what is that?" she said.

"You answer nearly every question with another question!"

"Do I?" Her eyes sparkled with mischief. But I saw that one hand lay protectively across the pocket of her apron.

"Show me your notebook," I said.

"Will you show me yours?" she said.

"Aack!" I squawked in frustration. She put up a hand to calm me.

"I do sometimes tease too long," she said. "The result of having brothers. Never let them think they've won. Always have the last word."

"You have brothers?" I said.

"Three. But we are not here to trade family stories. You and I want the same thing, and we're both struggling to find it."

"What do we both want?" I said.

"Two murders," said Verity. "Isn't that right?"

I lowered my face to examine the pattern on the towels in my arms. "It's an awful thing to want," I said. "Even if it makes a good story."

"I tell you, Aggie Morton, you are cut out to be a reporter—or a detective. It might have taken me another whole day to think of visiting the undertaker if you hadn't put the idea into my head. And, fear? As a weapon? That's bloomin' brilliant! Also, I've learned that being a chambermaid is an excellent way to collect information. There can be no better apprenticeship for either job, if you want my advice."

"I do not imagine my mother would be pleased to have me pursue an occupation that involved snooping." I pretended to resist the commendation, though secretly held onto her praise with both fists. There was plenty to be said about Mr. Fibbley that I would not want said about me. He was duplicitous and disrespectful and relentless. In truth, my (hopefully well-concealed) admiration was growing. He wrote a story in the newspaper every day. Every day! Sometimes a segment of a serial already unfolding, sometimes a new tale intended to hook, tantalize and inform the reader. He never shirked his duty to research, though he did play with the facts on occasion—or, at the very least, shaped their telling to support his own opinions.

"There comes a time, Aggie Morton," said Verity, "when a mother's opinion matters only if we ask for it. Unbidden judgment must not bar the path to your dreams."

As she turned, the keys clinked on the ring at her waist.

"One more thing," I said.

She tipped her head, her silly maid's cap looking like a dollop of cream about to slide off.

"Does one of those keys open the door to the Wellspring Spa & Clinic?"

CHAPTER 24

A RISKY TRESPASS

IF HECTOR AND I HAD learned anything from our previous adventures as detectives, it was that no one should venture out alone at night to a questionable location. By day, the Wellspring Spa & Clinic did not qualify as questionable, but in the dead of night, it was *sinister*.

We waited until Grannie Jane was snoring and Mummy mumbling to herself, as she often did while dreaming. I liked to imagine that she met Papa in the land of Nod, and they walked by the sea, holding hands, or shared an hour in the library before daylight burst in like a rowdy dog, ending the encounter for another night.

Hector and I dressed silently and carried our shoes to the passage, tiptoeing to the stairs before tying them on. Our riskiest obstacle was the location of the night clerk, who assumed the Buzzard's duties during the late hours. We'd never seen him, and did not know his name, but we had heard the Buzzard complain that he left the kiosk untidy, a dish of plum stones inside a drawer, or the circle of a teacup marked on the registration form of a guest. From our room to the clinic there was no route that avoided his domain of the darkened lobby, so we had devised a plan for unavoidable encounters. Hector would be suffering from a toothache and seeking an emergency remedy. Hector had earlier shredded half a page of writing paper from the escritoire in the room, forming it with diligence into a ghastly wad of moist pulp. He inserted this between lower gum and cheek to produce a look of swollen misery. It also impeded his speech, so that he slurred as if he'd been nipping whiskey.

We crept down the stairs and surveyed the lobby from behind a column in the arched entry. An odd rumble came from the direction of the kiosk. Hector and I exchanged happy hand-dancing. The night clerk was asleep and snoring! Hector extracted the wad of paper from his mouth and slipped it—*ew!*—into his pocket. We made our way across the carpet, alert to every snuffle from the snoozing man. A line from the Christmas poem ran through my head: *Not a creature was stirring, not even a mouse . . .*

The walkway was sheltered and the breeze fresh and warm. I pulled Verity's key from my pocket. It turned easily, making a faint click. I looked at Hector. We did not know that our actions would yield results, nor really what results we sought. There were many words for what we had chosen to be this evening. Trespassers. Invaders. Burglars. Criminals. Furtive. Interlopers. And, finally, Just Plain Naughty.

Between the nurse's desk in the reception area and the door to Dr. Baden's office was a small room like the pantry of a kitchen. This was the dispensary where the medicines and balms were blended and packaged. A small window provided a square of muted moonlight. But not enough. Hector turned on his torch and let me hold it. Here were many glass-fronted cabinets full of jars, boxes full of powders, tonics and tablets. On the stone counter was a cutting block, an array of measuring instruments, a pair of scales, dozens of empty bottles and a small sink. I opened the first cabinet and my spirits sagged. The nurse and doctor were not so orderly as to alphabetize their cupboards. I opened each cabinet in turn and ran the torch light over the labels—especially made for the Wellspring clinic, with a watery blue band around the border and the contents written in a tidy script.

Soothing Syrup, Fruit Salt, Bromide of Potassium, Calisaya Bark Elixir, Quinine, Pepsin, Chloroform, Calendula, Hazeline, Lavender Oil, Malt Extract, Cod Liver Oil, Clove Oil, Beef Wine, Iron Wine, Acid

Phosphate, tinctures of liquorice root, echinacea, tea tree oil and many more . . .

I knew next to nothing about chemistry, but—aside from chloroform, which I had learned could occasionally be dangerous—none of these mixtures suggested poison.

"You imagine she has a bottle with the label ARSENIC?" said Hector.

"I suppose that *is* what I was hoping." Optimistic, I saw now. "And are poisons not meant to show the image of a skull and crossbones at the very least?"

"If such a bottle exists, will it be stored in a cupboard with common items?"

"We did not properly think it through," I admitted. "Either they keep the toxic blends in a locked cupboard . . ." I scanned the dispensary with no success. "Or the poison is masquerading as a more ordinary powder? And only the nurse knows what is what, among her curatives."

"A bottle that says Epsom salts is, in truth, strychnine?" said Hector.

"Something like that. But we did not come prepared to take samples from every jar . . ." We left the dispensary and I leaned on the desk. "And would it not be too risky to mislabel medicines in a cupboard also used by the doctor? *Oof!*" The nurse's chair had wheels and rolled as I sat. "Would she perhaps keep the lethal powders in her desk?"

"Open and find out," said Hector. "Check also for a secret drawer." The surface of the desk was bare, its polish reflecting circles of torchlight.

The shallow, central drawer revealed spectacles, two handkerchiefs, a row of pencils, a tin of throat lozenges, a small bottle of scent and a packet of caraway biscuits.

"Are you listening for someone coming?" I opened the tin of lozenges to check that it did not hold powdered poison.

Hector peeked into the passage. "All is quiet."

Under the desk, on one side, was a sturdy set of file drawers. I rolled the chair into position to examine these files and met, with surprise, the bumpy girth of a closed umbrella hanging from the hooks meant for coats and hats. Closed, but not properly furled and fastened, because its sides bulged. I hopped up from the chair and pulled the umbrella from its hook.

"Hector!"

He came at once. "Do not open indoors! It is bad luck for seven years!"

I handed him the torch. "Hold this." I reached carefully amongst the spokes to discover what the bumps might be. The first item was as familiar to me as my own nose.

"Mummy's indigo scarf."

Hector's eyes were faint glimmers in the torch light, round with astonishment. I next withdrew a man's silk handkerchief, and then another. A tortoiseshell comb inset with ivory flowers. A brooch in the shape of a crescent moon. A tiepin with a jade bead. A lady's silk handkerchief edged with lace, a silver pencil with a cap, an enameled pillbox and two gold rings.

"What *is* all this?" But I already knew.

"She is a thief," said Hector. "You uncover her cache."

"She is robbing the patients!" I couldn't believe my own eyes. "Is this the secret Sidonie Touati held against her? Nurse McWorthy is a thief! She lied to Mummy's face about not finding her scarf!"

The door flew open with a whoosh. My heart jumped. Hector snapped off the torch. Light from the hallway spilled across the floor. The figure, in silhouette, wore a long skirt and a frilled cap. The beam of *her* torch swept across to find my face. I put up a hand to avoid being blinded.

"Ha!" said the intruder.

"You made my heart stop!" I protested.

"You can't blame me for being curious," said Verity. "What might twelve-year-olds wish to burgle from a hotel spa?"

Hector's arm moved ever so slowly in the dark, below the dancing torch beam. His hand closed over the object nearest to him and slid it into his pocket. Without looking down, I followed his lead, first wrapping Mummy's scarf about my waist, then laying my palm on the spiky form of the jeweled crescent brooch and tucking it into my sash.

"What are you doing?" said Verity. "What have you found?" Her torch jumped here and there, never landing long enough to reveal our mischief. At the desk, we swiftly confiscated all the evidence we had uncovered. A bang in the outside walkway made us all gasp.

Verity's head yanked around to look. "Blast." Her torch went out. In the darkness, I found the handle of Nurse McWorthy's umbrella and slapped it back on the hook of the coat stand. Heavy footsteps thudded outside, and then a hollering voice.

The night clerk.

Were we selfish or wise in what we did next? Our brain cells had little to do with our actions. Like bunnies in the path of a fox, Hector and I dove—and miraculously both fit—under Nurse McWorthy's desk.

"Thief!" shouted the night clerk. "Caught red-handed! You deceitful little—"

Verity made enough noise at the door to cover any scuffling of our own. "Keep off, sir!" she cried, and, "I've stolen nothing!" and "Do *not* touch me!" as if she were the victim and not the perpetrator of a trespass.

"Owww!" cried the night clerk. "You bit me!" A thud, a nasty oath, what may have been a slap, further scuffling, and a grunt as the man must have tripped—or been tripped? More footsteps, but escaping ones this time, the tread light and quick. Verity had slipped away.

Hector and I were frozen and sweating at the same time. The night clerk huffed and heaved himself up off the floor. After a few bumps, we heard him close the door. Verity's key was folded into my sash, along with other booty from our few minutes of plundering.

We crept as far as the lobby like nervous mice, but the night clerk had abandoned his post, we guessed to chase Verity. Our good fortune and her bad. We climbed the stairs with no obstacle. In the passage outside room 201, we caught our breath, and made a quick inventory of the items we'd swiped from the nurse's umbrella.

"Remember," I whispered, "how she said her umbrella was broken, but then we saw her using it the next day from our window? I did not think of that until just now."

I worried for a moment that we had dropped the crescent pin during our flight, but it was hiding between the folds of Mummy's scarf, which I moved from my waist to my neck. We bundled everything into one of the men's handkerchiefs and knotted the corners. We turned the door handle ever so carefully, and arrived in the shadowy room in utter silence.

"Hello, my pets." Grannie's voice was unusually gentle, perhaps to avoid waking Mummy. "I was beginning to worry that something had happened to you beyond mere naughtiness."

CHAPTER 25

A SHOCKING DEVELOPMENT

IT WAS MILLY WHO brought our breakfast tray the next morning, a little later than usual.

"What has happened to Verity?" said Mummy. "Do you trade rooms on Wednesdays?" She was already seated at the little table by the window, eager for her tea and currant scone. I had stayed in bed as long as I dared, to postpone meeting Grannie Jane's gaze by light of day.

"That little cow—" began Milly, and abruptly stopped. I flung on my clothes and went into the sitting room in the hope that Milly would be indiscreet. It might be acceptable for a chambermaid to gripe with her fellow hotel workers, but certainly not with the paying guests. Milly's cheeks flamed. "Begging your pardon, ma'am," she said, and then, "Ma'am," nodding also to Grannie

Jane. "But Verity is no longer working at the Wellspring Hotel. She was let go in the middle of the night." Her effort to refrain from gossiping fell short. "On account of being found burglarizing the clinic."

Mummy's hand froze halfway to the teapot. "I beg your pardon?"

I risked a peek at Hector, who sat next to Mummy staring at an empty plate.

"After me training her for all those hours," said Milly, "it seems she was only here to steal. Medicines and such."

Grannie, with a back as straight as a wall, *tsk*ed in surprised sympathy, as if she hadn't dragged (some of) the story out of us last night.

"Oh dear," said Mummy. "And she was found by Mrs. Upton yesterday, poking about in poor Mr. Hart's room, wasn't she, Aggie? Do you suppose she'd helped herself to a few of his trinkets after all?"

"Well, she's gone now," said Milly. "Sorry I'm late with your breakfast, madam. Let me know if I've forgotten something."

Mummy expressed her surprise more than once during the next half hour, until finally she gathered herself to depart for her treatment. Yes, we all agreed, we'd see her at lunchtime and best wishes for a restful morning at the spa. Our own morning was about to become the antonym of restful. *As fraught as a council of war. Like the holding pen outside a slaughterhouse. Drenched with the nausea that descends after being revealed as a sneak and a thief* . . .

Grannie Jane's method of punishment was never swift. She imposed the burden of prolonged reflection, merely by choosing not to thrash us with a leather strap and having it over in a thrice. I was accustomed to this anguish, though only occasionally had I erred so egregiously. Hector, however? I would have felt secure in a wager that he had not slept for more than five minutes during what must have seemed like an endless night.

Even now that my mother was well gone, Grannie silently passed the muffins and poured Hector's chocolat and sliced off the top of a boiled egg with the precision of a surgeon. I could not help but believe that she was enjoying herself.

"Madame?" Hector ventured, but was ignored for several more painful heartbeats.

"If I understand your explanation correctly," she finally said, "you felt you were performing a mission to aid the chambermaid in fulfilling an obligation."

I nodded, and Hector did too, though not as vigorously.

"Her obligation, you said, was to—"

"One of the reporters," I said. "He convinced her to

peek into the spa where the dead woman had spent so much time. To see whether there might be evidence of poison."

"And in the process of assisting a reporter who had no compunction in asking children to be spies, you happened upon your mother's missing scarf?"

"Yes, Grannie."

"And you have reason to believe that the scarf's presence in the nurse's domain was not a coincidence?"

"I do not think it was," I said, "having heard from a reliable source that there is no such thing as a coincidence when two bodies appear on two park benches in the same week."

"It is a little early in the day, Agatha, to introduce sarcasm," said Grannie.

"I must tell you, madame," began Hector, "it is a heavy burden to deceive you, when your kindness and generosity has shown no limit."

Could he be about to tell her that the break-in had been our idea?

"We assist in this venture because we, also, are curious. It is so simple as that."

We were treated to another extended period of silence. Hector, for whom breakfast was usually the glorious start to a new day of eating, managed only a few spoonfuls of oatmeal and then a spoonful of marmalade. My own worry had been erased by Hector cleverly telling the truth and withholding the truth at the same time. I slathered marmalade on thick strips of Irish bacon and had quite a feast, while ignoring Grannie's reserve.

Milly came back to remove the tray of breakfast things. She was gone in about six minutes. How had I not noticed when Verity had dawdled so, the other morning? She'd been devising her plan of action as well as her next newspaper story with every word we uttered.

"You will remain in the room until lunchtime," said Grannie Jane.

She gathered her knitting and left us to stew. Little did she know that we'd been waiting for this minute.

"Her displeasure when crossed is not to be borne by the weak of heart," said Hector. "Shall we not tell to your grand-mère what we suspect? That we have some proof of Nurse McWorthy—"

"She'll only try to stop us!" I said. "We can get a little closer to solving the puzzle before we ask for help, do you not think? Let's look again at the stolen loot. Perhaps we'll be inspired as to what we do next." I pulled his Sunday-best shoes from beneath his cot, where he had hidden the handkerchief full of bits and bobs collected by Nurse Lizzie McMagpie. "I feel as if we're missing something. A small but obvious connection between all this thieving and the murders."

"I will not dare to say the word *coincidence*," said Hector.

"Maybe Mrs. Shelton caught the nurse in the act of stealing? Did one of these handkerchiefs belong to her? Or the comb, or the pillbox? That would be a motive, wouldn't it? Trying to stop Mrs. Shelton from calling the police?"

Most of the items we did not recognize. "But this—" I held up the diamond-sprinkled crescent moon—"must be the brooch that Mrs. Upton lost. I believe we can put this to use."

Hector looked momentarily alarmed. "I hope you do not intend for us to sell it? I do not think a pawnshop is a wise idea."

"Silly Hector," I said. "We'll use it to *buy* something. We'll use it to acquire the truth."

At lunch, Hector's appetite was back. Mummy's face was rosy and her mood content. She'd not made any comment about a murderer lurking in our hotel, and I did not remind her of it. She did, however, bring us news from the scene of the crime.

"Poor Nurse McWorthy," she said. "She's a bit off-kilter this week, with her mother's birthday party, the death of a new patient, and now all a-flutter in the aftermath of the burglary."

"Was anything stolen?" said Grannie Jane, assisting our inquiry without realizing.

"The night clerk arrived in the nick of time," said Mummy. "The nurse and Dr. Baden were both concerned about the medicines, but everything was in order. Nurse McWorthy was unsettled by the invasion of her privacy more than anything else."

Hector's foot met mine under the table.

As we finished our meal, Alberto came to say that George and his nurse were at the entrance, asking if they might stop by the table momentarily? Despite Mummy not knowing them especially well, she graciously invited Nurse Touati to join us for a glass of rosehip tisane.

"No, no," said the nurse. "Thank you, and I apologize for the intrusion, but George insisted on saying a quick hello to his friends."

George brought his chair close to mine. "Drop your napkin," he whispered.

I did so. "Oops," I said.

George leaned over the side of his chair with swift grace, catching the linen cloth between his fingertips. Straightening, he returned it to my lap, a sloppily folded bundle.

"Er, thank you?" Inside the bundle was an envelope. I waited exactly ten seconds before asking, "Mummy? May we please be excused?"

Hector and I were released and walked to the garden gate with George and his nurse. I had the envelope tucked safely in my sash but was obliged to walk with Nurse Touati, while Hector pushed George behind us. Their muttering was too quick and low to catch, especially while listening to the nurse suggest that we might like to visit Ripley Castle if we got another bright day. What I wished to ask was, *How did it feel to kill a living creature? Had she been exploring medicines and gone wrong? Or had she been refining poisons—and got it right?*

"And you will tell me everything that happens between now and when next I see you," said George.

We had barely waved them off when Hector said, "George delivers a letter? From the new tenant at Mrs. Woolsey's lodging house?"

I tore the seal and found three folded papers.

"We should have known." I showed him the first letter. "She's so sharp she'll cut her own tongue."

Dear Miss Morton,

As you may know, my employ at the Wellspring Hotel has been terminated due to my curiosity over-stepping itself. If you are clever enough, and lucky as well, I wonder if you might retrieve my (brother's) belongings from room number 207, formerly used by

Mr. Benedict Hart? It was briefly convenient to have an empty room for my transformations, but my hurried departure has reduced me to only one shirt and one pair of trousers. You may find me at Mrs. Woolsey's boarding house on Beulah Street.

Sincerely, Verity Slye

"She's using the name Slye?" I crumpled the page in disgust.

"Mr. Hart is deceased," said Hector, "and suddenly Miss Slye, she has a room in which to change her disguise, so her roommate Milly is no longer distressed by the pretend brother. Mrs. Shelton is deceased, and suddenly a room is available in which Miss Slye may sleep. She is most adept at using the opportunities, is she not?"

"Yes, she is," I said. "But how does she imagine we will retrieve her clothing? 'Excuse me, Mrs. Upton? Those trousers that fit a man half the size of your uncle? I believe they belong to someone we know . . .'"

Hector laughed. "'Pardonnez-moi, madame? The maid you discover loitering in your uncle's room? You are fortunate to find her wearing a dress at all.'"

"Hector!"

"You have two more letters," he pointed out.

I unfolded the smaller one, its first line written in Verity's same script, followed by boldly printed words.

This is the transcript of a letter folded, but not sealed, in the writing case of Mr. Hart, now in my own possession. I regret not asking whether by chance you knew of a dead cousin? G.F.

My dear Gerald, I am dismayed to write that I have learned a worrying fact about your sister's death. Could you reply by return post with a number where I might reach you by telephone? I hope this finds you well. Your cousin, Ben

"'Your sister's death'?" I said. "Meaning Mr. Hart's cousin's sister's death?"

"Phoebe," said Hector. "The new bride who dies on her honeymoon."

"He told us she died of food poisoning," I said.

"Food poisoning?" said Hector. "Or only poison?"

"What did Mr. Hart learn that made Phoebe's death suddenly suspicious? Was it hearing Mrs. Shelton's symptoms? Or something else?"

"Does Mrs. Upton see also the letter to Cousin Gerald?" asked Hector.

"We'll need to ask Mrs. Upton," I said, "without actually asking her, of course."

"Mr. Fibbley says the real letter is now in his possession," said Hector. "Nurse McWorthy is not the only thief on the premises."

The evening I met Verity in the linen room, I'd asked what she'd taken from Room 207. Her hand covered the pocket of her apron. I'd guessed then that she was hiding her notebook, but it must have been the letter written, and not yet mailed, by the doomed Mr. Hart.

"Why does Mr. Fibbley choose to tell us *now* what the stolen letter says?" asked Hector.

"I expect he wants us to do something for him," I said, "more than simply fetch his clothing."

The third piece of paper was covered with words, front and back.

Dear Miss Morton, I have dictated this story to my editor over the telephone. It will be published today in the Torquay Voice*. These notes are to spare you the two-day wait for your sister to send. G.F.*

"Handwritten notes," I said, "for Augustus Fibbley's next article."

"Read, please," said Hector. He was already leaning

close, trying to get a better view. I spread it out between us on the bench so we both could see.

For _Torquay Voice_

Scared To Death???
Harrogate Bench-Killer Still At Large!!!

New evidence shows that the second unusual death last week in Harrogate, Yorkshire, may not have been the result of a diseased heart but of a different sort of attack altogether. Mr. Benedict Hart (46) of Nottingham died while a guest at the Wellspring Hotel & Spa. His death followed that of another visitor, Mrs. Lidia Shelton, who was systematically poisoned during a period of some weeks. The investigation into Mrs. Shelton's death by arsenic has made no substantial headway, and police dispute the idea that Mr. Hart's death was a homicide, leaving the public dissatisfied and even afraid. But this reporter has questions. Why did two such different, unexpected deaths take place so close to the hotel? If Mr. Hart died naturally, why was he lured to his place of collapse by an unidentified tele-phone caller? Was that call made from inside the hotel? Is it possible that his fragile health was used *against him, that fear caused his heart attack? And who better than an employee or guest of the hotel to know of the victim's health condition? Information exclusive to the <u>Torquay Voice</u> has revealed that a piece of tragic family history may be connected to the current events. Further details in the Late Edition.*

"He heard us guess that Mr. Hart was scared to death," I said, "and suddenly it's a headline!"

"Which employee or guest is he suggesting?" said Hector.

"Also . . ." I again skimmed Mr. Fibbley's notes. "'Information exclusive to the *Torquay Voice*'? Because *he* is the one who stole a letter from a dead man's desk! That's one way to keep information out of anyone else's hands!"

"And now, 'a piece of tragic family history may be connected'?" said Hector. "He makes a story—as your grandmother says—out of thin air."

"But, is it thin air?" I said. "Or is he seeing links that we have not yet seen? What do you suppose Mr. Hart learned at a hotel in Yorkshire about his cousin Phoebe's death in Spain?"

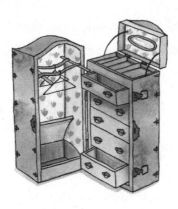

CHAPTER 26

A DEVIOUS MANEUVER

WE KNOCKED ON THE door of Room 209 and were greeted by Mrs. Josie Upton, in some disarray. Her sleeves were pushed up, her hair was missing pins, and her face showed a sheen of perspiration.

"Hello, you two," she said. "Your timing is perfect! The maid has just returned your mother's clothes, freshly sponged and pressed." Mummy's dresses hung on the back of the wardrobe door.

"Wonderful," I said, with a sinking heart. If she simply handed over the borrowed clothing, we'd have no excuse to ask chummy questions.

"We are also come to offer assistance," said Hector. "Perhaps you require someone to fold the garments of your uncle?"

Nice work, Hector! I nodded my head too many times, to show this had been part of our mission.

"Oh." Mrs. Upton looked doubtful.

"I assure you," said Hector. "I am indisputably a tidy person."

Mrs. Upton laughed. "In that case, I shall not dispute," she said, "though it seems an odd pastime for children on a sunny afternoon. But, I confess, a little help will be most welcome. Come in, come in."

The room was as disarranged as its inhabitant. An empty trunk sat open on the floor, with a standing travel-wardrobe next to it. The wardrobe was empty too, while every piece of clothing owned by either of the Uptons was heaped upon the bed.

"My uncle's room is the same." Mrs. Upton pointed through the connecting door of the suite where a similar pile lay higgledy-piggledy across the bed and the chair next to it. "I took everything out, flung it on the bed and haven't had the courage to go further. I'm a bit overwhelmed," she said. "The moment I was married, my husband lost the ability to pack his own suitcase. It became one of my wifely duties, in the absence of servants."

"That doesn't seem fair," I said.

"And now Uncle Ben's as well," she said.

"If you will permit?" said Hector. "Aggie may assist you in this room, as I begin the organization of Mr. Hart's belongings? This way, you will not become disconsolate."

Clever Hector. It would be my task to distract Mrs. Upton while Hector removed Mr. Fibbley's second pair of trousers and his shirts. The changing room secretly used by the reporter, after being hired as a chambermaid, was no longer needed.

"What would you like me to do?" I asked Mrs. Upton.

"Would you have a quick peek inside the drawers and cupboards to see that I haven't missed anything? I'm still looking for my wedding brooch from Uncle Benedict."

And you will soon get it back from our stash of stolen goods . . . after we've used it to its best advantage.

"Have you heard from your parents since their telegram?" I said. "I dread being an adult for exactly the reasons you now are facing. So bewildering! Would your father's cousin possibly help?" I remembered at the last second that I could have no reason to know his name was Gerald. "The brother of Phoebe, who died? Does he live near to you?"

"He lives in Coventry," said Mrs. Upton. "About fifty miles away. He did come to our wedding, with his wife, Ann."

"That's nice!" I said. "He'll feel better, won't he, that he had a final visit with Mr. Hart?"

I heard the door in the connecting room open and then shut. Hector must have found Mr. Fibbley's shirts and trousers—and hurried down the hall to hide them in our room. "Have you written to tell him the sad news?"

Mrs. Upton nodded as her eyes filled with tears. "I had a letter back from him this morning. He is devastated." She retrieved an envelope from the desk, its edges printed with a black stripe to indicate mourning. The note inside was written in brown ink, in a looping script.

"'My dear Josie,'" Mrs. Upton read aloud, "'Your news has come as a shock, though I know Ben's health was not tip-top. It is small comfort to say that he was as proud as a father at your wedding, but it is true. As we are still recovering from poor Phoebe's passing, this fresh loss is hard to bear. May he rest in peace. With heartfelt condolences and affection, Gerald.' That's all."

"Oh dear." My words were false, for my spirits swooped up. The letter of condolence did not mention an urgent note from Mr. Hart, expressing suspicion. Cousin Gerald had no cause to notify the authorities or try to learn what Mr. Hart had uncovered. And Mrs. Upton herself did not realize she'd been burgled, which was best for now, under the circumstances.

"Perhaps you'd like a moment to yourself? I will take Mummy's dresses to our room." I hastily dislodged the hangers from the hook and scurried out.

Hector was coming toward me along the passage. "Mr.

Fibbley's clothes are under my bed," he said, "wrapped in a towel."

"Mrs. Upton is weeping again." I lifted my armload so that the hems of Mummy's dresses wouldn't brush the floor. "Cousin Gerald's condolence letter did not mention any ominous correspondence from Mr. Hart," I whispered, "meaning that Verity stole the original, I think. Mrs. Upton seems to know nothing, thank goodness. One less thing for anyone to worry about." We grinned at each other, our sleuthing abilities feeling rather impressive.

"But now we're stuck helping to pack their trunks!" I said. "Do *not* mention that we've got the crescent brooch! We will put it to use as soon as we're done, and Mrs. Upton can have it back afterward."

The minute we had dutifully completed our act of snooping-disguised-as-kindness, we put the next phase of our plan in motion. Step One: collect particular items from Room 201.

Grannie Jane looked up from her knitting and raised her eyebrows.

"Has something happened?" she said.

"Where's Mummy?" I said. Hector slipped behind the screen that sheltered his cot, as well as a growing store of other people's possessions.

"Did you not hear my question, Agatha? Or do you imagine that your evasion will go unnoticed?"

"We're going to return the indigo scarf to Mummy," I said. "Do you know where she is?"

"I believe she is enjoying an afternoon treatment," said Grannie Jane. "Followed by a rendezvous with the doctor in the tearoom."

"A *private* rendezvous?"

"As private as a hotel tearoom permits, I suppose." Grannie rested her knitting in her lap, the needles crossed neatly like tiny swords. "Perhaps this is the moment when you hear an important truth, Agatha. Your mother is still a lovely woman, and not suited for solitude. It will not hurt to let her be admired here and there—by a Mr. Hart, or a Dr. Baden—until she meets someone she truly cares for."

"Stop!" I cried. "How can you say that? Papa—"

"She will always love your Papa best," said Grannie Jane, "but . . . a lonely widow is not who anyone wishes to be." She picked up her knitting and pushed her needle through the next loop. "We'll leave it there."

A lonely widow? Cold prickled my arms. Grannie was a widow, but also old. She must expect to be lonely on occasion. But she was suggesting that Mummy was lonely too. Mummy had me, didn't she? And my sister, Marjorie, with a baby coming, though she did not live nearby. Was Grannie thinking of a time when I, too, might live elsewhere? Or did she mean *now*, that Mummy might like other friends *now*?

Hector emerged from behind the screen, his pale face pink as he tried to pretend not to have heard Grannie's words. He held up Mummy's indigo scarf. "Shall we go?" he said.

"I should like to know . . ." Grannie Jane peered *very* closely at her knitting, before her eyes caught mine, "why your mother's scarf needs to be delivered rather than waiting here for her arrival?"

And our escape had been so near! I sighed. Hector's face reflected defeat in the glare of Grannie's inquisitive persistence. Our situation was a delicate one. If the person we accused of being a likely killer was one of the people who was caring for Mummy, my grandmother would have no choice but to make a noise and call the police. If Mummy were in actual danger, naturally we would alert the police ourselves. But . . . we'd rather like to investigate just a little further, before crying for help or causing noisy trouble.

We plunked ourselves down, side by side on the sofa, and took turns telling slivers of the story, further to what she already knew—yet hurrying, so as not to get behind on our schedule. Nurse McWorthy seemed to have a thieving problem. What if Mrs. Shelton, or possibly Mr. Hart, had caught her in the act? What if the nurse was so afraid of being exposed that she . . . well, we didn't know. But we did know that a telephone call had been made, and the Buzzard—excuse us, the bell captain, Mr. Bessel—could not say if the caller was a man or a woman. Also, Nurse McWorthy dispensed three bottles of Rejuvenation Tonic to Mrs. Shelton the day before she died. Wasn't that simply too ironic? And there was more, but did Grannie see why we were compelled to satisfy such specific curiosity?

"Does Nurse McWorthy not live in a little house somewhere with her mother?" said Grannie. "And goes home to care for her each night? What leads you to think she was on the premises during the evening when Mr. Hart died? There is a great distance between keeping a lost scarf for oneself and murdering a gentleman."

Hector and I looked at each other. The Uptons had been with us on Wednesday evening, and Mr. Smythe, and Dr. Baden. We hadn't seen the nurse, it was true, then or earlier.

"A killer would make a point of not being seen," I said. "Would she not?"

"The facts you have listed are all facts," said Grannie Jane, "but they are not the *only* facts. The orchard is full of facts, and you have picked from only one or two trees. Do you see? It is quite likely that a fellow has got a cartful over there somewhere . . ." She waved a hand vaguely toward the window. "His fruit are of a more obscure variety and might give an entirely different flavor to the pie." She winced. "That was a bit clumsy, I'm afraid."

"Not at all, Madame Morton," said Hector. "You are saying we do not yet have all the ingredients for the most fulsome pie."

"Very good, Hector. You have caught my meaning."

"Is the nurse skulking in the garden with a croquet mallet when Mr. Hart dies of fright? Or is she elsewhere? This is an apple we must not discard."

"Otherwise known," I said, "as an alibi."

Our timing could not have been better. Hector and I arrived at Nurse McWorthy's desk just as my mother appeared from the spa area.

"Hello, my dears." She put an arm around each of us. Hector beamed and I did my best to mimic him. "To what do I owe this surprise encounter?"

"Madame Morton," said Hector. "We are so happy to find your precious indigo scarf." He held it out, folded neatly, as if it were a rare book signed by the author.

"Oh!" Mummy's cry of joy nearly diverted attention from my official position as Nurse-Watcher. But I kept my gaze on Nurse McWorthy's face even during Mummy's hug and her all-important question, "Where did you find it, you clever children?"

The nurse was speechless in her bafflement, mouth gaping in imitation of a panting hound. *Ha!* Act One of our plan had worked perfectly.

"It turned up," said Hector. "We may accept no applause."

"Possibly the maid found it," I said, "in some odd place."

"The maid?" repeated Nurse McWorthy. "The burglar maid?"

"And now you have it back." I ignored the nurse's revealing remark. "Wouldn't Papa be pleased?" I could not help reminding Mummy of Papa, before her meeting with the doctor in only a few minutes. But she simply wrapped the scarf about her neck, its color making her eyes sparkle.

"Mrs. Morton." Dr. Baden came out of his office with a cheery hello for us all. "I wonder," he said, "if we might have dinner later this evening instead of tea now?"

Mummy glanced at me, but I ducked my head, not wishing her to see that I felt every bit as sour as Nurse McWorthy looked.

"That will be fine, Doctor, thank you. My family will do without me for an evening."

"That's a lovely scarf, if I may say," Dr. Baden said. "The color suits you beautifully."

Blech. Her smile.

"Aggie? Hector? Shall we go upstairs?"

We had not had the chance to ask the nurse our question about her alibi for last Wednesday evening.

"You go on ahead," I said. "We're going to visit the garden."

We reached Mr. Hart's bench and sat, not looking at each other.

"The nurse was every bit as discombobulated as we hoped," I said.

"But," said Hector, "we still do not know if she is a killer or merely a thief."

"It's a good thing we have our second act ready," I said.

Hector reached into his pocket for Mrs. Upton's pretty moon-shaped brooch.

CHAPTER 27

A DISASTROUS TURN

"HELLO!" GEORGE WAS calling from the street. Nurse Touati opened the gate so the chair could pass through, but then she waved at us and disappeared.

"I made Sidonie bring me back," said George. "I know you're scheming and deducing and ready to catch a killer, and you keep forgetting about me."

"No, no," we said, but he was right. He hadn't been part of our plan, and why was that?

I winced to think how I'd allowed his chair to limit my notion of his ability to help. He had a brain, didn't he? It wasn't as though we needed to climb over fences or run through bracken to capture the killer of the Bandstand Corpse. I wouldn't be much good at that either, and Hector . . . well, he'd be Hector. But, the *unmasking* of the villain required wits and determination—two things George possessed in plenty.

"Today is a week," said George, "since the man died."

"On this bench." Hector patted the armrest.

"Do you know who did it?" said George.

"Not quite yet," I said. "But we have a very short list."

George eyed us closely. "You're in the middle of something right now, are you not? I knew it! I told Sidonie to leave me alone for an hour, so she's not here to follow us about. What can I do?"

Hector and I consulted with a nod. We filled George in on our campaign to torment Nurse McWorthy, and showed him the cracked urn.

"Let's get the mallet." I said. Hector retrieved it from where it lay hidden under the picnic blankets in the games shed. It fit perfectly on the wheelchair, tucked in beside George's thigh, with the battered head out of sight under his rolled-up jersey.

"You'd best remove the grin, George," I said. "It might be a tip-off that you're doing something other than looking for a glove."

"And please also to remove a glove," said Hector.

George's grin grew wider as he pulled off one of his gloves and shoved it under his bottom.

The handles on the back of George's wheelchair prevented the clinic door from closing properly behind him. We could hear his first words.

"Please, Nurse? I think I've left one of my gloves in the change room."

"Go on, then," she said. "I'll be turning off the lights and shutting down the steam valves in five minutes."

I imagined his angelic smile thanking her. My mind's eye followed as he rolled along the passage to the area with the Turkish baths and steam room, the hot and frigid pools. We counted slowly to two hundred and entered ourselves. For us, Nurse McWorthy's welcome was not warm. She was, no doubt, still recovering from the reappearance of Mummy's scarf an hour ago. Was she as frantic as we hoped? Wondering whether we knew she'd accumulated a collection of missing objects?

"What now?" she snapped. "It's closing time."

"Good evening, Nurse," I said, in my friendliest way. "We wonder if you would check the calendar for us? Mummy wanted to know, was it Tuesday or Wednesday evening when she came in to ask about the mud masks?"

"I do not recall that conversation," she said. "But Wednesday is our night out, my mum and me, so I never stay late. We have fish and chips with old Miss Lemon next door and listen to Sousa's band on the phonograph.

It's a jolly time and we never miss it. Your mother must have come by after I left."

Inwardly, I groaned. Would we need to visit old Miss Lemon to verify the story?

"This sounds like much fun, your little party," said Hector. "Do you remain a long time with Miss Lemon?"

Nurse McWorthy seemed confused at Hector's interest. "My mother goes to bed at nine o'clock," she said. "But on Wednesdays, we're sometimes a little later than that. If it's any of your business."

"And on this past Wednesday?" pressed Hector.

"It was the night of the murder," I said.

Hector sighed.

"I mean, the night when Mr. Hart died."

The nurse glared, a livid flush creeping up her neck. "That'll be enough of that," she said.

We'd lost a bit of footing. *Sorry, Hector!*

I spoke up before she could send us away. "We found something caught in the folds of Mummy's scarf." I held out my hand, with Mrs. Upton's sparkly brooch lying on the flat of my palm. "We wondered if, by chance, it was the one a guest was asking about last week?"

Nurse McWorthy's face was now mottled with red blotches. "I wouldn't know," she said. "I never saw that before, not never. Take it away."

"Away?" I said. "But didn't Mrs. Up—"

"Then give it to *her*!" The nurse's voice became more shrill. "Or Mr. Smythe. Or anyone else but me!"

The door to Dr. Baden's office flew open and out he came, stopping short when he saw us at the desk.

"Nurse?" he said, very concerned. "What is the trouble here?"

Nurse McWorthy, eyes moist, face splotched, took in a deep, wavery breath. "A misunderstanding, Doctor. Nothing for you to be bothered about. We're sorry to have disturbed you, aren't we, children?"

That's the moment George chose to wheel into sight, steering the chair with one hand and waving the green-striped croquet mallet above his head. The nurse did not turn pale or clutch her throat or quake with guilt. She shook her head in confused disbelief.

"Good gracious, George," she said. "What is this nonsense?" She became more like a proper nurse every second. "Put down that stick and behave yourself."

George did not put down the mallet. He waved it and poked the air while Nurse McWorthy clapped her hands as if scolding a naughty dog. George ignored her because he was staring at the doctor. Time seemed to slow in the most unnerving way.

Dr. Baden took a single step, to put the desk between himself and the boy with the weapon. His face, usually so pleasant, showed an unguarded look of apprehension, like a cornered badger surprised by sudden exposure to the light.

George hurled down the mallet and used both hands to roll his chair away from the doctor. As the path to the door and the hotel was blocked by us, he wheeled backward into the eerie cavern of the Turkish baths.

"Not the nurse!" cried Hector. "It is the *doctor* who uses the mallet to frighten and kill Mr.—"

Nurse McWorthy made a noise, like a cat gagging on a fishbone. Her sharp gaze followed George's exit and sped back to study the doctor's dismay. Her own face showed distress quite clearly, as the truth sank in that Dr. Baden did not deserve her reverence.

That, in fact, he was a *dangerous* man.

My legs would not work, but Hector began to move. The doctor's foot shot out to send him sprawling. The nurse leaned over, I thought to help Hector upright. But instead, she picked up the mallet, using her fingertips as if the handle was sticky or hot. She inched toward the door that led to the hotel.

"Nurse!" growled the doctor. "Stop there."

She did not stop. "Help," she whispered. "Getting help."

Hector took my offered hand and scrambled to his feet. "Let's *go*! She must not remove the murder weapon!" He tugged at me, that we should hurry after Nurse

McWorthy. But, George! I snatched the nurse's umbrella and brandished it toward the doctor with deadly intent—or, at least, wildly enough to get us past him.

I cried out, "George!" and ran, knowing Hector would follow. We couldn't leave George alone to face the wrath of a madman. And he *must* be mad! Behind us, I heard the noise of the nurse's chair being shoved aside, banging against a wall with a crash.

"George!" We hurtled into the underworld of swirling mosaics and dark, still pools. Our feet clattered on the tiles and from behind us came a bellow of rage.

George had got to the other end of the spa. "Just hide!" he called. "He won't attack a cripple!"

The first door we came to was the women's changing room.

"No!" cried Hector. He would soon regret his modesty. We raced past the icy pool and I pulled open the next door, and Hector cried out again—not a word, but a grunt. The villain had caught us up! He yanked Hector's jacket, spilling him to the ground. This gave me clear aim to ram the doctor *hard*, in the chest, with the tip of the umbrella.

"You. Silly. Girl." He wrenched the umbrella from my hands.

Hector and I hurled ourselves through the open door beside us and slammed it shut, panting. We found ourselves in the steam room, with Dr. Baden's ugly leer visible through the small windowpane. The door shuddered, while I held it shut with every bit of quivering strength. But through the glass I saw the doctor laughing, then felt the handle jump before the villain backed away. Was he tempting us to chase and tackle him? No, he had toyed with the door—and it *would not open*. I pressed my face to the window and saw the evidence just below the frame. The umbrella was jammed through the outside latch and securely locked our prison.

Inside, it was warm and moist, but not steamy, as the spa day was over and the facility ready to shut down. My head spun from the suddenness of our calamity. If only I had poked the evil man more fiercely!

"Are you hurt?" I said.

"Not at all," said Hector. "Only my pride, not seeing the truth."

"Dr. Baden." I hadn't warmed to him, I confess. Likely because Mummy had—but was that also the reason that I had not seriously imagined him to be despicable? Because how could Mummy admire a murderer? "Dr. Baden and *women*," I said, as other pieces of the puzzle clicked into place. "He was wooing Mrs. Shelton. Their special friendship upset Nurse McWorthy!"

"The Rejuvenation Tonic," said Hector. "He adds arsenic each time the nurse mixes the recipe for Mrs. Shelton." The picture was grimmer every moment.

The villain had planned the lonely widow's demise with meticulous care. First, he wooed her, having assured himself that she was wealthy and without ties. Then he introduced a tiny dose of arsenic into her daily tonic, slowly increasing the amount as days went by. Blast her for being intelligent enough to eventually suspect his crime! He was forced to kill her before she'd become his wife, making the entire exercise for naught. Blast the man who'd recognized his motive! And blast these children, who tried to ruin everything. His menacing glare turned to smug elation when he realized he was holding a Hart's umbrella with an unbreakable shaft—the perfect tool to trap them, with no chance of escape.

"I think—" said Hector, but then a *whoosh* of sound, and a belch of steam from a pipe near the floor. A very few moments later, we were rather warmer and inside a fog that threatened to make us invisible to each other, despite being a mere foot or two apart. I wiped off the window and peered into the chamber beyond. George had advanced his chair and stationed himself on the walkway between pools, challenging the doctor with a grim face.

"George!" I banged upon the door. It did not budge even a hair's breadth.

"If it is Dr. Baden," said Hector, "who kills Mrs. Shelton, we must consider also cousin Phoebe—"

"We can't think about her *now*!" I said. "Right this minute, Dr. Baden is trying to kill George!"

The doctor lunged at George, hands outstretched, pushing at his shoulders, forcing the chair to skid along the edge of the ice-water pool. George's hands gripped the wheels, his eyes blazed, and the line of his mouth was, incredibly, a smile.

The air around us became thicker and hotter every minute.

"He turns up the steam." Hector pulled off his jacket. "To the highest degree, I think."

I could not take a full breath for the sting when I tried. I kicked out of my shoes and tore off my wool stockings, using one of them to clean steam from the glass.

"Ha! George is ramming his chair into the doctor's shins!"

But the rage on Dr. Baden's face was terrifying. His snarling mouth spat words I could not hear. And then *whoomph*! The chair toppled. George fell sideways, his hands grabbing air.

CHAPTER 28

A VERY WET HERO

HORROR CLOSED MY THROAT. Hector nudged me aside so he could see for himself what had struck me mute and shaking. He stood on tiptoe to look out.

"The doctor leaves," he said. Faintly, there came the slam of a door as the villain escaped.

Hector wiped condensation from the little window. "But where is George? His chair—"

His chair lay on its side. The upper wheel spun, and then slowed down like something running out of breath.

"He's in the ice water," I whispered. Tears burned my eyes. Hector tugged on the door handle in a fury, as if we had not already done that a hundred times.

"Let me have another look." We traded places, and I again used my sodden stocking to wipe the glass. The wheel on the chair was no longer spinning. The surface of the icy pool swirled gently, showing no sign of where our friend had sunk. I had a chilling flash of Nurse Touati's beautiful face, ravaged with sorrow, holding the lifeless body of this funny boy.

But then, "I see him!! His head is above water!"

"Bravo, George!" said Hector. "The water is not deep."

"*But he can't stand up!*" I wept.

I turned away from the door, weak from the unbearable weight of George under water.

Goodness it was hot, scorching hot. My stocking did nothing but smear more moisture on the glass. The pipe that pumped steam into the room made huffing, hissing noises, like the snorts of a fiery dragon. There was not a single thing in the room with which to smash the thick pane of glass in the door. I pushed the wet hair from my face, willing myself to look again for George.

But Hector was there, straining to see. "*Ohh,*" he said.

"What?"

"He puts his hands . . . ooh la la!" cried Hector. "C'est incroyable!"

"What?" I said. "Put his hands where?" It took all my strength not to shove Hector out of the way. "*Tell me what's happening or move over!*"

"He is a marvel," said Hector. "He puts hands on the tiled edge; he pushes with the big muscles and *whoosh!*

See? He sits on the side of the pool!" Hector ducked down to let me look. George was indeed sitting on the edge of the pool, his legs dangling into the water. He slapped himself with extreme vigor.

"He must be freezing," I said. "While we are about to be cooked."

Behind me, Hector moaned and collapsed to the floor.

"Hector!" He'd fainted! "Hector?"

No sound. I dropped to his side. Too hot. Had he hit his head?

I jumped back up and kicked the door. We were baked through. We had to get out. I wiped the glass and was astounded. How had George done that?

"Hector!" I pushed his leg with my bare toes. "Wake up!"

A very quiet groan. "Oh, thank you!" I squatted beside him. "Can you sit? I think George—" I jumped back up to check on George.

With sopping clothes, plastered-down hair and a look of gritty resolve, George somehow . . . How? Had managed to haul himself back into his chair, though he struggled to settle himself in the right position. I banged and knocked and pressed my face against the glass. George's eyes searched the air and then found mine. His shoulders seemed to double in size; he yanked himself a little straighter and rolled awkwardly forward, right up to our door.

The steady, scalding steam and the limited vantage point through the small window blocked my view of what George was doing.

"Please, please, please, Nurse McWorthy," I said. "We're sorry we ever suspected you of murder even for one minute. Please fetch help! For George, if not for us."

"For us also," said Hector, rallying, "though she may not be the most dependable—"

The door swung open. Steam billowed and swept past us in a hot gust, turning us blind for the moment. Hector clutched my hand, but when I tried to take a step, I found that George's chair was blocking our escape. We were bumbling, sodden puppies, newly released from a sack intended to drown us.

"Thank you, George, thank—"

"You are not injured?" said Hector. "The doctor is gone?"

"When you came in, wielding that mallet!" I said. "Like a Viking with a spiked club!"

"His face!" said George. "You devised the perfect trap!"

"He is so careful and patient in the poisoning of Mrs. Shelton," said Hector, "but under pressure, all calm evaporates!"

"Mrs. Shelton, and we think cousin Phoebe was a victim too," I said. "That's why Mr. Hart—"

"Is there a valve for the steam?" said Hector. "Are you able to move from our path, George?"

More fumbling and shifting and dripping. The steam room pipe was shut off and the hissing stopped with a hefty sigh.

"Did he strike you?" said George. "Are you hurt?"

"Are *we* hurt? *You* were the one dumped into a—"

We each made certain the others were intact, with no loss of blood. George had a bump on his head and a serious case of the shivers. We rolled him into the steam room to catch the leftover warmth, and we knelt by the ice water pool to splash our own necks and faces.

"And now," I said, a minute later, "let's get on with catching Dr. Baden before he gets away!"

"Will we enter the hotel lobby so wet as this?" said Hector. "You are barefoot!"

I began to laugh and could not stop. After everything that had occurred, Hector could not bear to be seen as untidy! Soon, we all were laughing.

And that is how they found us.

Nurse McWorthy had run as far as the lobby, she told us later, and then stopped in her tracks.

Mr. Bessel, the bell captain, was nowhere to be seen,

nor Mr. Smythe, though she knew he would, in any case, be useless. Where might she find a brawny man? Not a guest in sight! The children! The children! Should she fetch Mummy and Grannie, whose room number she did not know? The croquet mallet was still in her hand. She dropped it, and kicked it under an elegant sofa, where it lay until quite a while later. Oh! The police! Of course, the police! She'd find a telephone. Wait, thank goodness! There was Mr. Bessel, arguing with the skinny young reporter, trying to put him out on the street.

"But I tell you!" the reporter was saying. "I'm here as a friend, not as a reporter!"

"I'll need you both," Nurse McWorthy broke in with renewed purpose. "One to fetch the police, and the other to assist in rescuing the Morton girl. She and her friends are in mortal danger."

("Well," she said, in her report to us, "*that* lit a fire under their bottoms!")

But still there were some hiccups.

"You'll need to tell me more," said the bell captain, "if I'm to summon the police. Mr. Smythe will chop my head off if that inspector shows up again for no reason."

"It's not no reason!" cried Nurse McWorthy. "He's chased them into—"

"Where?" cried Mr. Fibbley (though the nurse did not yet know his name). He bounced up and down, until finally interrupting her tale to Mr. Bessel. "Stop blithering, woman! WHERE ARE THE CHILDREN? And have you alerted Aggie's mother?"

"Room 201," called the bell captain, as he scurried off to telephone the constabulary.

"Follow me," said Nurse McWorthy to Mr. Fibbley. "We should hurry. It's the doctor, you see, and—"

"But isn't that the doctor now?" The reporter pointed to the glass front doors.

"Heaven help us!"

Dr. Baden, carrying his medical bag, rushed past the entry of the hotel, with a wave from the poor, ignorant doorman!

"He's making a dash for it!" cried Nurse McWorthy. "Stop that man! He must have killed the children too!" Mr. Fibbley raced to the door, but the doctor was already gone from sight. He threw up his hands in exasperation and came back in.

"Tell the police which way he went," he called to Nurse McWorthy, as he flew past. "I will find the children. Inform the Mrs. Mortons that they are needed at once!" He dodged Mr. Smythe, emerging from his office, and sped along the passage that led to the clinic and the Turkish baths.

To us.

CHAPTER 29

A WHOLE LOT OF NOISE

WE'D FOUND WHERE the towels were kept and were wrapping George, who now shook *like a leaf in a gale wind, like an old woman with palsy, like a boy who'd been plucked from the Arctic Sea.* My own clothes were soaked through as well, clammy and itchy, but not cold. My braids were two thick, sodden cords, swinging heavily with every movement. I caught them up in turn and wrung them out like face flannels, water drizzling to the tiled floor.

"I should've taken my shirt off first." George's chattering teeth made it sound as if he stuttered. "It feels like a newspaper that's been used to scoop snow."

"We'll start over," I said. "We've plenty of towels."

"A return to the steam room?" said Hector. "It remains warm, even without the steam." That's where

Mr. Fibbley found us, as Hector awkwardly pulled off George's wet shirt, and I stood ready with a stack of towels to bundle him up.

"You're alive," said Mr. Fibbley. "A much better ending to the story than the one I've been afraid of, these past few minutes."

"We are alive," I said, "thanks to George."

"Your mother's coming," said Mr. Fibbley, "but the doctor—it *was* Dr. Baden who threatened you? Did he also kill Mrs. Shelton?"

"Mr. Hart too," I said, "*and* Mr. Hart's cousin Phoebe, a year ago on her honeymoon."

"Well, he just scarpered," said Mr. Fibbley. "Heading for the railway station, is my guess."

I gaped at him. "What are you doing here? You must stop him!"

"I wanted to check that you were—"

"Go!" I cried. "We're fine. Mummy's coming, right?"

"Inform the police!" said Hector.

"We've done that."

"Get the story!" I said. "Before Mr. Thomas does!"

Mr. Fibbley grinned. Then he squatted beside George's chair. "I want to hear your story too," he said. "If Miss Morton says she is alive because of you, that's a tale I want to write. Save it for me, will you?"

George nodded, even as he shivered. Mr. Fibbley hopped

up and ran away. Hector and I returned to the task of draping and tucking towels around George until he looked like an enormous ball of yarn with a human head. His arms were trapped, so Hector pushed the chair and I held open the door. And then Mummy was there, with Nurse Touati right behind her, and Grannie Jane as well, each of them making a different sort of noise, so that it sounded as if a flock of worried geese had entered the Wellspring Spa.

"George, George, George," Nurse Touati said, about fifty times. "My dear, dear George." Mummy and Grannie retrieved more towels and piled them around Hector's shoulders and draped more on mine, clucking and fretting, without listening to a single word we tried to say. First, they saw only that we were alive, and then, that we were utterly wet.

"Dr. Baden is the killer!" I finally cried.

This inspired a swell of gasps and squawks, and Mummy said, "Upstairs, all of you. Hot baths before anything else."

We got as far as the lobby and were suddenly in the midst of a sizeable crowd of curious guests eavesdropping on Nurse McWorthy's broken explanation to a befuddled Sergeant Rook. We had missed the arrival and hurried exit of Inspector Henry and his constables in pursuit of the doctor, but the sergeant had remained behind to uncover what facts he might.

Nurse McWorthy, on seeing us cloaked in white towels, emitted a raspy cry and fell into a swoon. An actual swoon! How wonderful! The Buzzard, standing (this time, usefully) closer than necessary, was well-placed to catch her, and soon had her lying on the nearest sofa. Sergeant Rook turned a page in his notebook, prepared to consider our part in the drama.

"Please, my dear ladies and gentlemen!" Mr. Smythe was nearly dancing in agitation. "The fine sergeant will ask his questions while you each enjoy a glass of champagne in the lounge. Courtesy of the Wellspring Hotel." His face gleamed with perspiration. "Will someone take these ill-dressed children away?"

As shivery as I'd begun to feel, I did not wish to leave this theater.

"You!" said Mr. Smythe to Nurse Touati. "You're a nurse. Can you not do something about a fainting spell?"

Nurse Touati sighed and rummaged in the kit bag that hung from the back of George's chair. She extracted a vial of smelling salts and held it under Nurse McWorthy's nose. During their previous encounter, one of these women had publicly accused the other of murder. But now, Nurse McWorthy awoke with a jolt and gazed up, remorse burning from her squinty eyes.

"Sid," she said.

"Sid?" murmured George.

"I am sorry all over." Nurse McWorthy's words gushed out. "You've no cause to forgive me, I know that. I had no cause to say what I did. I'm all of a jumble, and here the doctor's gone and broken my heart, being evil, as it turns out."

Nurse Touati patted her arm. "Never mind all that for now."

"Will you sit up!" said Mr. Smythe. "No feet on the furniture!"

Nurse McWorthy blinked and next saw me. "Not killed after all! Well, that's one good thing." She pushed herself up to sitting. "But you've plenty else to answer for, missy, sneaking about, taking what I'd collected, and—"

How dare she accuse *us*? Hadn't *she* just left us in the clutches of the killer?

George sneezed, to save us. Hector and I bugged eyes at each other. We had very nearly been exposed as thieving tricksters! Sergeant Rook woke up, and arranged for Nurse McWorthy to be accompanied home by a constable, to await further questioning when it suited Inspector Big Joe Henry.

"We'll take the children now," said Mummy. "They've had their fill of drama for today."

"On that point, madam, could you say a few words?" Mr. Frank Thomas had appeared, despite the ban on reporters, and had his notebook open.

"Goodness! Is it true?" Mrs. Upton and her husband came out from the Champagne Lounge, flushed and breathless. "Everyone's saying that you caught my uncle's killer!"

"Sadly, we do not *catch* him," said Hector.

"He hared off for the train," said George.

"*After* he attacked us," I said.

"The train?" said Mr. Thomas. "That rotten Fibbley told me the police had him hidden in the hotel somewhere! Told me to wait right here!"

Hector and I laughed. Conniving Fibbley. Scooped his competition and kept the capture to himself! Mr. Thomas stomped out the front doors in a right pique.

"Who?" cried Mrs. Upton. "WHO killed Uncle Benedict?"

Many voices told her. Mr. Upton held her tightly so she wouldn't fall over.

"When I see that man again!" Mrs. Upton declared, "I swear, I'll—"

George sneezed again, this time a genuine blast, I think. I, too, was chilled and jittery. The towels draped over my shoulders were no longer comforting, but heavy with water that cooled further every minute.

"Not another word until these children have had warm baths." Mummy spoke with unusual resolve. "Especially George!"

Nurse Touati was briskly rubbing George's shoulders through the swaddling of towels, and muttering in a language I had never heard.

"Nurse, you may not take the boy home in this condition," said Mrs. Upton. "Come upstairs and use the tub in my uncle's room."

"I should have some woollies that will fit," said Mr. Upton, "or we'll arrange to have his own clothes delivered by the time you've finished."

This gave tasks to Mr. Smythe and to the Buzzard, who could finally be occupied elsewhere. The Buzzard went to telephone George's parents, to arrange for dry clothing and a motorcar to carry him home. Ignoring a renewed kerfuffle at the front door, Mr. Smythe led George and his nurse to the lift, which Hector and I had not known existed! It was just big enough to squeeze in the chair, with the nurse crammed against the side.

"We may not see you until tomorrow," said Hector, bowing gravely to George. "I thank you for performing a most estimable rescue."

"If not for you . . ." I said.

"Save your gratitude for next time," said Nurse Touati. "Pity to be rescued and then to die of pneumonia."

The Uptons used the stairs, and Mummy went along to help, and to start the bathwater running in our room too. We'd have to toss a coin for first turn. Grannie said she'd bring us up in just a few minutes. The moment that Mummy and Mrs. Upton disappeared up the stairs, Grannie turned us about to view the lobby. All thoughts of a bath vanished. Shivers vanished too, replaced with the heat of outrage. Inspector Henry and Dr. Baden walked like comrades across the marble floor toward the passage that led to the billiard room. The doctor wore no hat. He looked rumpled and even scuffed, with a bruise darkening one cheek.

Behind them, Mr. Augustus Fibbley was in a similar condition of dishevelment, but his grin was as cheering as sunshine in November.

"Is it possible that Mr. Fibbley actually fought the doctor?" said Grannie Jane.

"And won?" I said. My bare toes were numb on the cool marble floor.

"Why is the villain not wearing handcuffs?" said Hector.

"And why have they returned to the hotel," Grannie said, "rather than continuing across town to the Harrogate constabulary?"

"Perhaps it is closer to bring him here?" said Hector.

Inspector Henry turned before entering the passage. He pointed a finger at Mr. Fibbley and jabbed the air while speaking words we could not quite catch. The reporter raised his hands and backed away a few steps, before quick-stepping across the lobby to where we waited.

"We got him," he said, not able to hide his smile. "One of my better moments, I confess. Like an American cowboy on a bucking steer."

"Mercy," said Grannie Jane. "Are you aware that your face is bloodied? It is most disconcerting." She excused herself to go to the dining room to request a damp cloth. But she had barely stepped away when Mr. Fibbley leaned in and spoke in an urgent whisper, pulling an envelope out of his jacket.

"Take this." He handed it to Hector. "I daren't stay here much longer, and if anyone has a chance to use it, it will be you and Aggie Morton. The inspector has fiercely warned me off. He was mighty irked that I got to the doctor before he did."

"What is inside?" Hector slid the envelope into the damp waistband of his trousers.

"I, er, borrowed the letter, remember? From Hart's writing case. To his cousin? The other item was in his bedside table. I didn't realize what it was until—you'll see. You might need it."

Grannie Jane was back, carrying a teacup and a napkin, which she presented to Mr. Fibbley. "Are you able to tend to your own injuries?" she said.

"Yes, Mrs. Morton." Mr. Fibbley's cheeks colored below his spectacles. "Thank you."

"Thank *you*, young man. You have displayed bravery, as well as affection for my granddaughter. Neither is to be dismissed. However, we have an urgent appointment and must not be delayed. If you'll excuse us?"

The reporter retired to an armchair with the cloth and cup. I hoped Mr. Smythe would not evict him.

"It is unfortunate, Agatha," said Grannie Jane, "that your shoes and stockings appear to be missing. Since we haven't much time, we must proceed as if I hadn't noticed. Just this once."

I stared at her, hope speeding my heart.

She pulled the woolly shawl from around her shoulders and settled it on mine in place of the now-damp towels. She turned to Hector in consternation.

"I am merely damp, madame," he reassured her, "and, otherwise, most eager to hear the cause of your urgency."

"I feel rather strongly," said Grannie Jane, "that the inspector's interview with the villain must not unfold without your own contribution to the conversation."

CHAPTER 30

A STUBBORN VILLAIN

WE CREPT ALONG THE passage to the billiard room, feeling bold. Grannie Jane had declared herself chaperone, but in truth she could not bear to miss a scene that might prove to be enlightening.

"Oh, to be dry and unrumpled," Hector whispered. "One must dress with dignity in order to be treated with dignity."

"At least you have shoes on!" I whispered back, my toes colder every moment.

Grannie deemed that simply bursting into a police interrogation was not permissible. We must wait for the right moment. Her ethical standard softened, however, when we spotted a two-inch crack where the door had not been properly shut.

"Move closer!" she mouthed, nudging us into position for best listening.

It was the villain who spoke, not quaking in fear as I'd hoped, or puffing with fury as when he'd assaulted us, but in the plummy, congenial voice he used to put his patients at ease.

"I've had concerns about her for some time, Inspector," he was saying. "She is erratic in her behavior, exhibiting signs of a disturbed mind that go beyond petty thievery."

"What you're saying, Dr. Baden, is that the nurse is responsible for poisoning Mrs. Shelton?"

Hector and I gaped at each other. He was blaming Nurse McWorthy!

"Sadly, it would seem so. I suspect . . . forgive me if this sounds self-important, as normally I'd prefer not to mention it, but I suspect that the nurse had a misguided affection for me . . . and perhaps felt insulted by my attention to the charming widow?"

"Insulted enough to kill?" said the inspector. "That is a powerful affection."

"As I say, she is disturbed, Inspector. I hope she has been confined?"

"You're also suggesting that it was she who attacked the children this evening?"

"Well, to that point, Inspector, who can say if there even *was* an attack, as you call it? These particular children are a bit unruly, have you noticed? With a penchant for poking their noses into matters that do not concern them?"

It seemed a bit wrong to feel huffy about such slander while my nose was an inch from a door conveniently open for spying . . . However! How dare he!

"Youngsters get themselves into scrapes," the doctor was saying, "and, when caught, they make up lies to divert attention from their own bad behavior. Surely you and I remember incidents from our own boyhood, eh? Blaming someone else was the best way out!"

But that's *exactly* what he was doing to Nurse McWorthy!

"There may have been an incident or two," agreed Inspector Henry. I glanced at Grannie Jane, whose mouth turned down in disgust.

The doctor chuckled. *Chuckled!* "You see? Boys will be boys."

"You're *FIBBING!*" I could not bear his smug way of speaking for one more instant. "You dirty *rat!*" I kicked open the door and bounded into the room. Hector followed so closely that when I halted to reconsider, he crashed into me and stumbled foolishly back. Poor, mortified Grannie had no choice but to join us, doing her best to look like a refined old lady and not a sneaky low-down eavesdropper.

Inspector Henry stood beside the felt-topped table, idly rolling a yellow billiard ball under his palm. Dr. Baden sat on a low stool at the far end of the table, his back straight, his feet firmly on the floor. Sergeant Rook loomed behind him, but jumped at the sight of us. The inspector merely cocked his head with interest.

The briefest show of alarm flashed in the doctor's eyes when his gaze met mine, but it was gone as quickly as a falling star. I had imagined coolly staring this ogre down, but my heart had begun to hammer.

You nearly killed George!

I tried to make my eyes pour hatred into his. *You locked us in a furnace and left us to cook! Hector fainted and we were trapped and George's legs don't even work!*

"Good evening, Inspector Henry." Grannie stood with one hand clamped on my shoulder and the other on Hector's, her grip so firm I guessed it was more to prevent herself, rather than us, from going anywhere. "Please excuse our hasty entrance. It does not diminish the significance of our report. Agatha and Hector are equipped to enlighten you on critical points."

"Will you sit, Mrs. Morton?" The inspector indicated a row of high-backed seats used normally for ladies viewing their husbands using long sticks called cues to poke wooden balls into pockets in the corners of the table. Grannie declined the offer to sit, replacing the old lady persona with that of protector and dragon. Hector and I stood close enough together that the backs of our hands touched as we waited to learn what our intrusion might cost.

Dr. Baden had shifted his focus away from me with no sign that he'd received my message of wrath. He looked impatient, shaking his head with a sigh.

"Shouldn't the children be in their nursery by now?" His amiable voice was a sickening sham. "What can you hope to achieve by allowing—"

I felt Grannie Jane bristle. Or was that my own skin, crawling with fire ants of loathing?

"You've made rather a noisy entrance, Miss Morton." Inspector Henry was calm and curious, as if remarking on an outing to the zoo. "Is there something you wanted to add to our discussion?"

While the doctor smirked, the words spat and blinked inside my head like damp firecrackers, with no chance of becoming sentences.

Hector nobly took a turn instead. "We wish to adjust the record, Inspector. We understand the doctor claims he does not harm us? This we know to be false."

Dr. Baden sighed loudly, a belittling hiss.

"In addition, he makes the claim that Nurse McWorthy is the poisoner of Mrs. Shelton. This, also, we know to be false. Both these acts are performed by the doctor himself."

Dr. Baden prepared to stand, putting his palms on the edge of the billiard table and causing a purple ball bearing the number 12 to hop slightly. Sergeant Rook tapped the doctor's arm, urging him back to his seat.

"Thank you, Sergeant," said Inspector Henry. "I see no harm in hearing a little more." His lips pressed together in an ominous smile. "As much as I dislike the fad of *sleuthing* as a juvenile pastime, so popular since the advent of Sherlock Holmes, there are times when children notice things not meant for them to see or hear." This was his first admission of possible value in what we had to say, and it gave me a boost.

I addressed the inspector directly. "Hurting George and feeding arsenic to Mrs. Shelton are only two of the doctor's crimes. He also killed Mr. Hart, we know that now, and—"

"Good God, Inspector!" Dr. Baden tried again to rise, and again the sergeant kept him down. The doctor batted away the policeman's hand, but remained sitting. "Does it amuse you to listen to pointless accusations?" His tone became less pleasant. "Made by a *girl*? Why would I go about killing Wellspring patients? That would be very bad for business, would it not? I'd hardly met this man, except for a brief encounter in the lounge." He looked over my head to my grandmother. "You were there, Mrs. Morton, were you not? You saw the old fool. He was infirm. He died of a heart attack before I had a chance to help him in the clinic."

"I *was* one of that party, Dr. Baden," said Grannie Jane. "I believe Mr. Hart spoke on that occasion about his dear, departed cousin Phoebe."

Oh, thank you, my darling grandmother.

"Your wife," I said.

"Your late wife," said Hector.

The inspector, finally, was stirred to full attention. The yellow ball beneath his hand skidded away as he straightened up and surveyed we three accusers.

"Well, now," he said. "This is something new."

The doctor's eyes had closed for a moment, but now he shook his head. "This has gone beyond a child's prank, Inspector, when my private grief is trodden on with no regard."

"You married Mr. Hart's cousin Phoebe," I blurted, "and you took her money and maybe had insurance on her life as well. You were courting Mrs. Shelton, and you hoped to inherit her money, too, but she became suspicious, didn't she? You killed her before she—"

"I think we're finished here." Dr. Baden looked around at Sergeant Rook. "Step back, Sergeant, will you?" But Inspector Henry's head was moving side to side, telling his sergeant, *No, the interview is not yet over.*

AND! I did not say out loud, *You intended to seduce my mother! Did you plan to kill her, thinking she had money to steal? But Mummy is not alone, as those other poor ladies were.*

Mummy has me! And Hector and Grannie Jane, and Papa in Heaven, and you were never, ever going to win her heart.

Instead, I said, "Mr. Hart recognized you. He saw you in the clinic that morning and knew straightaway you were the man his cousin had married, a week before she died."

"The symptoms of food poisoning, they are similar to those of Mrs. Shelton," said Hector. "The stomach unrest, the terrible pains."

"Mr. Hart must have spent the day wondering what to say, how to ask you what happened," I said, "but when the moment came, in the lounge, he only hinted at what he believed—that his cousin's death was suddenly more suspicious when sharing the light with that of Mrs. Shelton. With you being connected to both women—"

"Inspector!" the doctor broke in.

"You're not enjoying this, Dr. Baden?" said the inspector. "Whereas I am finding it fascinating. Stay right where you are. Please go on, Miss Morton."

"Mr. Hart bought drinks for everyone," I said.

"But soon you leave our company," said Hector, "and within minutes you place the telephone call from your apartment, to inform this devoted uncle that his niece is come to harm."

"At once, he was full of fear," I said. "He raced out

322

into the dark night, taking the shortcut through the hotel garden, just as you guessed he would."

"His heart . . ." said Hector, "is fragile."

"You were there before him," I said, "armed with a croquet mallet from the games shed, ready to conk him over the head."

"I wonder, do you speak with him?" said Hector.

"Whether you spoke or not," I said, "you threatened him, and scared him badly. You swung the mallet and hit the urn, and you hit the bench . . ."

"Your aim is not so good," said Hector.

This brought a little noise from Inspector Henry.

"But there was no need to hit him," I said, "because his heart was seized with fright! And that is why he died. Was it not?"

"Of *fright*?" said the inspector.

"A lucky break," said Hector, "as you say in English."

"D'ya hear that, Inspector?" said Sergeant Rook. "Total rubbish, if you ask me."

"Aye," said the inspector. "It does seem we've just cut ties with real police work."

"Thank you, Inspector," said Dr. Baden. "Will you stop their chatter now?"

"Next . . ." Hector stepped forward and raised his voice, "you hide the mallet."

"And then you lurked about," I said, "waiting for someone to find the body."

"Is this little bit of theater complete?" said the despicable Dr. Baden. For a man who'd been so rattled by George's trick with the mallet, he now displayed nerves of iron! "These children have spun a lengthy yarn with no connection to reality. This nonsense is on your head, Inspector Henry. If you continue to allow it, I shall have you reported."

"Did you say you have been married, Doctor?" said the inspector.

The doctor glared at Inspector Henry, and then cast a scowl at Hector and me.

"Though it is no business of yours, sir, and nothing whatever to do with these children, I will tell you that, yes, I have been married. I took the position at Wellspring as a way of recovering from a broken heart. My wife died during our honeymoon a year ago."

"Phoebe," I said.

The doctor shook his head. "No," he said. "Her name was Penelope."

CHAPTER 31

A PRICKLY RESOLUTION

PENELOPE? HAD WE MADE a mistake? Were all our deductions based on the wrong premise?

Questioning someone's sorrow seemed the lowest form of insult. I was momentarily silenced.

Or . . . was he telling more lies? Hector's hand moved to the envelope tucked into his waistband. The letter!

"I beg to interject," said Hector. "We are entrusted with a letter from the desk of Mr. Benedict Hart."

Entrusted? Ha! The flexibility of words to tell different stories!

"This letter, it is written to the brother of cousin Phoebe. She who, alas, is dead."

"What's this?" said Inspector Henry. He signaled that Sergeant Rook should fetch and bring it to him. The doctor appeared to be frozen, his mouth half open. The envelope was not sealed. The inspector flicked it open and pulled out a folded piece of writing paper, the contents of which we already knew from Mr. Fibbley's transcript. But, along with the paper, he also withdrew a photograph mounted on a stiff white card! Hector and I inhaled as one. I heard Mr. Fibbley's pleading voice as he'd handed the precious envelope to Hector. *I found something else in there too. You might need it. I didn't realize what it was . . .*

But I knew what it must be. Mr. Hart's cousin Phoebe had sent him a photograph of herself and the man she was about to marry. Mr. Hart would not meet that man until one morning in the clinic of a spa hotel in Harrogate. He had looked across the room and recognized the doctor from the picture he carried in his writing case. Sticky-fingered Mr. Fibbley had guessed its value and swiped it along with the letter to Phoebe's brother.

Inspector Henry stared at the image in his hand and then at Dr. Baden. He turned the card around, to show the picture. "This seems to be a likeness of you, Doctor. With a fetching young woman."

"Th-that's my wife," said Dr. Baden. "That is Penelope."

"And how did it come to be in the possession of Mr. Hart?"

The doctor shook his head. "I cannot begin to guess," he said. "It makes no sense."

"I expect," said Grannie Jane, "that Josie Upton will be able to clear up the matter when she is shown the photograph. There need be no confusion."

"My dear madam . . ." began the doctor.

"I am not dear to you," Grannie said. "It will be more efficient if we do not waste time on being nice."

"Sergeant?" said the inspector. "Will you please summon Mrs. Upton? A small matter of identifying property." Sergeant Rook made his way importantly around the billiard table and out the door.

"We will, for now, put aside the events of a year ago," said Inspector Henry, "and look more closely at what occurred last week. If you were not skulking about bashing garden furniture with a croquet mallet on Wednesday last, Dr. Baden, where were you?"

The doctor's chuckle this time was hollow. "A reasonable request that I will happily answer. I excused myself from the little Morton party, because I had an early start the following morning and wished to be well rested. Upon returning to my rooms, I found myself more tired than I'd realized, and fell into a deep sleep while still clothed and sitting in the armchair."

Hector's hand brushed mine, ever so lightly.

"How long did you sleep?" asked Inspector Henry.

"I can't say precisely," said the doctor. "Not long, I shouldn't think, though I don't recall what woke me. I'm told the boy came knocking." He nodded at Hector. "So likely it was that."

"I knock, but you do not respond," said Hector. "Three times, I knock."

"In any case," said Dr. Baden, "I roused myself and thought I'd take a quick turn about the hotel before turning in."

"First you are too tired to sit in the Champagne Lounge, and then you feel the need for exercise?" said the inspector.

"Nothing better than a stroll before bed to aid a full night's sleep," said the doctor, as if sharing a professional secret. "But I got only as far as the lobby before I was told of a medical emergency in the garden. I hastened there without delay and found the poor man collapsed on the bench, with his niece weeping as if refilling the North Sea."

A moment of silence, after so much talking. My arms tingled and I scarcely dared breathe, for if the next few sentences spoken were the right ones, Dr. Peter Baden was about to—

"Who told you?" said Inspector Henry.

The doctor tilted his head. "Who told me what?"

"Who informed you of an incident requiring your assistance?"

The doctor shrugged and flapped a hand. "I don't recall," he said. "Smythe? The bell captain? Does it matter?"

It mattered quite a bit. The inspector was only guessing, but he, too, had sniffed the air and knew we were close. He picked up the nearest billiard ball, a green one, and balanced it on the flattened palm of his hand.

"I am confused, Dr. Baden," I said. "Hector and I were with Mrs. Upton when she found her uncle's body. Hector went to find you and could not."

They all were watching, waiting.

"I am obliged," said Hector, "to convince Mr. Smythe instead, of the crisis in the garden."

"I suppose I came along right then or shortly after," said the doctor. "Word travels quickly, eh? The lobby was buzzing."

"Au contraire," said Hector. "*No one* knows. Mr. Smythe is most insistent on this point. No person in the hotel knows yet what occurs."

"What I think is this," I said. "You threatened Mr. Hart. You even tried to hit him, but missed and smacked the urn. He was so upset that he suffered a heart attack. You watched him die. You then went to hide the croquet mallet and returned, under the pretense of helping."

His face twitched, but he caught himself. "I don't think so," he said.

"You do not come from your rooms in the hotel," said Hector. "Nor through the lobby."

"What does it matter where I came from?" snapped the doctor.

"Mrs. Upton can easily confirm," I said, "that you came through the gate. From the street. And we know what you were doing out there."

"Certainly not killing your Mr. Hart," said Dr. Baden, his face turning red. "Not whacking iron benches or lurking around Valley Gardens Park hiding croquet mallets behind trees in the dark. I was taking a quiet stroll before bed, after a long day! And why are you not asking Nurse Mc-blasted-Worthy what she was doing last Wednesday night?"

I used every thread of my frayed willpower not to gloat with a wide, ravenous grin. Hector squeezed my hand. Grannie Jane squeezed my shoulder. I was going to be black and blue if the inspector didn't step in.

But he did. A new glint in his eye lifted my heart. He tossed the green billiard ball into the air, making the number 6 spin before he caught it again.

"Dr. Baden?" he said. "I believe Miss Morton is about to sink the last ball."

"No one mentioned Valley Gardens Park." I looked straight into the doctor's eyes. "Or anything about a tree. Only the person who hid the mallet could know where it was found."

Deathly silence, for one, two, four, six heartbeats. And then he lunged, with a terrible snarl, scrambling around the side of the table, meaning to tear me in half. Hector and Big Joe Henry jumped to block him, but it was Grannie Jane who scooped up the red billiard ball from the table and hurled it with a keen arm, catching Dr. Baden on the bridge of his nose for a knockout.

An Epilogue

I STAYED AN EXTRA WHILE under my blankets on the morning after our long journey home. Rain splattered the window, and Tony was curled at my feet. Sally brought me a tray in bed, a soft-boiled egg and toast fingers brushed with butter. Also, a pot of cocoa, which made me miss Hector. Despite traveling for hours and hours on the train together, we had, as ever, much more to talk about. Like whether George would find someone else to match Hector's skills in croquet? And who would replace Dr. Baden, now that he sat awaiting trial? Had Inspector Henry been applauded for solving the double murder? Or made to feel foolish for sharing the spotlight with children?

Would Nurse McWorthy seek counsel from the vicar about her thieving inclinations, so that she might remain working in the clinic? Among our pleasant and woeful farewells, we'd had one onerous encounter before leaving the Wellspring. I had objected violently, and even Hector was reluctant, but Grannie had firmly insisted that we must confess our wrongdoing and make amends to Nurse McWorthy for having removed the items from her umbrella.

"But she stole them first!" I said.

"Which does not give you permission to be as depraved as she," Grannie said.

Mummy intervened to say that naturally my grandmother was correct, and thus should accompany our mission. *Ha!* It was not often that Mummy bested my grandmother, but on this occasion . . . Who was most uncomfortable during the ensuing attempt to teach us a lesson? Nurse McWorthy's podgy pink face looked anywhere but at us, while we took turns stuttering our apologies. (If we should ever perform a similar misdemeanor, we would not be so foolish as to confess!) Grannie Jane appeared to be holding her breath until we left the clinic—if the magnitude of her disapproving sniff was any indication.

As we shuffled along the passage, still glowing with shame, we came upon Mr. Smythe in conversation with Mr. Bessel, the bell captain. His back was to us, and yet his pontificating voice carried very clearly.

"I always knew there was something off about that fellow. You get a sense of who people really are, working in hotels. And there he was, bold as brass, saying as how there'd be no need for the police. With a dead man lying right in front of us! I should have followed my instincts and insisted on a full investigation. I knew there was more to that corpse than met the eye . . ."

Hector's eyebrows rose so high they nearly met his perfectly combed hair. I blurted half a laugh and coughed at once, to cover myself. Mr. Smythe turned sharply in our direction, but we gazed innocently back.

Eventually, on that first day home, still a bit stupefied by travel and fatigue, I ventured down to the drawing room to join Grannie and Mummy. The morning post had brought a letter from Marjorie.

Owl Park

Dear Family,

Welcome home! I assume you've landed back at Groveland with no mishap. I thought it wise to address this letter to Torquay rather than the hotel in Harrogate, for fear of missing you. I am eager to hear your versions of the unfolding drama, after reading Mr. Fibbley's accounts in the Voice. I have no doubt that Aggie and Hector will have wriggled their way into the investigation. (Thank you for your letter, Aggie. My reply is also in this envelope.) I am feeling fine and fat, with only eight weeks until the baby comes along to change the world. I am so pleased, Mummy, that Charlotte will be coming to Owl Park as nursemaid for the first few months. Thank you for allowing her to relinquish her teaching duties for Aggie. I trust my dear sister will not find that to be a hardship?

James sends love, as do I,
Marjorie

The letter to me was folded and sealed, with my initials, A.C.M., drawn on the outside. The seal meant she was keeping private her answer to my letter from the Wellspring. With an extra thump of the heart, I tucked it away for reading later.

"No hardship at all!" I agreed. No Charlotte and no lessons? I could not think of a lovelier summer. "But will we not go to Owl Park? To meet the baby?"

"We will, of course," said Mummy, "but you will likely need diversion elsewhere, for a portion of the summer. Reverend Mr. Teasdale has recommended some intriguing—"

"Thank you, but *ugh*," I said.

I excused myself and hurried to my bedroom to read what Marjorie might have to say.

Owl Park

Dearest darling Aggie,

I wish we could be together to have this talk. You are confused and worried and sad all mixed together—and most of that is because we still miss Papa every day. Our love and Mummy's love for Papa will never go away, I promise.

But in the meantime, aren't we lucky to have a kind and beautiful mother who inspires admiration in all who meet her? Aren't we lucky to have a mother with excellent judgment and a devotion to fairness that allows us to trust that she thinks of our well-being above all else?

Should the day ever come when a man enters her life, and manages to snag a small piece of her heart, we will have this conversation again. For now, I believe she is not so lonely as Grannie might imagine, and that she simply likes to be told—as do we all, from time to time—that she is a good and lovely person.

Your favorite sister,
M.

There came a tap on the door, and here was Mummy. She could not fail to see the tears bucketing down my face, or the letter, damp and wrinkled in my hand. She sat next to me on the window seat and pulled me into a long embrace. Tony came snuffling in, wondering why the air was tinged with salt. My tears ebbed, and we rested there a while longer, but Tony kept batting my knee, so we stopped feeling restful. Mummy reached for my hairbrush from the washstand and undid the messy night plait and stroked the hair away from my face in slow, gentle waves. When that was done, we hugged again and I told her, "Mummy? You really are a good and lovely person." After that, we got on with a morning of unpacking and laundering and playing in the garden with the best dog in the world.

The next few days brought news from Nottingham and from Yorkshire, so that we stretched our connection as tautly as we were able, for just a little longer.

TELEGRAM

TO: MORTON FAMILY, GROVELAND, TORQUAY
THIS BEARS PROOF CAN NOW SEND TELEGRAMS STOP MANY
THANKS FROM LADY BOSS STOP SET OF FOUR NEW UMBRELLAS
TO FOLLOW STOP BEST WISHES JOSIE UPTON STOP

May 9, 1903
Harrogate, Yorkshire

Dear Aggie and Hector,

Thank you for your letters, which arrived yesterday. I have been quite bereft without your company, but have regained my position as Top Player of Croquet in all of Yorkshire. To answer your questions:

1)   No other guest our age has shown up, but there is a pair of twins who are twenty-four and dress identically, usually in lavenders and pinks. They are both Miss Stretch, and the one named Edith likes to play croquet. The other one, Ellen, has only one arm, which is a bigger impediment than no legs.

2)   I retrieved the parcel you left for me with the bell captain, and delivered it, as requested, to Mr. Augustus Fibbley in care of Mrs. Woolsey, prior to his departure for Torquay. I understand he stayed an extra day to participate in a billiards match with Mr. Frank Thomas.

3)   The funeral for Mrs. Shelton took place at St. Michael's, with a beautiful choir and a fine eulogy spoken by the minister. Mrs. Woolsey has given me all Mrs. Shelton's books left behind, which is a good remembrance.

4)   Sidonie is well and sends her regards. She met with Nurse McWorthy yesterday for a cup of tea, in an effort to patch their long estrangement—and it seems to have succeeded! McWorthy has enrolled in a program at her church that assists those seeking to correct the wrongdoings of their past. According to Sidonie, she has petitioned the nursing college to reconsider both their dismissals as being the result of dishonorable action on her part alone, now being mended. Sidonie is content being with me, she says, but

McWorthy will go off to be a real nurse and bore people elsewhere than at Wellspring.

5) Sidonie and I have twice visited Napoli & ~~Son~~ Daughter. Miss Napoli has agreed to school me in anatomy. This is only the beginning. Also, she has submitted an application to replace the county coroner. Lots of people say a woman shouldn't do that job but no one else wants it, so maybe she'll be lucky and turn her secret hobby into a paid occupation.

I enclose a cutting from the <u>Yorkshire Daily</u>. As you'll see, Mr. Thomas has made quite an about-turn in his attitude toward Miss Napoli. She thinks it is due to his sudden recognition that her business provides an endless supply of story material, and he is merely trying to stay on her good side.

I miss you more than I can say,

George

THE YORKSHIRE DAILY

APRIL 30, 1903

Local Lady Undertaker
Decorated for Service to Community
Comely and Valiant
Not Afraid of Dead Bodies!!!

by FRANK THOMAS

Earlier this month, a Harrogate woman made a crucial contribution to the investigation into a double murder and, now, is being honored for her devotion to the needs of our city's well-being. Miss Eva Napoli [26] is the [woefully unattributed] daughter of the establishment of Napoli & Son, located in Old Lane. Following scientific intuition, Miss Napoli boldly broke open the case by testing the body of Mrs. Lidia Shelton for the presence of arsenic. The positive results led directly to the arrest of a reprehensible villain, masquerading as a doctor at the

Wellspring Hotel & Spa. At the request of the police, Miss Napoli analyzed three bottles of Rejuvenation Tonic, bearing the label of the Wellspring dispensary. Two were found, unopened, at the victim's lodging house, and showed no unexpected substance. The third was broken and held only dregs, recovered from a flower garden near the Valley Gardens bandstand. Nearby was Mrs. Shelton's ransacked handbag, missing since the day of her death and believed to have been stolen by hooligans. Miss Napoli's examination of the broken bottle showed evidence of the lethal poison. Questions are now being asked about the late wife—and possibly wives?—of this wicked man.

In an effort to redeem their formerly stellar reputation and recoup financial losses due to the scandal, the Wellspring has issued a statement denying any involvement in the crimes of their employee, Mr. Peter Baden [42], and offering any guest of the past four months [coinciding with Baden's perfidious activity] a complimentary treatment in the Turkish baths on the occasion of a second visit. Baden is being held at the York Castle County Gaol to await his trial this summer. Miss Napoli's testimony will be critical in proving his guilt. Our esteemed Mayor has seen fit to present Miss Napoli with a Key to the City and the gratitude of all its inhabitants.

We were also treated to a summation of our holiday in the *Torquay Voice*.

It happened that I was nearest to the tea trolley when Sally wheeled it to a stop one afternoon in the drawing room. Hector was there, and Mummy and Grannie Jane, and a slightly lopsided chocolate cake with buttercream icing. I reached for the newspaper tucked in next to the napkins, and unfolded it to read the headlines.

"God's nose!"

They all protested my swearing, but I began to laugh and then to read aloud. "'MISSILE-LAUNCHING TORQUAY GRANDMOTHER BRINGS KILLER TO HIS KNEES!!!'" I said. "'CANNY KIDS CONQUER ALIBI!!!' by Augustus Fibbley."

Silence.

Three dropped jaws. Four, including Sally's. Grannie Jane, in particular, looked thunderstruck.

"Well?" said Mummy. "Do go on."

And so:

Residents of the Wellspring Hotel in Harrogate, Yorkshire, will rest more easily tonight, according to Detective Inspector Henry, thanks to the swift action and original thinking of three Torquay residents. Two guests of the hotel were murdered during the month of April, and the perpetrator was none other than the (possibly fraudulent) doctor and director of the Wellspring Spa.

"I'll skip over the blah-blah that we already know," I said, "about the murders and the tonic and the lethal croquet mallet . . ." I hopped down several lines.

In a rapid series of events on Wednesday, Peter Baden was confronted by the evidence of one of his crimes and ruthlessly assaulted three children in a panicked effort to escape justice.

"Ruthlessly," repeated Hector.

Baden was then involved in a street scuffle with this reporter, who tackled the villain on the platform of the train depot. During the questioning that followed his apprehension, Baden caused a disruption, attempting to attack his 12-year-old accuser (Miss Aggie Morton of Torquay). He was promptly and heroically brought to a halt by Miss Morton's grandmother. Mrs. Jane Morton picked up a billiard ball and threw it at the killer's nose with such precision that the man crumpled to the floor, unconscious to the world.

Hector began to applaud. "A great moment, madame."

Instead of bristling, Grannie Jane exhibited every sign of being tickled pink by Mr. Fibbley's description.

"I will confess to you an untold secret," she said. "There was a summer, in my youth, when my brother Cameron was home from university, with a friend named Rashid and another named Laidlaw. Usually, such a men's club would have denied entry to a younger sister, but an affection was blooming between myself and Laddie—"

"My grandfather!" I said.

Grannie Jane smiled and nodded and touched the watch pinned to her bodice. "Even Cameron was forced to be tolerant," she said, "as Laddie taught me to toss darts, alongside the boys. None of them liked it, though, when I won the tournament at the end of the summer and was named champion."

Mummy laughed. "I've never heard that story," she said.

"That summer of the darts," said Grannie, "was butter on bacon all the way through." Her way of saying that it held one good thing on top of another. "It ended with our betrothal."

"So you don't mind having your name in the newspaper?" I asked her. "You always seem a bit vexed when mine appears."

"Gracious, child," she said, with a hint of a smile. "I was being commended for making an excellent shot, not for merely tripping over a corpse!"

"To darts and bodies," Hector said, raising his teacup. "Let us toast to memorable summers."

"May this one coming up be another," I added, "for whichever of those pleasures it might hold."

Author's Note

CLARISSA MILLER, THE MOTHER of mystery writer Agatha Christie, died in the spring of 1926, causing profound sadness for the daughter who had always called her "Mummy." In August, before Christie had recovered from the anguish of losing her mother, her husband, Archie, announced that he had fallen in love with someone else, a woman named Nancy Neele. These two life-altering blows, so close together, affected Christie deeply. She was, by now, 36 years old and the famous author of six popular novels. Early in December that year, Christie left her young child in the nanny's care; wrote notes for her secretary, her brother-in-law and her husband; and drove away with only a small case of clothing and papers. The car was discovered the next day a few miles from the Christie home, close to a place called the Silent Pool. The puzzling disappearance of a famous mystery writer provoked a massive hunt and wild speculation in the tabloid newspapers.

Where had she gone? Was it a publicity stunt? Had she killed herself in a fit of unbearable grief? Had she been murdered . . . by her cheating husband?

Ten days later, Christie was found a long distance from home, in the north of England, at the Old Swan Hydropathic Hotel in Harrogate, in the county of

Yorkshire. One of the musicians who played in the hotel orchestra had recognized her photograph, printed each day in the newspaper as part of the national hunt. Archie Christie declared that she had temporarily lost her memory, but had no explanation for why she had registered at the hotel using the last name of Neele. Christie never discussed the episode in public—and included no mention in her autobiography.

When first considering the possible story of a third novel about Aggie Morton, I was intrigued by the idea of a hotel with a spa attached. Partly, I was thinking of poor Mummy, whose health and spirits needed uplifting after her husband's death. Partly, I was thinking of myself, wishing very much to spend time doing research in such a setting! What about the south of France? Or perhaps a visit to Hector's home country of Belgium, where the town of Spa had given its name to a series of resorts that tapped into curative mineral waters and hot springs all over northern Europe.

Then I remembered Harrogate, a fashionable destination at the turn of the last century—and the place to which Agatha Christie had fled for solace in a time of crisis. What if, as a young girl, she had visited Yorkshire and had an adventure she would never forget? What if she was drawn back, recalling how her sad and languid mother had been rejuvenated by the effect of the Turkish baths?

Under usual circumstances, I would have visited Harrogate to research the town's history and its former distinction as a destination for taking the waters. The pandemic was raging, however, during the time I might have traveled, and I was left with my imagination. I stopped worrying about getting things "right" and began to make up what was needed for the plot involving Aggie. As always with historical fiction, the author's job is to offer an invented story inside the framework of a world that is close to what really existed. In the Aggie Morton books, I have created a girl whose childhood circumstances occasionally overlap with those of Agatha Christie. By introducing Hector Perot, I am not insisting that this boy becomes the actual famous detective Hercule Poirot, but instead he is Aggie's inspiration for that character, in a future where she grows up to be our beloved writer of mysterious tales. The character of Grannie Jane allows an adult reader glimpses of Christie's other great sleuth, Miss Jane Marple, who possessed many qualities of Christie's own grandmother and her "cronies," to use the author's word. Throughout the Aggie books, I've taken care to show her growing interest in being a storyteller, alongside the Morbid Preoccupation that so worries her mother. Maybe when you read stories by the original Queen of Crime, you will think of Aggie Morton and the fictional insights I have put in her path.

SOURCES

AS WITH THE FIRST TWO Aggie Morton books, I began by
reading and re-reading many novels and stories by Agatha
Christie, always on alert for details or character quirks
that might turn up in young Aggie's world to inspire later
moments in her own writing. Part of the fun is giving my
character ideas for a title or plot premise that an adult
Christie fan will recognize and that a young reader will
discover by chance in a future page-turner.

I consulted an uncountable number of books and
websites to learn what I knew little about: the Victorian
custom of taking the waters, the business of being an
undertaker, how arsenic poisoning affects a person and
how its use is detected, how the disabled were treated or
supported 120 years ago.

The chair that George would be using in 1903, for
instance, would have differed greatly from the nimble,
lightweight wheelchairs of today. It would have been
cumbersome and heavy, likely made of wood or wicker
with iron wheels. The first self-propelled wheelchair was
invented way back in 1655 by Stephen Farfler, who made
clocks. When his mobility was severely compromised by
a broken back, Farfler applied his clockmaking skills to

developing a moving chair that could give unimagined motion to those who would otherwise be bed-bound.

Here are some of the books that helped me find out other things:

Baty Goodman, Jocelyn, ed. *Victorian Cabinet Maker: The Memoirs of James Hopkinson 1819–1894*. New York: A.M. Kelley, 1968.

Cooper, Gail and Adam Negrusz, eds. *Clarke's Analytical Forensic Toxicology*. London: Pharmaceutical Press, 2013.

Harkup, Kathryn. *A Is for Arsenic: The Poisons of Agatha Christie*. London: Bloomsbury Sigma, 2015.

Hempel, Sandra. *The Inheritor's Powder: A Tale of Arsenic, Murder, and the New Forensic Science*. New York: W.W. Norton, 2013.

Heos, Bridget. *Blood, Bullets, and Bones: The Story of Forensic Science from Sherlock Holmes to DNA*. New York: Balzer + Bray, 2016.

Lee, Edwin. *The Mineral Springs of England and Their Curative Efficacy*. London: Whittaker, 1841.

Parsons, Brian. *The Undertaker at Work 1900–1950*. London: Strange Attractor Press, 2014.

As a minor sidenote, I have come across only one creation, apart from the Aggie Morton Mystery Queen series, where Agatha Christie and her invention Hercule Poirot appear as characters together. The movie *Murder by the Book* was written by Nick Evans and directed by Lawrence Gordon Clark. Ian Holm plays Poirot and Dame Peggy Ashcroft is Christie.

Acknowledgments

Thank you, as always, to Lynne Missen, Margot Blankier and Shana Hayes for superb editing and extreme patience.

Thank you to my literary agent, Ethan Ellenberg; to my screen agent, Rena Zimmerman; and to the team at Tundra Books for pushing Aggie even further into the world.

Thank you to Isabelle Follath (yet again) for your clever and glorious illustrations.

Thank you to Sarah English for your precise and hilarious audio interpretation of Aggie's world and the many characters who live there.

Thank you to Robin Chadwick for being my musical guide (and a marvelous violinist).

Thank you to Dr. Elena Cunningham for certain forensic details and for a shared Morbid Preoccupation that has seen us through some dark times.

Thank you to Tara for starting things off.

And thank you to my various covens of friends and writing women who have listened, read, suggested, brainstormed, fixed, written from the backseat, and considered Aggie worth the trouble I've begged of you. Most especially Hadley and Judy, who truly got me through this one. Lucky me.

More mystery,

more murder . . .

COMING SOON IN THE NEXT

AGGIE MORTON

MYSTERY QUEEN

And don't miss Aggie's

other adventures!